The Devil's Luck

RUN LIKE THE DEVIL

JAYCE CARTER

Run Like the Devil
ISBN # 978-1-80250-539-9
©Copyright Jayce Carter 2023
Cover Art by Kelly Martin ©Copyright May 2023
Interior text design by Claire Siemaszkiewicz
Totally Bound Publishing

Published in 2023 by Totally Bound Publishing, United Kingdom.

RUN LIKE
THE DEVIL

Dedication

To my coffee and the lies it tells me about just how productive we're going to be today!

Chapter One

It doesn't matter how deep you bury the past — it'll always climb back out.

And with some fancy-ass wings, no less.

My brain struggled to make sense of the sight before me. Part of me wanted to sag in relief at the sight of Gorrin there, alive and well — or as alive as anyone in the Chasm was.

The other part wanted to drive that dagger into him another time because of all the lies he must have told me. Those flashy wings sure as fuck said he'd kept things from me.

And yet another part wanted to wrap my arms around him to convince myself that he was real. Or let him stab me in a way we both would enjoy...

Before I had a chance to pick any of those, however, Gorrin caught my arm and the world disappeared around me, plunging me into darkness so the only thing I could see was Gorrin, as if I couldn't bear to lose sight of him for even a moment.

When everything came back into view around me, I tried to glance around, to figure out where I was. As soon as I did, warmth pressed against my lips.

No, not pressed. That implied a sweet kiss, something lovers did for the first time when testing out chemistry and whether or not the man would get slapped for his attempt. That was *nothing* like this. Instead, the kiss was ravenous, angry and desperate. He delved past my lips with his tongue, devouring me, while his hands grasped my arms so tightly I'd no doubt sport bruises by the end.

And the idiot I was returned his kiss with every bit of that same need. I took my conflicted feelings out on him, letting him bear all the pain I'd suffered while mourning him.

When he held me tightly enough that I couldn't touch him back, I used my new strength and powers to knock his arms away from me, to free myself.

His wide golden eyes said he hadn't thought me capable of that, but I didn't care about impressing him. I pounced at him, wrapping my arms around his shoulders, clinging to him, my legs tight around his waist as I reclaimed his lips.

I swallowed down a deep, masculine groan from him, letting it soothe and excite me all at once.

I tilted my head to deepen the kiss, and grasped his face with my thumb at his jaw and my palm against his cheek. It was far from a gentle touch. Instead, it was controlling, tilting his head to let me deeper, to give me more.

Something hard hit my back, knocking the breath from my lungs, but I didn't give a fuck. Who cared about petty things like breathing at a moment like this? I lived off Gorrin, could subsist solely on his touch and his heat. Fuck, I could breathe the air from his lungs and that would suit me fine.

He pulled his body back just enough to reach between us, and the loud rip told me what he felt about my clothes. Any other time it would have pissed me off—ruining my shit was not the way to my heart—but for now it was in my way, too.

My shirt was gone, and quickly my pants followed. Gorrin didn't take even a moment to check out my underwear, didn't pull back to marvel at how lovely I looked in my black lace, and that was fine with me. He paused when his fingers found the front of my bra, as if sense had suddenly returned to him and he feared my reaction at ruining that.

Bras were off the fucking table normally—no woman enjoyed the headache of finding ones that actually fit—but now was far from normal. To make that point clear, I took his hands and used my own strength to tear the front of the bra, the rip loud even over our combined panting.

He let out a low sound so close to a growl that I shivered, then broke the kiss to pull my panties down my legs.

Of course, that left me naked and him totally dressed, which was one-hundred-percent not okay. He wore the same clothes as always, that stupid blue jacket so familiar that my eyes stung at seeing it again.

But I pushed that ugly feeling away and shoved at the fabric.

Gorrin rose up, which made me realize we were on the floor, though I didn't recognize where.

The room was dark, but not like the Chasm. A breath in told me we were on Earth, that familiar freshness I'd recognize, but beyond that?

I didn't know and I didn't care.

We could have been on a football field at halftime and I'd still be taking Gorrin's pants off. What was an audience compared with what I wanted right now?

Gorrin tossed his jacket aside, the action surprising me. He was generally so careful, but it seemed he didn't give a fuck about things like wrinkling his jacket right now. Buttons popped off his shirt as he yanked it, the discarded items flying around before the shirt joined the jacket as he straddled me. He toed his boots off, then unfastened his pants as he raked his gaze over me.

And I'd *never* seen a look like that on his face before. I'd seen him angry, annoyed, even mildly amused, but never had this sort of heat rested there. Had he hidden it all this time? Locked it away somewhere deep inside him so I couldn't even glimpse it?

If so, why?

Would things have been different if he hadn't? If he'd shown this to me? Would we have been different? Would I not have—

Before that thought could fully form, he grasped my thighs in his large hot hands. "I don't want you thinking, little fish, not right now." He tugged, the action scraping my back against the hard floor, tiny stings implying it left small wounds, but the desire in his eyes drugged me enough that I didn't care.

Especially once he pulled me up, drawing my hips from the ground, the position strange, but the way he leaned in had me more than willing to ignore that. He didn't use his words to tease me, not like Hale did. He didn't declare feelings like Tyrus did.

No, Gorrin was a man of action, so he simply leaned in and pressed his seeking lips right to my cunt, dragging his tongue up my slit. The touch burned, lighting some uncontrollable fire inside me, my back arching in response to the overwhelming sensation.

But he didn't stop. Instead, he delved deeper with his tongue, as if he wanted to drown in me. I looked at him, my body entirely on display because of the position. That might have embarrassed me if I were myself right then, might have made me nervous, but the way his golden eyes locked on mine made that impossible.

Instead, I melted, my entire body going molten at every touch of his. He moved between sinking his tongue deep into my cunt and sliding it against my waiting clit, and he kept me from guessing his next move with ease.

I would have never thought Gorrin capable of this, never thought he'd feel this way, that he'd have this sort of passion inside him. He'd always looked at me with such stone, always unmovable, but I almost couldn't see that man in the one who pleasured me now.

His grip remained on me, tight and unflinching, and the first orgasm that struck me happened so fast that I couldn't stop my eyes from squeezing shut at the intensity. It rushed over me in crashing waves that made my entire body tense, my back arching impossibly more, my hands drawing into fists, even my feet twisting as if I could grasp some semblance of control.

All I could do was endure, though. It went on forever—especially because Gorrin didn't pull back or stop—until I felt as if I might really die. It seemed like an eternity later when my body finally went lax, when all that tension released.

As soon as it happened, Gorrin pressed a strangely sweet kiss to my cunt, then the cool stone floor touched my sweat-soaked back as he lowered me.

If I thought it was over, though, I was *dead* wrong. Instead, his weight rested over me and his wet lips found mine. I tasted my own sweetness on his lips, and I happily cleaned it from him.

The blunt head of his cock pressed against my still twitching pussy, and he waited for only a moment. Part of me wondered if he'd ask, if he'd check in. It seemed like a Gorrin thing to do, since he was always responsible.

Perhaps it was a testament to how out of control he was, because instead, he wrapped his fingers in my hair, drawing his hand into a tight fist as if to hold me still, then plunged his impossibly thick cock deep into me in a single hard thrust.

It threw me headfirst into another orgasm, or maybe they were aftershocks from the last? I couldn't tell anymore, didn't know where one ended and the next started. It felt like wading from the beach into the ocean, where the water moved nonstop and I couldn't tell apart the individual waves.

Each thrust caused his grasp in my hair to tug against my scalp, and *fuck* did that do it for me. I moaned, not caring about how I looked, how I sounded or what he thought of it. Who cared about pride at a time like this?

So I wrapped one leg around his hip, not wanting him to pull out at all, not willing to lose any of this for even a heartbeat. I dug the heel of that foot into him, forcing him to grind into me deeper, harder, to give me more.

And Gorrin did exactly that. Pain in my back said his thrusts shoved me against that rough floor, and I knew I'd be a mess of scrapes by the end, and that thought made me grin against his lips. The wounds felt like some tangible proof that this had happened, that I hadn't just lost my mind and made it all up. They said this was *real*, that he was here, with me, no matter how impossible that seems.

He took me with wild abandon, as if he'd lost himself entirely to his need, as though I'd reduced him to something animalistic. He sank his cock deep into me each time, and the action ground his pelvis against my clit, each time drawing a gasp from my lips.

His huge wings blocked out the outside world, the white of them so pure in what felt like such a filthy moment that it didn't seem like they belonged here at all. Not that it mattered—I did all I could to ignore them.

They made me think about our past, about all the secrets between us, about everything I didn't want to intrude on this moment. So I shut that out, keeping my eyes closed to focus instead on the sensations arcing through my body, the electric feeling that ran through all my nerves from each place he touched me.

It went from where my nipples rubbed against his chest, from the sting in my scalp when he tugged on my hair, from the deep almost-ache in my cunt as he fucked me. My body felt like one single nerve, so each place he touched me lit up and threatened to catch fire.

His lips never stopped, his motions becoming even more frantic. I dug my nails into him. I was sure I drew blood, but fuck it. I'd cried for him—he could bleed for me.

Tears for blood—it felt like our normal exchange.

Gorrin rested his weight on the forearm of the hand fisted in my hair, his other hand grasping my hip as if even the slight movement from me was too much. It was as if he wanted to take over me entirely, wanted me totally at his mercy.

And to remind him I was not that woman, that I would *never* be that woman, I bit down on his bottom lip.

Gorrin shuddered as he delved in as deep as possible, his body stilling as he came. The copper tang on my lip from his blood threw me over that same ledge, let me leap off it with him. After how much I'd missed him, after feeling so fucking alone, I didn't like the idea of him moving away from me in the least. So I held on to him and sank into that bliss right along with him.

When my body started to settle, when his softening cock slipped from me, when his kiss slowed and changed from the frantic madness from before, exhaustion took over. I could have fought it, could have shoved it away, but right now?

I let it take me, because a part of me still feared that this was all a dream, and I sure as fuck didn't want to wake up from it. So, instead, I let myself drift off in the arms of a man I loved, a man I'd killed, a man I never thought I'd get to see again.

* * * *

Consciousness came to me slowly, and when I blinked, I squinted against a bright light that assaulted my eyes.

The Chasm was *never* this bright, which had me ready to snap at Gunnar for fucking around with something and waking me up. When my vision started to clear, it wasn't Gunnar I found there.

Gorrin's face, his eyes closed, brought back everything.

I'd gotten the agreement of the other Demon Lords to overthrow Hubis, and Gorrin had shown up with his

Jayce Carter

fancy fucking wings. My cheeks burned as I thought about what had happened *after* that.

Which made me realize all the aches and pains in my body, a sure sign that I hadn't imagined that all.

And a naked Gorrin in bed beside me also helped sell that point.

I gulped hard, and in response, Gorrin's eyes snapped open, the familiar gold of them almost startling.

It was one thing before, when we'd both been so taken by passion, but now? Now reality crept in like that fucking sunlight and lit up the truth.

Gorrin isn't dead.

I reached out and touched his chest, unwilling to fully believe it still.

He set his hand over mine and squeezed, saying nothing. Still, the touch let it finally sink in.

I hadn't killed him. I'd spent all that time blaming myself, hating myself, suffering with guilt so deep I didn't think I'd ever escape it, but I hadn't killed him at all.

The thought brought back all my suffering, the panic attacks, the times where I wanted to close my eyes and never wake up again.

And in response to those memories?

I curled my hand into a fist and punched him.

Fuck him, and not in the fuck way we already had.

"You never change." Gorrin didn't react at all to the hit. Despite his already darkening skin, despite it having to have hurt, he hadn't even flinched.

Show-off.

"I thought you were dead." I shoved away from him.

He let me go, choosing to sit up instead. It let me get a good look at his body, and boy had I left my share of

15

marks on him. He had small bite marks and deep scratches all over him, signs of my need. Not that he was the only one.

One glance down at my front showed the same, like we'd been animals desperate to leave our claims on one another.

"I know you did."

"Don't give me that shit," I snapped. "How are you here? I *saw* you die!"

"You wounded me severely," he admitted. "But you didn't kill me."

"You told me that dagger would kill anything. I *watched* it kill Azael." Just saying that took me back to Azael's corpse lying on the floor, unmoving. It also brought back the memory of Gorrin's body turning to dust before my eyes, collapsing in on itself.

It hadn't occurred to me before, but Gorrin's body hadn't reacted the same, had it?

"The dagger is bound to you, so it only works based on your feelings, your desires. Some part of you hesitated, so while it injured me, it didn't kill me."

I pressed my lips together and kept my hands in tight fists, wanting to strike him again, to make him understand just how much he'd hurt me. Instead, I used my words. I'd learned that beating sense into a person never worked. "Why did you let me believe you were dead, then? Do you have *any* idea how much I suffered!"

He let out a sigh, the first sign of him feeling a damned thing. "You stabbing me at all said you wanted me gone. How was I supposed to face you after that? I'd pushed you so far that you stabbed me. I did enough that you snapped, that a part of you broke, that you did something you would have never done otherwise. You believed me dead, so it seemed a kinder choice to leave you be. Clearly, I was only hurting you."

I dropped my gaze, unable to look at him and think at the same time. "And the wings?" They were gone now, but that didn't erase my memory. "Demons don't have wings like that, which means you've been lying to me from the start, right?"

He sighed, the sound loud in the silent room. "There is no reason to hide it anymore, I guess. Yes, I'm an angel."

"Since when?"

"Since always. I was the first angel that Hubis made, back before he created humans."

"So you were never a demon at all? It was all a lie? Why would you do that?"

"Because I needed to. Souls began to go to the Chasm, souls cut off from Hubis, but there was no order there. I thought I could do something, could make something of that place, so I went to the Chasm and set myself up as the first Demon Lord. It wasn't a lie, not entirely. Just like Hubis takes a human form, just like you have a demon form, I took a demon form as well. It is why I could bind souls to me and rule there, and it is why when you stabbed me, when you destroyed my demon form, you gained my position and power. You killed the part of me that was demon, that had a connection to the Chasm."

I tried to make sense of his story. In some ways, it made sense. All the details I'd heard, the fact that he had been a Demon Lord the longest, the way he didn't seem to fit with the others—being an angel made it all fit.

Still, I couldn't accept it. It was like he changed everything about him then, like he turned it all around.

Instead of looking up to him, instead of thinking of him as the best of us, it turned out he wasn't even one of us.

Which also took me down another path. I recalled the way Azael had followed Hubis, his loyalty to him.

Asking if I could trust a man who had lied to me so much was probably a stupid question, right?

"Where are we?" I asked.

"A place I have on Earth. I thought if we remained in the Chasm, we would get found and interrupted faster."

"And why did you come back?" I asked, my voice quiet. "You let me think you were dead for so long, you let me mourn alone, so why come back now?"

"Because you, as always, chose the most difficult path. If you had chosen to simply do your duty as a Demon Lord, I would have watched over you as I have since I left. I would have allowed you to live your life as you pleased, content with merely serving as a shadow. You, however, can never do things the easy way. When you made the choice to gather the other Lords to do the unthinkable—attack God—I had no choice but to step in."

Which told me what I'd been pretty sure but too afraid to say out loud.

Gorrin had heard our plans. He knew exactly what I intended to do and had shown up for that reason.

I met his gaze head-on. There was no reason to hide from it, to slink away. If he wanted to face me, there was nothing I could do. I wouldn't run, though. "Are you going to kill me?"

He tilted his head, the action so familiar to the man I'd known that it took me back to all the fights we'd had before, all the times when we'd butted heads over what we each thought was right.

Was this the end of it? And the sex? Just some weird parting gift? I'd faced off against Azael and he had nearly killed me — if Gorrin wanted me dead, I doubted I could do a damn thing to stop him.

He let out a soft breath as though disappointed in my question before shaking his head. "No, Loch. If I haven't killed you yet, that should show you I don't intend to. Even after you lied to me so many times, after you worked against me, after you tried to kill me, if none of those were enough to make me want to end you, I doubt there is a thing you could do that would make me willing to lose you."

"What does that mean?"

"I call you little fish because you always seemed so fragile, so insignificant compared to the sharks around you. You said your mother called you Salmon because you always swam upstream, always went against the current no matter how difficult. Well, little fish, trying to stop you has never worked. It seems I will swim upstream with you, no matter how foolish."

And fuck me, because I would have sworn my heart just skipped a beat…

I am in so much trouble.

Chapter Two

Well, isn't this awkward?

I never thought I'd have to sit through another meeting with Gorrin, and suddenly I missed the months he'd been gone.

Don't get me wrong, I was glad I hadn't actually killed him, but somehow being forced into another tense meeting where he would probably be incredibly annoyed with me was not the reunion I'd wished for.

And if I could have, I'd have just stayed in bed longer. It was hard to think there were any better ways to spend our time than another roll — well, not in the hay but on the hard floor? *Damn my vagina for not being able to keep up!*

The spirit was willing, but the body was bruised and exhausted.

So here we were, in Tyrus' place since we'd already pushed our luck by meeting at my place once. It was far less suspicious for us to come here this time.

Yazmor hadn't looked surprised at Gorrin's arrival, but I had no idea if that was just because he generally enjoyed the unexpected or he had some inkling that Gorrin wasn't as dead as I'd thought. I could never put anything past Yazmor.

Hale and Tyrus were a totally different matter, though.

Neither man appeared happy about the turn of events, and their gazes kept flitting to just above Gorrin's shoulders, as if they could see the wings that were safely hidden away.

In fact, other than when he'd shown up—and the time after that—he'd kept his wings out of sight.

Why?

I didn't dare ask, especially not in front of everyone.

"You should have stayed dead," Hale muttered.

"Rude." Yazmor looked toward me, as if checking in. "Right?"

"Yes, Yazmor, that's right. That's pretty rude."

Yazmor's grin was like a wagging tail of a puppy who'd just gotten praised for good behavior.

"Yeah, well, I *meant* it to be rude. We were one fucker down, and now he shows back up like the last few months didn't happen? Like his little game didn't almost fucking crush you?"

An ache started in my chest at his unexpected care.

And just as quickly he put an end to it. "Now he's going to get pity sex all the damn time. It's fucking unfair."

I blew out a long breath, sending up some stupid prayer for patience. It probably wasn't a great idea to be asking shit from a god I planned on overthrowing.

But maybe it was like sex before a break-up—one last bone tossed before it all ended.

"Back to the point," I said.

"Should we really discuss this in front of him?" Tyrus' voice made me aware of just how little he'd said thus far. At my look, he went on. "Gorrin lied to us all about what he truly was. He is connected to Hubis and must have returned to the Plains after what happened. How do we know he wasn't feeding Hubis information this entire time? How can we trust he isn't doing so now? How many times have you ended up in the wrong place at the wrong time, Loch? You can't tell me that his appearance at *this* time isn't suspicious?"

I opened my mouth to tell Tyrus he was wrong, but no words came out. I *wanted* to trust Gorrin, but I really had no good reason to. Everything Tyrus had said was right, after all.

What we were here to do was unprecedented. It was dangerous and difficult and having an unknown involved only added to that danger.

When I said nothing, Gorrin spoke up, his expression showing no signs of hurt. Then again, distrust in the Chasm was pretty much the name of the game. "I understand your concerns, and as much as I wish I could tell you to trust me, I know those would be empty words and nothing more. I have no proof of my intentions or loyalties, after all."

"Are you really trying to say you're loyal to us?" Tyrus lifted his dark eyebrow to call Gorrin an idiot.

And Gorrin's soft snort in response said he read it that way. "Of course not. I still have no issue destroying every one of you three. My loyalty is to Loch, as it has been since she arrived."

"So says the man who almost tore her fucking mind apart," Hale all but snarled, his tone drenched in anger and violence.

Which meant this meeting was headed *way* off course. I knew better than to butt in, though. They had to work this out.

Better they pulled weapons and fought here than ignore it all and have it happen in the middle of our plan, right?

"I know exactly what her mind could take. I would have never pushed her far enough to do any true damage."

"Doesn't change that you hurt her. I don't exactly trust your fucking loyalty when you do that. I've done a lot of shit to her, but I sure as fuck never hurt her like *that*."

His words struck me as *far* less innocent than they sounded. They took me back to the rough sex we'd had a few times, to the way he touched me, the way things often ran that line between pleasure and pain.

I tried to wipe the thought away before anyone could read it on my face, but a glance at a smirking Yazmor said the bastard had noticed.

"I know exactly what this place does to those who are not prepared to survive here. You three understand it as well, have seen others destroyed by it. I did all I did to make her strong enough to survive here," Gorrin said.

"And how'd that fucking work for you?" Hale's lips tipped up on one side, the lopsided grin as good as an insult.

"I may have been short-sighted," Gorrin admitted, his voice softening just a hair. "She has done well for herself in my absence. I am not saying I made the right choices, only that I made the one I believed was right for her best interest. Unlike you, I don't coddle her. You prefer to be the good guy, to have her like you rather than to have her safe. My actions may have been harsh, but they were done for her, no matter how distasteful I may have found them."

And there went that 'I'm wrong and sorry' tone from Gorrin's voice. Honestly, he'd managed it longer than I thought him capable of. Now he'd gone right back to that arrogance, as if challenging Hale to respond.

"You picked what was easiest for *you*." Tyrus had his gaze locked on Gorrin, a threat resting in the darkness there.

I could have drowned in the testosterone in this room.

"You believe it was easy for me? You think I *wanted* her looking at me like I were her enemy? That I enjoyed that distrust in her eyes?"

"I think you liked her keeping a distance, that you enjoyed having control over her," Tyrus said.

"You never had control over her. She ain't yours!" Hale rose to his feet and slammed his palms against the table between us, the sound echoing off the walls.

And, just like that, Tyrus and Gorrin all stood as well.

It left Yazmor and me seated, beside each other.

"Boys will be boys, won't they?" Yazmor shook his head as if watching kids at a park instead of fully grown, immortal men. "It doesn't matter how old they get or how mature they think they are — throw a girl they like into the mix and they turn into elementary school children again."

"Children with blades," I added on.

"At least that makes it interesting."

The three had moved away from the table, standing close enough to not need to yell — not that it stopped them from still raising their voices.

"They're not going to kill one another, right?"

"No." Yazmor paused and pressed his lips together. "Well, *probably* not. No Lord has killed another directly.

It's too difficult and it would throw the balance of power off too much."

"Gorrin isn't a Lord anymore."

He sat up slightly, as if cheered up by that thought. "You're right! Well, then maybe someone *will* kill someone else! I put my money on Tyrus winning."

"Over Hale?"

"Hale's a lot of bluster. Tyrus fights dirty, though, and, since he doesn't look like it, people underestimate him."

I went to argue that but realized what we were doing. "Wait a minute, I'm not taking bets on who gets killed."

"Of course not. We hadn't put up anything yet. We could, though! I'm willing to bet anything. Wait, no, not my crocodile. It doesn't matter how sure I am, I never bet Smiley."

"You named your crocodile Smiley?"

"Of course. We have the same smile."

And, try as I might, I couldn't exactly argue the point... Something about Yazmor's smile always unnerved me, as if he had too many teeth.

Also, had I just accepted he owned a crocodile so easily? I really had gotten myself drawn into the depth of his madness, hadn't I? I no longer even questioned his nonsense.

"We don't have time for this, do we?"

"We're all immortal. Time is the one thing we have in spades. Besides, if you don't let them work this out, it'll just keep coming up. Think of it like siblings bickering. Mommy can come in and tell them to stop it, but the moment she turns her back, they'll just pick it right back up."

"Don't call me Mommy. It's a total mood killer."

But, on the plus side, at least that let me know there were for sure kinks I had no interest in. Somehow that reassured me.

Just then, Hale took a swing at Gorrin, one Gorrin dodged with ease.

I went to stand, but Yazmor grasped my arm to keep me sitting and beside him. "Let them go. They've got to work this out themselves."

I ground my molars together but did as he said. Without something like my dagger, it wasn't like they were likely to kill one another too fast.

"You don't deserve her, not after what you did," Hale shouted.

"You have no say in what happens between Loch and me," Gorrin answered, her voice calm enough to enrage Hale further.

"I've been here the whole fucking time, so I do have a say. I helped pick her up after what you put her through. I saw her fucking destroyed."

Tyrus got between them, but that worked as well as was to be expected. What had started as an attempt to separate them quickly turned into just a very violent threesome when Hale swung again and caught Tyrus.

And just like that, the three gave up pretenses.

I could hardly keep track of the fight, their movements were so fast. They each fought so differently, too.

Hale was all brawn and reckless fury. He hit hard and never backed down, as if his movements were controlled by his anger and little else. Gorrin, however, fought with foresight and consideration. He dodged and countered, each move well thought and executed. He managed to fight without seeming to feel a thing.

And Tyrus did exactly as Yazmor had claimed. I'd never seen him this way before, as a man who actually fought. He'd always used his brain and his power, and the few times he'd physically engaged with anyone, it had been so quick and decisive that it had been over before it really started. Now I got a glimpse of him like this, and Yazmor had nailed it.

He fought dirty. He waited for the other two to get distracted, then took advantage of every opening. He delivered a strike to Gorrin's side when he blocked a hit from Hale, then swiped Hale's foot from beneath him when Hale had kicked at Gorrin.

"You see? Despite that fancy suit, Tyrus grew up having to protect himself. He's tougher than he looks and doesn't mind using that to his advantage."

Sure enough, after a few more moments, Tyrus had both other men on the ground. Not that it hadn't cost Tyrus—he looked exhausted, panting hard like I'd never seen before.

Tyrus shifted his gaze toward me, a fire there that made me shiver. It held a promise, a need as if we were thousands of years ago, just animals who wanted to fuck after a good fight.

Except Yazmor broke that moment—as he so often did—by tossing his arm over my shoulders. "Nope. We already postponed this meeting once for a quickie. If we put it off each time you all got turned on, we'll never finish. I mean, I guess *you* will."

That seemed to wake Tyrus up, because he blinked slowly then shook his head. "This is foolish," he muttered as if to chastise himself and took his seat again.

Hale and Gorrin picked themselves up, but a flicker in their eyes said they weren't quite finished. No doubt one reason Tyrus had taken the top spot was because they'd both been more concerned about each other than him. Next time, that wouldn't go quite the same way.

Once everyone had sat again — bruises, busted lips and all — I tried to get us back to the task at hand.

"Look — we all need one another. What we're wanting to do here, it won't be easy, and like I said before, it isn't even possible if we don't all work together."

"You need the four Demon Lords," Tyrus corrected me. "Gorrin is no longer a Lord, thus holds no souls. That means he doesn't actually add to this."

I sighed at his short-sighted view. No doubt that was more because of his own personal feelings rather than the facts, since only an idiot would claim that Tyrus wasn't a phenomenal tactician. "Are you really going to tell me that if we're going to the Plains, if we're going to attack Hubis, that having an angel isn't useful? Because last I checked, none of *us* have been to the Plains. We don't know shit about it, about Hubis, but Gorrin does."

I'd hit the nail on the head there, since Tyrus pressed his lips into a tight line and dropped his gaze to the table. He might not admit I was right, but his actions proved that he knew it.

I'd take that as a win.

"We've got enough shit we're fighting against here — the last thing we need is to fight between us as well."

Thankfully, the three of them at least managed to look ashamed. I doubted they actually felt it, but it was like a fake orgasm.

I appreciated the effort, at least.

"We can fight again when we're done, but for now? We're in this together."

"And just what is *this*?" Gorrin asked. "You have decided on a rather aggressive idea, but I have yet to hear an actual plan. Do you have such a thing or is this all wishful thinking?"

"I figured we'd work out a plan together. Five heads are better than one, right?" At the look I got in return, it didn't seem they agreed. I sighed and gave up the whole, 'fake it till you make it' thing. "Okay, I admit I don't know much about the Plains or how exactly you kill a god. Will my dagger work?"

"Yes," Yazmor answered. "The dagger can kill him. The problem is getting close enough. Hubis has the same amount of power of all four of us put together, so facing him one-on-one wouldn't work. He could probably stop you before you could use the weapon. You'd have to get close enough to take him unaware to stand a chance."

"Kylie said he'd come here to deal with Azael's death. What about then?"

Gorrin shook his head. "Hubis is exceedingly careful when he comes here. He will have an angel with him, and he will be on guard. This is enemy territory to him—you'll have no chance here."

"Does he go to Earth?"

"No. He dislikes Earth nearly as much as he dislikes the Chasm."

I let out a long breath when the only option became clear. "So it has to happen in the Plains?"

Gorrin nodded. "That is the only option. However, you going there is a larger issue."

"Can't I just go through that nifty little arch in the meeting room?" As I said that, I recalled the way Azael had passed through it, the light that had come through it, the strange desire to follow.

"No. Because you sold your soul, that path is blocked to you."

"There *has* to be another way."

Gorrin said nothing, and his expression suggested it was bad news.

Yazmor spoke up, his voice soft. "There *is* another way."

Gorrin swung his gaze over, narrowing his eyes. "No."

"It's the only option."

"It isn't an option—it's suicide."

"Perhaps—perhaps not. That's up to Loch, isn't it?"

The two stared at one another as if they had their own private conversation with that look. The tension said they knew *exactly* what the other meant.

"You care to let me in on this?"

Gorrin sighed and yanked his gaze from Yazmor, staring instead at the floor, making it perfectly clear he didn't intend to answer but also wouldn't stop Yazmor from doing so.

"There's another way to the Plains. Just like the Forgotten Caves exist outside of our reality, like little pockets, there's another route that anyone can take. We call it the Path."

"And, given Gorrin's reaction, I'm going to guess it isn't a flower-lined road with bunnies and shit, right?"

"I've heard there are bunnies," Yazmor said, "but the bunnies are carnivorous and only eat prey while it's still alive."

"Are they still bunnies then?" Hale's expression had twisted into disgust.

"They're actually cuter than regular bunnies, believe it or not. Fluffier. I hear you can make sweaters from their fur!" Yazmor tapped his finger against his chin. "Maybe we can shear a couple on the way..."

"Focus," Gorrin snapped as thought entirely over Yazmor's nonsense. "The Path exists at the far end of the known Chasm."

I looked over at Tyrus. "You said there was no end, that anyone who went that way either didn't come back or came back mad."

"I've heard rumors of the Path, but I know of nothing specific or reliable."

Gorrin went on, each word slow as though he had to fight himself to get them out. "The Chasm isn't endless. It exists here, and at either end, there is a walkway in the rock wall. One goes to Earth and one goes to the Plains. If the Path were easy to traverse, damned would constantly attempt to make the trip and go to the Plains. Instead, the Path is perilous. However, if a person can survive it, they will arrive in the Plains no matter the state of their soul. At least, that is the story."

I considered that, the story sounding like some bullshit fairytale where to get through a forest a person had to stay on the road.

Then again, I'd learned that every fairytale, every legend came from some kernel of truth.

"So we have to go through that Path to make it to the Plains, then attack Hubis when he isn't expecting us? Well, when can we leave?"

"Not yet," Gorrin said. "Hubis will come to the Chasm in the next few days to deal with the aftermath of Azael. If you are not here at that time, he'll know something is wrong. Instead, we have to set things up so he won't miss any of you. This will not work unless we can take him when he isn't expecting it."

"Still, we have a plan, right?"

"A bad plan," Gorrin muttered.

I grinned at his complaining tone. "That's fine. I am an expert in bad plans!"

And the groans of each of the men said they didn't disagree at all.

* * * *

Gorrin

Walking through the halls of what had been my home for so many years struck me as odd. I never really believed I'd return here, not after everything that had happened. In fact, if I'd have been forced to discuss my feelings about this place before coming back, I'd have said it didn't matter to me.

Stone and walls and barren floors had meant nothing to me. It had been a place where I kept things, a place from which I went from, a base of operations, but nothing else.

Or so I would have said.

Why was it then that walking through these familiar halls made my chest tight? Why did each turn feel oddly familiar? Why did they make a strange warmth grow inside me?

Even more than that was the sight of Loch walking ahead of me.

I had, of course, known she'd taken over. I'd watched over her, seen her flailing, but somehow that was different than actually standing beside her now. It forced me to recognize that she had truly taken my place.

It wasn't jealousy that I felt—at least, I didn't believe so. I had no animosity about it, didn't want to take it back, yet it made me consider her in a different way.

She had been someone I had felt the need to protect. I had wanted to save her from herself, from the pain I knew had waited for her, but now?

Now she could stand on equal footing with me.

I still recalled the pain of the knife she had buried in me, the agony as it had nearly killed me. No, not just the pain, but the shock. I had never thought she would have that will inside her.

Leave it to Loch to manage to outsmart me, to go further than I would have ever thought her capable of.

She had planted her feet where she stood, and no matter how hard I pushed, how much force I exerted, she had refused to move. I couldn't help but respect that level of fortitude.

And yet watching her in her new position made me feel nostalgic. I wore my old outfit, the one I had from my first days as an angel, the one Hubis had given to me. I had cherished it so much at first, as if it were a promise to myself, a command of who I was to be.

Yet, as years passed, no matter how I put it on each day, I struggled to feel that same pride. I had lost myself along the way and wearing this uniform did not help at all.

We crossed into my office—no, Loch's office, I reminded myself. The room was much the same, with the basic items all as they had been before.

The well in the corner, the desk, the shelves, the couch.

A twitch in my cheek threatened to turn into a smile at the memory of that couch, at how Myers had given me a sharp look when I'd asked for it. Never before had I cared for having any true furniture in my office since I didn't want anyone to stay long enough to need it.

Yet somehow, soon after Loch had arrived, I'd asked for it. The sight of her standing had bothered me, especially when it forced her to leave before I wanted her to. She hadn't mentioned the arrival of it, though a line in between her eyebrows had said she'd noticed how strange it was.

"I thought you would have changed more." I noted a few missing items, such as books and pieces of décor. "Though some things have been moved."

"I didn't get rid of it," she said, voice soft in what almost sounded like an apology. "It's all packed safe and sound."

"Why? It wasn't as if you thought I would return for it."

"It felt wrong to get rid of it. It was like…like doing that admitted you weren't coming back."

Which brought me to another topic. "You visited my grave."

She flinched, and it took me back to the sight of her on her knees, to the pained words that had left her. That had tested my resolve more than anything else, the desire to take her into my arms nearly having overcome my good sense.

"You saw that?" As soon as she asked, she paused, then let out a quiet laugh. "I felt like you were there, like you could hear me. It's rude to eavesdrop, you know?"

"Is it truly eavesdropping if you were talking to me in the first place?"

"You just love to twist things to make yourself right." Even though her words chastised me, her tone lacked any true censure. "Do you have any idea how much pain I was in?"

I shook my head. "I believed you would rebound quickly. I was certain you would feel some guilt, since you have always been soft-hearted, but I thought it would only take a few days to move past it."

She peered over at me, her expression dubious. It was strange to think she still truly didn't understand. After everything we had been through, did she still think she didn't matter to me?

Then again, Loch was a stubborn woman. She excelled at failing to see anything she didn't wish to see, at believing the world was whatever suited her fancy at that moment.

"You really don't get it," she whispered.

Her words, so similar to what I had been thinking, surprised me. "What do you mean?"

"You don't have any idea how hurt I was, do you?"

"You would have gotten over it. Time heals all wounds, or at least removes the memories so the wounds no longer hurt. If I had stayed out of your life, I knew you would recover. Any guilt you felt would drift away and you would move on. So I kept my distance, giving you that time. When I saw you had gone to the grave, I risked it. I didn't expect to see you still so bothered."

"Then you're a fucking idiot," she snapped. "I was drowning. I barely left my room for a month afterward. I closed my eyes never wanting them to open again, praying to a God I knew didn't give a fuck about me to let the darkness swallow me up. I actually thought if that happened, maybe I could follow you and see you again somewhere."

Her words sliced into me, worse because I could hear the truth in them. Had I been so wrong? I'd expected some sadness—mostly due to guilt—but the depths of her agony shocked me.

How could I so misunderstand things? Had she truly suffered that deeply?

One look into her face told me the truth of it.

I wanted to reach out, but I stopped myself. Somehow, I didn't feel as if I had a right to do so.

The moment of madness I'd felt when I'd slept with her, when I had allowed my passions to take me, to blind me to reason, that had retreated and now I had my impeccable good sense again.

I had no right to touch her.

She sighed, as if she read my thoughts, and turned her back on me. "You really are an idiot."

At the moment, I struggled to deny her claim.

Instead, I went to the well, peering into the familiar surface, the place where I had spent too many hours before. "You've done well here."

"I don't know about that."

"You have. Well, other than allowing a stuffed animal to hear petitioners for a while, at least."

She lifted one of her eyebrows. "Was that a joke?"

"Of course not. I don't joke." While my words came out deadpan, she smiled, telling me she heard the truth beneath it.

And it warmed me, made me feel as if we still had some connection between us, some understanding.

"You even managed to survive Azael."

"Only because someone helped me."

"Kylie only did so because of you. She would never have shown herself in that way if it wasn't for your influence, for what you had done and risked. Do not take that lightly—she has run and hidden and avoided her past and her truth for a very long time. Her stepping up when she did was nothing short of a miracle."

Which again reminded me of the true strength Loch had.

She changed others. She led not by force or power or manipulation, but by behaving in such a pure way, others had to face their own truths.

She altered each person she came into contact with— me included.

"I don't know how to act around you," she admitted softly.

"You never cared about that before."

"Before it was clear. You were the Demon Lord and I was owned by you."

I snorted softly. "You never behaved as if I were your master, no matter how much easier on us both that might have been." Even as I said that, I knew I never wished for her to behave in that way. I had never wanted her to be a slave, even if I had worked so hard to force her to accept her place. "We are equals now. This"—I waved my hands to indicate not just this room but the entire residence—"is yours. You gained it rightfully."

"I feel like I stole it, like I don't deserve any of it. Fuck, I don't really *want* it."

"Too bad. I don't want it back, and I couldn't take it back even if I did. Unless I wished to take a demon form again, I would be unable to truly rule here. Besides, you don't need me anymore. You have grown into your own, have learned to rule it in your own way."

She blew out a sharp breath, then sat on the couch. "So what now?"

"Now?"

"You're back, but what does that even mean?"

"I don't know," I admitted and sat beside her. "I am not a man used to uncertainty, yet you make me uncertain. We have a plan on how to proceed, but I don't know what that means between you and I."

"So I guess we're both in it together, huh? Both lost as fuck."

I reached out slowly, my gaze forward, unwilling to look directly at her. She felt like the sun, something too bright for me to stare at, something that would destroy me if I forced myself to do so. Instead, I set my hand on top of hers and squeezed. "I am not used to being lost, but if I have to be, I think being lost with you doesn't bother me so much."

She turned her hand and laced her fingers with me, returning my touch by squeezing my hand back. The touch was hesitant, yet reached deep into me.

It wasn't a clear answer, but I'd take it. It was certainly more than I thought I could ever have.

Chapter Three

I never figured having Yazmor by my side would make me feel better. He wasn't exactly what I'd call a comforting presence most of the time.

In fact, thinking back on everything that had happened, I was pretty sure he usually made things far worse. The memory of our trip to the pharmacist's house came back to me, when he'd chased a cat while I'd fought off a pantsless pervert.

Still, walking through the dark toward the cavern where I needed to take Kylie's necklace made me admit— *I miss him.*

If nothing else, he gave me something to focus on other than the sound of my own steps echoing off the stone.

However, I was supposedly a Demon Lord, so I should have been brave enough to do shit on my own. It meant I'd tucked the innocuous-looking necklace into my pocket and headed for the Forgotten Caves all by my lonesome.

The trip felt as if it took longer than it had before, probably because each little noise made me jump. I hadn't seen anything the last time — such as cave spiders or bullshit like that — but that didn't mean they weren't here.

Maybe they saw Yazmor as one of their own and had left us alone, but with me by myself now, they were more than willing to take a chunk out of me.

Stop freaking yourself out!

The Chasm was scary enough without me needing to come up with new things to fear.

According to Kylie, all I had to do was toss this thing into the right cave and everything would go back to the way it had been before. Of course, that wasn't quite as easy as I'd hoped, since the Caves weren't exactly easy to figure out. It seemed that wherever a person wanted to go would appear — eventually.

What a shitty system. Why couldn't the doorway appear right when I entered the Caves instead of making me wander around like a religious nut job for hours first?

At least I knew I wouldn't miss it, though. It seemed that only the places I wanted to go would light up, giving me access to them.

Finally, a familiar light glow caught my attention up ahead.

About time.

I jogged the short distance, then crossed the threshold as I had before. The same strangely colored sun, the same weird grass all told me I'd found the right place.

The necklace felt oddly warm in my palm still, and when I pulled it from my pocket, I got a good look at it for the first time. It looked like a crystal, and I rubbed my thumb over the top.

Why would Kylie risk so much for something so small? Coming here had been risky enough but taking this had caused the real problems. Her words came back to me, when she'd said it was because she needed a reminder of who she had been.

I wanted to push that away as stupid, but I couldn't quite do it. I wasn't nearly as old as she was, hadn't lost as much, yet I could sort of understand. I recalled going back to Earth, seeing Kylie for the first time after so many years.

That reminder from my past had hit me hard, made me feel less lost. It had been like a punch from a life that had ended for me, and it had meant something to me.

Was that how Kylie felt? Had she been adrift until she'd held this? Lost in a world that wasn't hers, with everything moving around her but nothing to hold on to?

There was still so much I didn't understand about Kylie, like her connection to Hubis, but I knew better than to pry into it. She'd done more for me than I had a right to ask her for already.

I could have chucked the necklace, but that felt wrong. Instead, I kneeled and cleared the leaves away from a spot on the ground. Once I made a neat little circle, I carefully placed the necklace in the center. Even if it wasn't exactly real, even if Kylie couldn't keep it, this mattered to her. It deserved that respect.

After setting it there, I rose to my feet and took a few steps backward. This would help prevent any more issues with the possessions of humans, which bought us time. Kylie had sacrificed this for us, for our plan, and I wouldn't let that go to waste.

I took a deep breath, then turned to leave. There was nothing else for me to do here, nothing but watching the echo of a dead world. It was like staring at a corpse and it only made me consider my own future, the future of my own world. If we overthrew Hubis, what would that mean? Someone else would take his position, but would our world eventually end up just another cave here?

I stepped out of the cavern, but before I turned to head back toward the entrance, a light farther down caught my attention. It was so dim I wasn't sure I even saw it at first.

I couldn't make sense of it. Kylie had explained that only the places we wanted to go would appear, and I was pretty fucking sure I didn't want to go anywhere else but Kylie's world.

Then again, I often didn't think I wanted to drink water, but once I did, I realized I was one dehydrated bitch. Was that the case here?

Before I'd even come up with whatever reasoning I'd use to convince myself that heading for some weird light in the Forgotten Caves of hell was a good idea, my feet already took me in that direction. The light was farther away than I would have thought, given the light that spilled from the doorway was usually so muted.

It took a good five minutes of walking to get to it— I'd stopped expecting hell to make any sense. Just like before, only a general light spilled from the doorway, not showing me what occurred past there.

"Sure," I said to myself, the sound of my voice making me feel as if I weren't alone. "Go into the creepy cavern that appeared out of nowhere when you're all alone. What could possibly go wrong with that?" Even as I chided myself, I drew my hands into fists and stepped through the doorway.

Hubis and Kylie's world had been impossibly bright, making me squint against the sun. That was a far cry from what I now found.

Instead, the entire landscape was bathed in darkness, so even the colors that did appear were deep and saturated. The ground was rocky and uneven, with sharp edges jutting out and cliffs everywhere. The sky was black, making the Chasm seem cheerful in comparison.

In fact, this world seemed more hellish than even the Chasm.

In the distance, things moved in the darkness. They were spindly, elongated and moving with a fluidity that unnerved me. It was like everything in my body said, 'fuck this nonsense' on an instinctual level.

A snap to my left had me twisting to find a huge creature, something that dwarfed me and reminded me of an ancient gnarled tree. It was black with deep red streaks and violet eyes.

I felt like I'd seen those eyes before, but I would have remembered the fuck out of something like *that*. It was a nightmare creature, something someone thought up on some bad acid trip.

It didn't look at me — thank fuck — but instead at a smaller creature that scurried along the ground like an unreasonably large spider.

The large creature reached out with a hand that looked more like branches than the limbs of a living thing. Everything started to short out, as if the world melted around me. Sound popped and clicked, like static on a bad television channel.

I *knew* I'd experienced this before. It had been outside of that pharmacist's house. My heart pounded hard as I put it together, as I experienced the same fear I'd felt back then.

No, that can't be it.

I forced my legs to move, backing away from the thing, from the truth that was so obvious all of a sudden.

The power he had. The way he didn't fit in. How he knew so much more than he should have.

I wanted nothing more than to get out of here, than to rush back to somewhere safe, than to forget everything I'd seen here even if I feared the sight had tattooed itself onto my brain so deeply I couldn't ever rid myself of it.

I bumped into something, stopping my retreat and making me spin in a panicked rush.

"So you know the truth." Yazmor smiled down at me with that grin with too many teeth, as he blocked my escape path.

This is very, very bad.

Yazmor

Somehow, seeing Loch amongst the ruins of my world struck me as more meaningful than I expected. It was a strange juxtaposition between my past and my future, between what came before and what was yet to come.

Around her stood an echo of my world, the place I had come from, the place that had formed me. The jagged rocks, the deep hues—it all spoke to my core. It called to me, whispered for me to release my hold on the current world and let it all drift away.

She stumbled, her foot catching on one of the many cracks in the rocks. I reached out to catch her, but she yanked away as though I were far more frightening than falling.

And when my gaze moved to the side, to sight of another of my kind, I could hardly blame her.

She hit the ground and scooted away, the green of her hair standing out against the other colors. In fact, *all* of her stood out. The drab colors, the harsh lines, it was nothing like her pale skin, her bright green hair. She was a beacon of light in a place made of darkness.

Her chest rose and fell as she panted, moving away until her back struck a rock, until she had no more room to run.

I had never wanted her to look at me like this, to know the truth, but we had moved past that. I knew better than to fight against the impossible. While so much of the universe was in flux, time wasn't. What happened could not be undone—people couldn't go backward, no matter how much we wished it.

The sight of my old world spoke that well.

I lowered myself until I sat on the ground, trying to show I had no plans to harm her. I could have waved my hand and sent away the echo of another of my kind, but why?

She'd seen it. Getting rid of it wouldn't erase the memory. If anything, terrors like that grew in a person's mind, becoming more terrifying with time.

"Why didn't you tell me?" she asked, her gaze locked on my chest.

It was as if she wanted to keep me in her sight but couldn't bear to truly look at me, either.

"Why would I? You never told me if you were born vaginally or by C-section. You never told me the hair color you had at birth. What we are when we are born, where we come from, those things don't really matter after a while."

The narrowing of her eyes said she didn't agree. Except, rather than her telling me off as I expected, she remained silent.

The silence hurt. It was born of fear, and it tasted of ash and rot. I didn't care for it one bit. I missed her sass, her snarky retorts, the way she had looked at me as if I were safe.

Still, pressing too hard would only make her more fearful, so I kept my tone light. "I told you I was old."

"I thought that meant like, a thousand years or something." She paused, then let out a hollow laugh. "What's happened to me when a thousand years isn't a big deal? So, just so we're all on the same page, you're a remnant and this is your world, right?"

I nodded, seeing no reason not to come right out and tell her the truth. "Yep. This was home sweet, fiery home for me." As I said that, I forced myself to once again look around. "It's been a long time since I've come here."

"You never wanted to?"

"I wouldn't say that. I've spent a long time looking in the Forgotten Caves, but I never saw much of a reason to return to my own. It always felt pointless. This is gone — reminding myself of it would be like keeping an amputated limb just to look at." I shrugged. "Besides, each time a remnant returns the echo of their own world here, it becomes harder to leave it, harder to adjust. I've always excelled at letting go of what is lost."

"You don't miss it?"

The question surprised me, though I wasn't sure why. It was a perfectly normal question, wasn't it? It took me a moment to figure out why.

Because no one had ever asked me that — the reason being that I'd never spoken to anyone else about it. I'd never truly sat down with anyone and explained my past, discussed what had happened.

Others knew, of course, but knowing was difficult from talking about it.

"I miss it," I admitted, my voice so soft that I worried at first she might not have heard me. Still, I went on. "Missing it is pointless, though. It's gone."

"Are there any more of you?"

I shook my head. "No. There were when it was first destroyed, but they were lost with time. Most gave up, the change too extreme, the loss too great. They just…let go. The one who remade the world survived, but only until the next took over."

"You mean Hubis?"

A soft laugh escaped me at how sweetly naïve she seemed. "No. I'm not from the cycle before Hubis. I told you there had been countless iterations where someone decided they knew best, where they reshaped everything according to their whims. Some made it longer than others, but they came down to the same fate. The only thing that's constant is change."

She ran her tongue along her bottom lip, the action leaving a shine there. "How many worlds have you seen, then?"

I shrugged. "I have no idea. I stopped counting by the time it hit triple digits. It didn't seem worthwhile to keep track any longer. Some I participated in, some I just watched. The reason I've seen so much of the Forgotten Caves is because I lived through most of it. I doubt there is a remnant that exists who has survived more than I have." The words stuck in my throat, the truth I rarely acknowledged. "None alive even know of my world. I am completely alone and have been for longer than any other being has even existed." Even saying that out loud hurt.

I'd spent so long hiding this fact, so long running from it, that to admit it so clearly felt like tearing away my flesh and exposing raw nerves to the air.

I expected Loch to tell me off, to rush past me and out of this glimpse of the real me, of the place I came from. I wouldn't stop her, nor would I blame her for it. It was, by all accounts, the smart choice.

I kept my gaze down, trying to free her to do so, giving her the chance to escape.

She rose to her feet, tiny rocks grinding beneath the soles of her shoes. *Of course she'll run. Who wouldn't?*

I closed my eyes, wanting to block it out, not wanting to have to watch it at least. If I watched, could I let her go?

Except, a weight settled into my lap, causing my eyes to snap open. Loch set her palms on my cheeks, staring into my eyes with a determination that shows just what a threat she could be.

"You're not alone," she whispered, then rested her forehead against mine. "I won't let you be alone, not again."

And just like that, for the first time since I'd lost everything, I *felt* like I wasn't alone. A future with Loch almost seemed worth the time it had taken to get here, as if all the pain and suffering along the way had been worth it.

If it took waiting an eternity to get here…well, she was more than worth it.

Chapter Four

Loch

Walking toward the meeting room felt like I'd gone back to high school and was making my way to the vice-principal's office.

Never the principal. Good kids went there for praise, and that sure as fuck hadn't been me. Instead, I got the dreaded call to the vice-principal, who dealt with the screw-ups like myself, the lost causes where, after a while, he'd stopped even scolding me.

He'd just hand me a suspension notice, finding me not even worth the effort of trying to reform.

I really wish Hubis would think the same.

Somehow, I doubted I was getting off with a few days at home for this stunt.

I could almost hear the other Lords in my head.

"You will be fine, just hold your temper."

"Chin up and show 'em why they shouldn't fuck with you."

"Did you know dolphins use pufferfish toxin to get high?"

It was easy to guess who would have said what...

Except I couldn't actually hear them since I was by myself. No matter how much better I'd have felt if we had arrived together, I'd known I couldn't do that.

I needed to stand on my own. I'd gained power equal to the other Lords, so I needed to behave that way. Hale and Tyrus didn't go to meetings together like girls going to the bathroom.

Yazmor would have arrived together, but he did as he pleased no matter what.

Not to mention that we didn't need Hubis to get suspicious, and arriving like some little gang would let him in on the fact that we were getting along better than he was used to.

The path to the meeting room had never felt quite so long, and I swallowed down my anxiety over it. Hubis wouldn't let me off too easily. He wouldn't show up and say, "oh well, not a big deal!"

Kylie seemed sure he wouldn't kill me, but who the fuck knew? We were talking about someone who had destroyed his entire world, everything he knew. Why would he give a fuck about taking out some green-haired annoyance?

I tugged softly at my shirt, sighing as I looked down at my outfit. I'd fucked off with the whole dressing-up thing. I'd tried it a time or two, but as it turned out, a fancy set of clothes didn't change who I was. It didn't make me smarter or stronger or better able to handle all the shit that got thrown at me.

So instead of forcing myself into clothes that didn't suit me, I'd told myself — *'self — fuck that nonsense.'*

It left me in a baggy T-shirt knotted at one side and a pair of boyfriend jeans that hung loose on my hips, leaving a strip of skin between the two items. I might not *look* like a ruler in hell, but I did look like myself, and I was *far* more comfortable than I would have been in something else.

That counted for something, didn't it?

When I finally arrived at the meeting place, I found myself the last to arrive of the Lords. In addition to the four of us, Myers was already there, as was Kota. Hale and Yazmor hadn't brought anyone, but they usually didn't, so it didn't surprise me.

I forced myself forward and to the open seat, ignoring everyone else. For once, they did the same to me. Even Yazmor stayed quiet, not chiming in with any smart-ass comments.

And fuck, but I missed that. It made me feel alone, even when I knew I wasn't. We'd discussed this beforehand, had gone over how we needed to act in a certain way to prevent Hubis from raising an eyebrow.

Normally, the Demon Lords wouldn't give a fuck about one another. They never had before. If we suddenly acted all buddy-buddy, it would make Hubis suspicious and, worse, might even have him placing some of the blame on their shoulders.

I had made the choices that led us here. I'd wanted to save Jay and had gone there. I'd faced off against Azael. Even if I hadn't been the one to actually kill him, if I hadn't gone, he'd never have died.

So even if the others wanted to bear some of that responsibility, I couldn't allow that. Instead, I kept my gaze forward as I sat in the uncomfortable chair and waited.

Of *course* Hubis would be late. Then again, the last time the meeting had been unexpected, only announced when he'd arrived. This time we knew about it.

It took another long, tense few minutes before the archway lit up. Just seeing that made me want to rush forward, to go through that. Was that something instinctual or was it just me that felt that way?

I had a feeling that plan wouldn't do much for me, though, so I stayed put. A shadow appeared in the doorway, indistinct at first, but slowly taking form until a person I didn't recognize walked through and into the room.

Large wings told me it was the angel Gorrin had said would come. It took me back to Azael, to the memory of him as he'd snapped that woman's neck, his glee as he'd hurt me.

My immediate response was balanced against the memory of Gorrin, of the way he'd touched me so gently. As much as I wanted to hate all angels, to see them as the cruelty of Azael, Gorrin reminded me that wasn't fair.

It was like blaming all humans for how shitty Gunnar and I were.

So I tried to hold back that immediate dislike.

The angel peered around the room in a quick sweep. Checking for danger? It reminded me of what Gorrin had told me, that there was no way to attack Hubis here. Clearly, he had his guard up, especially after Azael's death. Having someone's right-hand man die would put anyone on edge, even if they didn't particularly care for them.

If someone killed Myers, I might breathe a little easier as the nagging and stress in my life went down, but I'd also know to watch my back.

After another moment, Hubis stepped through the doorway, and just the sight of him made me tense.

He appeared the same, like a grunge band reject, but his eyes held a sharpness they hadn't before. Well, other than when he'd made the meeting room a blizzard last time.

He looked around the room, but his gaze didn't stop on Yazmor, Hale or Tyrus. Instead, he passed by them as though they were invisible to him, like they were nothing but furniture in the room.

The reason was clear when his gaze stopped right on me.

And *boy* was that a lot of hatred in his eyes. It wasn't hatred like an enemy, but more like a pest. It was the look I'd given to cockroaches when I'd seen them at night after turning on the light in one of the many filthy apartments I'd lived in back before I'd died.

I didn't flinch under that look, though—I refused to give him that satisfaction. I needed to walk the line between accepting whatever he wanted to do without looking weak. I had to appear worthy to hold the position of Demon Lord, strong enough to keep the order here, but not so strong or difficult to make him think I'd stand against him.

Of course, I'd juggled men's egos my whole fucking life, so doing it again now wasn't anything new for me.

Hubis said nothing as he went to his seat, the angel taking a spot behind him like a feathery guard dog.

No one spoke at first. Then again, what were we supposed to say?

This was the equivalent of Mom coming into the room to scold us all, and it would have been stupid for us to say shit. *Never* admit to anything.

I'd learned my lesson on that one after apologizing for things the other person hadn't even realized had happened.

So, nope, Hubis would have to get this party started.

Eventually, after using the silence like a weapon, he spoke. "I assume you all know why we're here?"

"Because you missed us?" Yazmor asked. If anyone else had said that, I would have glared, but what was the point of doing that with Yazmor?

Especially because it would seem weird if he didn't say something like that. Nothing would have been more suspicious or given us away faster than Yazmor acting like a mature adult.

Hubis didn't rise to the occasion. Understanding that Yazmor was a remnant now made me wonder if Hubis ignored him because he didn't care, because he was used to it, or because he knew just how old Yazmor actually was. Whatever the reason, Hubis went on as though Yazmor hadn't said a word. "Azael was slain. The cause for that sits here, in this room. Something like that cannot go unpunished."

"I didn't kill him," I blurted out, regretting the words the second they left my lips. Hadn't I *just* told myself not to admit to shit? By saying that I was already outing myself as knowing I was the one involved.

Then again, I'd never taken good advice, *especially* my own.

Hubis didn't smile, but a slight twitch in his cheek told me he'd caught my mistake. Why was it that I felt like a mouse scurrying around in front of cat who was just playing with me?

"It would not have occurred had you not been involved. Such errors in judgment cannot happen again, which means I need to ensure you understand the severity of your mistake."

And wow, I had never heard words that sounded so proper on the surface come across as quite so threatening.

Still, I tried to respond calmly so he couldn't tell my heart was beating like I'd downed a handful of ADHD meds. "All I did was try to deal with a problem. I got word that a bunch of people were dying and I thought maybe damned had possessed a bunch of humans. Isn't that what you asked me to deal with?"

He narrowed his eyes. *Oh, so he doesn't like people talking back?* Why did that make me want to do it all the more?

"You were told to send back damned—not to look into the cause. You kept ignoring your specific orders to do as you pleased, and because of that, an angel is gone."

And a lot of humans are alive.

If he wanted me to feel bad, well, fuck him.

Still, no matter what I said or what I thought, this would only go one way—with Hubis getting his pound of skin in retribution, so he could walk away feeling superior and like he'd regained his power.

Which meant arguing with him would do nothing. Kylie's words echoed in my head, her warning not to press Hubis. At the end of the day, Hubis had every ability to wipe me from existence if he wanted to, and he answered to no one. It meant I needed to shut up and stop making things worse for myself.

So I pressed my lips together and bowed my head slightly, a sign that I submitted to him.

I'd played this game before. I'd handed my pride to people on a silver platter because it was for the best. If I could do that with fuckwits who lacked enough brain cells to rub together, I could do it for God, right?

"I've considered what the correct response to this is. It is a rather unprecedented event. We have lost very few angels ever. It means I took time to evaluate the situation. This entire problem stemmed from you being careless, from you misunderstanding the world or your place in it. You opposed the order because you do not understand why that order was in place. I could simply punish you, but that would solve nothing. For that reason, I intend to educate you instead."

Well, that sounds ominous...

"If you kill her," Tyrus said, his voice blank and careful. No doubt he'd done that so Hubis didn't suspect he actually cared about me rather that the problems my absence would cause. "The souls bound to her will splinter and that power will no longer be consolidated. It would cause a significant amount of chaos in the Chasm."

Hubis shifted his gaze to Tyrus as though having just noticed he was even there. "I have no intention to kill her. In fact, she will not be physically harmed at all. Instead, it will be a much-needed re-education that will serve her well in the future."

And wow did I want to opt the fuck out of whatever he had planned. It felt like a creepy guy assuring me he had a wonderful date planned in his basement.

I would much prefer to not attend that.

However, I doubted Hubis was about to take "no thanks" as an answer, so I kept my mouth firmly shut.

"But—" Tyrus went on.

I shot him a loaded look, trying to tell him to shut the fuck up. We knew going into this that there would be a price to pay, one I would have to shoulder on my own. Him getting involved wouldn't save me—it would only ensure I suffered for nothing if we made Hubis suspicious.

He must have understood my meaning, because he pressed his lips together and went silent.

"Let's get it over with," I said. "I'm ready."

"I doubt that." Hubis said that with a level of menace that made me gulp.

Suddenly I didn't think I was ready, either, especially when everything around me went black.

Hale

Loch collapsed, slumping over in her chair and nearly falling from it. All the times we had discussed acting like we didn't give a fuck about one another went out the window at that sight.

I'd never been great at holding my temper or following a plan, but even my meager attempt was fucked the moment I saw Loch unconscious. I was at her side in a blink, catching her before she slipped entirely from the chair and hit the floor.

She still breathed, which let me do so, too. Still, the only time her passing out was okay in my book was if it happened after I gave her a particularly spectacular orgasm. That certainly wasn't the case here.

I pulled Loch into my arms, her head lolling against my chest in a lax way that drove my temper up. Fuck, I wanted to do something, which in my life meant to draw blood from whoever was at fault.

But, given the person at fault was the fucker seated in the seat there, I didn't have much I could do.

"What the fuck is wrong with her?" I asked, not bothering to tone down my accusation at all.

Hubis blinked slowly, as though coming to. That didn't bode well for whatever was happening. "She is learning her lesson."

"Which means fuck all to me," I snapped.

If Loch hadn't been unconscious, she would have kicked me for responding that way. Of course, that only served to remind me that she wasn't conscious and that it was all that fucker's fault.

Talk about a vicious cycle of blame there.

Hubis rose from his seat as if nothing had happened. He peered at Loch, and something deep in the recesses of his eyes that made me want to shield her from his view. "She will wake in a few hours." He didn't wait for a response before he turned and walked toward the arch, passing through the light there without another word. His feathery minion went with him, leaving Loch in my arms.

Loch flinched in her sleep, and a broken sound left her throat. It was one of fear, of pain, and it tore at me. I wanted to crawl inside her skull and destroy whatever would make her loose a sound like that, but I couldn't.

Tyrus approached, setting his hand on her forehead. Normally I'd have bared my teeth at that, but I was too shaken up to react. Tyrus brushed her hair from her face just as she made another sound, worse than the first.

I turned my gaze toward Yazmor—if anyone knew what to do, it was him. I wasn't above begging, it seemed, at least not for Loch. "What do we do?"

Yazmor pressed his lips together, his expression showing I wouldn't like his answer. "There's nothing to do. Until Hubis releases her mind, she's trapped wherever she is. All we can do is keep her body safe until it's over."

"Where the fuck is she trapped? What is happening to her?" I knew my words came out desperate, but I had no idea what else to do.

No one answered, but no one needed to. I recalled Hubis' eyes before he'd left, when he'd stared at her. I'd seen the anger, the hatred, those things were expected. They weren't what froze me, what made me clutch Loch tighter.

Instead, it was the flash of pity. If whatever Hubis was doing to her was bad enough for *him* to pity her…

I held her tighter, since it was the only thing I could do.

Chapter Five

Loch

I blinked, trying to gather my bearings. It felt like I'd had a few too many edibles, where the world sloshed around me and I struggled to make head or tail of anything.

Of course, this was a lot better than I thought it would be. Instead of torture or any horror my brain could have come up with, spending some in this blackness wasn't so bad.

My feet pressed against some sort of ground as I turned, and when I took a step, waves of black shimmered as if I walked on the surface of water. The darkness stretched out forever in each direction, with no horizon or break between land and sky.

There didn't seem to be a breeze, nothing to indicate air — well, other than the fact that I wasn't gasping or choking. It was neither hot nor cold, as if the place had no temperature at all.

All of it added up to make me suspect I wasn't actually in a place at all. Instead, I felt removed from existence, like some tiny pocket.

"This place is in my mind."

I spun at the voice, finding Hubis standing behind me. He looked different, but I wasn't sure why. He wore the same clothing, hadn't changed anything physically that I knew about, but something had changed.

"Why am I here?"

He shrugged, and that was when I figured out what was different. He didn't have that same disinterest. Was it because we didn't have an audience? Was this the real man?

The fact there was a real man freaked me out. Hubis was *God*. No matter that I understood how it had happened, that I knew he wasn't the only one, none of that changed that he had formed my entire world. Him having a personality and acting like an actual individual made me feel oddly unsafe. It was like seeing a surgeon out drinking at night—I didn't like to see weakness in the people I had to trust.

"You are here to learn your lesson."

"Are you going to give me a lecture or something? Because I have to warn you—I've always been a shitty student. There are a few classes I only passed because my teacher didn't mind giving me some extra credit." I lifted my eyebrow even as I screamed that making sex jokes *now* was a horrible idea.

Not that Hubis reacted at all. "No. I am going to show you the chaos of the last world, to help you understand why my order is so important."

"And we're talking first why?"

"Because I can do so now without worrying about the others. I rarely find people worth talking to anymore, so I could hardly pass up this opportunity."

"Didn't figure you had much you wanted to talk about."

Hubis approached me, and while I tried to back away, it didn't seem as if I could move the way he could. He circled around me, walking with ease where it felt like the ground stuck to my feet, making me slower. I sure as hell didn't like him behind me, but all I could do was twist my head to try to keep him in my sight.

Not that it mattered. Looking at him wasn't going to protect me at all.

"A lot of people have fought against the order I have created, but few had done so quite as fervently as you. Few have also done it from a position where they could actually oppose me. By the time they achieved any level of power, they had long given up fighting the order — people at the top no longer care about changing things if it risks their place."

"I've always been one of a kind," I muttered.

When Hubis came in front of me again, he leaned in so close that we probably looked like lovers.

And we were sure as fuck *not* lovers. Even I had my limits.

"Order is essential to the universe. Without it, people suffer."

"People suffer anyways — that's life."

Hubis let out a quick, annoyed breath. "It isn't — or rather, it doesn't have to be. Before I took over, before I imposed my will, the old world was full of pain and suffering and madness."

"This world is still full of those things!"

"You understand *nothing.*" The anger in that word took me by surprise.

Hubis hadn't seemed to care about anything, yet here he was, showing a glimpse of true feeling. Leave it to me to pull out an actual emotion from him and have it be anger.

Still, he pressed on, each word full of more fury than the last. "You believe you know anything of pain? Of what chaos can exist when order is abandoned? Then you truly need the lesson you are about to receive. You can experience what I erased, what I destroyed and replaced with my own order. Perhaps, at the end of it, you will better understand why I am unflinching in the face of protecting that order."

He reached out and set a hand on my forehead, and yet again the world lurched around me.

When I opened my eyes, the brightness of the sun made me squint. I found myself alone, with Hubis nowhere in sight. Instead, I was in a wide-open field, surrounded with the same strange grass I'd seen in the Forgotten Caves.

This was his world, right? It didn't feel the same as it had in the Caves, though. There, it had been dimmed, like the difference of looking out a window and looking at a television.

This felt real. The cool grass wet my bare feet and the sun warmed my skin. I reached out to touch a plant that grew, the orange of its leaves so foreign I couldn't stop myself. Except…

The hand wasn't my own. At least, it wasn't unless I'd turned blue and grown a long fucking arm in the time since I'd last seen myself. I peered down, trying to get an idea of what the rest of myself looked like.

All of it was strange, and it took a long moment for me to sort it out.

I'm the same sort of being as Hubis.

The weirdest part was that it didn't feel wrong. Despite having more limbs than I was accustomed to, I didn't stumble around. Instead, I moved with confidence, as if I'd always had this body. It forced me to realize I didn't quite feel like myself.

Something else was in my head with me — not specific thoughts but feelings. It eased me, calming me so nothing around me felt that scary even though it really should have.

I doubted Hubis had done this just so I could get a nice little peek of what came before. His words echoed in my head, where he talked about chaos, about violence.

Still, that other part of me didn't feel that fear. They seemed happy, content.

I spun, though I wasn't sure why. It wasn't a sound, but as if I *felt* something there. Was that a sense I didn't know how to identify? It was as though vibrations in the ground had alerted me, and sure enough, five other figures came from behind me.

No fear swamped me, though.

"Are you lost?" one of the five asked. The words weren't a language I recognized, yet the meaning of them struck me a heartbeat after they were uttered.

"Who are you?" The words were mine, not the other being. Was this a memory of some sort? I experienced everything as if it were me, I responded myself, but those feelings were like another person. Each moment that ticked by made me more fearful.

I highly doubted Hubis wanted me to experience something pleasant…

"You should know better than to leave the domes," another of the five said. It didn't have a mouth that seemed capable of smiling, but I could almost feel the amused menace leaking from it. Maybe some things like that transcended all cultures and creatures. "It's dangerous out here all by yourself."

"I don't know where I am," I said, a quiver to my voice.

"You look clean. Clearly you came from a dome. You think we're beneath you, huh?"

That same sense from before hit me as the five came forward, each strike of their feet against the ground echoing up and through my body.

"I'm not who you think I am." I didn't even try to sound tough. It wasn't like me, but something about that other being made me feel small and weak.

"Even the way you talk says it all. What? Did you come out here to laugh at us? To mock the primitives who live out here?"

I shook my head, trying to deny it even if I didn't understand. None of it made sense to me. I didn't know anything about this world, couldn't talk my way out of something I couldn't even come close to understanding. I had no idea what the fuck a dome was, or what these people wanted, or why they so clearly hated me. Without any facts, I couldn't argue, couldn't manipulate them, couldn't do anything but back away.

Something inside me said to run, like an instinct that better knew this world than I did. It had to be the being who had this body, and who was I to argue with good advice?

I turned and tried to bolt, but I didn't get far before something heavy struck me from behind. It forced me to the ground, my body sinking into the dirt beneath the weight.

I struggled, but the difference between my strength and the being that had pinned me became clear. I felt like an ant trying to take on a bear. Worse, all too fast there were more hands when the others joined in, and soon I couldn't even put up the smallest of resistance.

A face was just before mine, sharp teeth bared in the sort of anger that transcended everything. Them being from an entirely different world didn't mean shit when it came to understanding rage that deep.

Whatever reason they had for hating me consumed them entirely. I could feel each place they touched me — the hands that pinned my arms, the leg that held my leg in place, the sharp ache in my side from where I'd struck the ground. Even if this body didn't feel like my own, I experienced everything it did. No matter that this was some weird memory, an echo of something that had happened before my world even existed, it was real to me in this moment.

"Let me go," I snapped, thrashing even if it gained me nothing.

"Don't worry," the thing on top of me said, but his tone was far from reassuring. "We won't kill you. What fun would that be? You dome-dwellers are so soft that it isn't even sporting to kill you. It'd be like slaughtering babies. Instead, we'll just play with you a while, then send what's left of you back to your precious dome. Let *them* see what happens when you come out here to laugh at us, let your broken body be a reminder of how much less you all are."

Please, God, help me, I prayed out, even if it was stupid, even if that very God was the one who had put me here.

The being over me laughed, coming closer until they blocked out all the light around me. "God turned his back on all of us — you should know that by now. God doesn't care what any of us do, but hell, maybe your screams will wake him back up."

And all I could do was tremble at his statement, at the fear that swarmed through me.

* * * *

Tyrus

How had we ended up here again? I'd never believed in fate or destiny, but somehow it seemed as if such a thing were at play here. Unfortunately, it had me reliving a fear I had never wanted to experience again.

Loch remained unmoving on my bed, just as she had before, after she'd endured torture, after she'd somehow survived it and made her way to me. This time she lacked the blood and bruises, but the noises she'd made were somehow worse.

Hale and Yazmor sat outside the room, both of them having gotten shooed out by me a few hours previously. They'd refused to leave my apartment, but at least they'd given me some small semblance of peace.

Neither had proven themselves good at waiting quietly. Yazmor had kept spouting random facts — some of which were wrong and others that made no sense — while Hale had kept making a noise that sounded like growling each time he looked at Loch's still form.

The peace I'd obtained with their absence was welcome, even if I wished Loch would break it. Gorrin had also come, though he hadn't stayed. Then again, too long away—especially right after this happened with Loch—would look suspicious on the Plains. He still had to keep up appearances.

I rubbed my hands over my face, wishing I could scrub away Loch's fear. Her pained whimpers dug into me, but I could do nothing. Yazmor and Gorrin had both explained that Hubis had done something to her, had invaded her mind in some way. She was likely experiencing something he wished her to, and none of us could do anything to stop it.

It meant I could only sit beside her and wait for her to come out of it. I had done all I could, had talked to her, had run my fingers through her hair, had even held her hand. None of it had seemed to get through to wherever she was, but I kept them up. I had no choice but to wait.

Loch sat up so fast I jerked backward in surprise. It wasn't the clumsy coming-to people did when asleep, where a groggy person had to slowly wake. Instead, it was as if between one heartbeat and the next she was conscious.

Her eyes were peeled open wide, locked on nothing, her panting, frantic breaths loud in the quiet room. Had she ever looked so terrified? Even after her attack before, when she'd had every reason to be nervous, she'd never looked like *this*.

I reached out and took her hand. I wasn't a comforting man, not someone used to reassuring others, but I couldn't leave her like that, couldn't let her think she was alone with whatever went on in her head.

Loch had always reacted to such things the same way. She'd taken every bit of physical contact and wanted more. She'd move in closer, as if starved for touch. I expected the same this time.

That wasn't what happened, though.

Loch yanked away as if my touch burned her. It didn't stop there, though. Instead, she bolted off the bed, her motions nothing but blind panic, her legs tangling in the blanket so she tumbled off the bed and hit the floor hard.

I stood there, silent, no idea what to do or say.

The door opened so hard it slammed against the wall. *Of course it would be Hale to do so.*

Loch lifted her gaze to find Hale with Yazmor behind him, but no relief showed on her face. Instead, fear consumed her. She scooted backward on the floor until her back hit the wall, until she could move no farther away.

"Loch…" Hale said, trailing off, uncertainty in his expression.

"Don't touch me," Loch whispered, wrapping her arms around her legs, curled into a tiny ball in the corner of the room.

I got the feeling she wanted to close her eyes, but something inside her wouldn't let her. Instead, she watched us with a suspicion totally at odds with the woman I knew.

She had always known how dangerous we could be. She'd never thought us safe, never been ignorant of our powers or our darkness. She'd respected it, but never *feared* it. If anything, she'd always been quick to put us in our places, to mock us for our perceived strength and arrogance. I would have said she'd never been smart enough to truly fear us as she should have.

That wasn't the case anymore, though. There was no way to mistake her shaking as anything but unadulterated terror.

And as it turned out, I didn't like her fearing me.

"You are safe here," I said, coming around the bed to stand beside the other two without going nearer to her. Maybe this was like a nightmare—she needed to get her bearings, needing someone to remind her that whatever had happened wasn't real.

And I ignored the need to ask her what had happened. It burned at me, wanting to know what had put that fear in her, but I held back. Remembering it now wouldn't do her any good. She needed to ground herself in the present more than anything else.

She swallowed hard, peering around the room. Recognition starting in her eyes, telling me she remembered this place. Still, the shaking didn't stop.

"It wasn't real," Hale said. "Whatever that fucker made you see, it wasn't real. You've been here with us the whole time."

"It was real," she whispered.

Hale crouched to catch her gaze. Once he did, he went on. "It wasn't. It was just something he made you see—nothing else."

Her shaking got worse until even her teeth clattered. She blinked tears away, but even then, she refused to take her gaze off us. It wasn't *just* something terrible that he'd shown her.

Whatever he'd done had shaken her very sense of security, had made her doubt us, made her fear us as she never had before.

"It was real," she said. "It happened here." She tapped at her temple. "And it was real. I remember all of it." As she started to speak, she gagged.

Loch was off the floor and bolting for the bathroom before any of us could move, and the sound of her throwing up from there rooted me in place.

What the fuck?

"I'll go," Yazmor said, his voice surprisingly soft and serious.

"Why you?" Hale asked.

"Because I have a feeling I know what Hubis showed her, and if so, I'm the least likely to bother her right now." Yazmor didn't make a joke, which told me just how serious the moment was.

Hale remained still as Yazmor left and closed the bathroom door, shutting Hale and me out.

"What the fuck was that?" Hale asked as if I could answer.

"That was Hubis ensuring his own death. Even if I was hesitant before, that secured it."

"Why is she afraid of *us* though?" Hale drew his hands into fists, and I understand that sort of impotent anger. "Why would he make her afraid of us?"

I dropped my gaze to my own hands, seeing the rough skin, the calluses, all the signs of the things I'd done in my life. No, not just that, but the sheer size of them. "I don't know what she went through exactly, but there are only so many things that would make her fearful of us, of men even if she knows us well."

Hale jerked his gaze toward me, his blue eyes wide. Had such a thing truly never occurred to him? I never thought I would consider him naïve, but it seemed he could be.

"Yazmor is a good choice to look after her if my guess is correct," I explained. He was frustrating and random, but he also lacked a certain masculine edge, and as far as I knew, he had never had such a relationship with Loch.

"And we just sit back and do nothing? We just let this shit pass?"

"No. Hubis hurt something that belongs to us, something precious to us. We do not sit back — we get ready for the next part of our plan. Nothing helps pass the time or distract a person quite so well as revenge."

And Hubis had just ensured he would suffer every bit as much as Loch had.

Chapter Six

Loch

Throwing up always sucked. It didn't matter the reason, didn't matter when or where or how old a person was — it was no fun.

I wiped my mouth with a towel after dry heaving for a while, almost tempted to eat something just so I had something in my stomach to come up.

My head hurt and sweat made my shirt stick to my back. Even still, all I saw playing in my mind was what had happened in that memory.

And it *was* a memory. The longer I had been trapped there, the surer I was. I'd experienced what someone had gone through, and right up to the end, when I'd dragged my bloody, broken body through that grass and toward a huge domed city, I'd felt everything they had.

The pain as those others had gleefully hurt me in every way they could imagine, their laughter at my screams, all of it played in my head. It mixed with what Clint had done to me, but it was so much worse.

Clint had wanted answers.

Those things that hurt me had only wanted me to suffer.

They'd had such hatred when they'd touched me, as if I had been the basis of all the pain in their lives. Their words had cleared up more of *why* they'd hated me, not that it had helped me bear it all.

The world had been broken apart—those who lived in the domes and those who didn't. It seemed that age old story of the haves and the have-nots. Whoever's memory I had lived through had lived an easy life in the domes, but for some reason had ventured out.

Since I couldn't hear their thoughts or see anything except what happened right then, I had no idea why they'd do such a stupid thing. Clearly life outside the domes was dangerous, but they'd still risked it. Worse, given the way they'd reacted at first, without fear, it seemed they didn't really comprehend the danger.

I recalled the ones who had attacked me as they'd laughed at God, as they'd ensured me that God no longer gave a fuck about any of them.

I set my arm on the toilet lid, ignoring how gross I'd find that at any other time, and rested my face against my arm.

"You should bathe."

I didn't jump at Yazmor's voice, though I wasn't sure why. I recalled my reaction to Hale and Tyrus, the immediate fear even from the thought of seeing Gorrin. Yazmor, however, didn't make me feel that way.

"Sorry my hygiene isn't up to your very high standard," I muttered, lacking any real heat in my words.

Yazmor moved past me in the large bathroom, his steps causing a slight squeak against the floor. A rush of water echoed off the walls, telling me he'd started to run a bath despite my snark. "Hot water will help you feel better. The heat relaxes muscles which knot from anxiety and stress. You've also been sweating in your sleep."

I rolled to the side from my knees so I sat on my ass beside the toilet. It let me look over at Yazmor, who sat on the side of the tub, his eyes unbearably kind as he stared at me.

I hated that look—it told me he at least suspected what I'd experienced. I much preferred him being random to this sickening pity. I recalled the surprise on Tyrus and Hale's faces, the way they'd widened their eyes as they'd looked at me, unsure what to do.

Yazmor didn't act that way.

He said nothing while the water filled the tub, steam drawing sweat from my brow and making it harder to see. I didn't bother to fill that silence, letting it wrap around me like the hug I for sure didn't want.

All too soon, the pouring of water stopped. "Come on, Loch, it's time."

His hand appeared in front of me, but he didn't grab me. Instead, he waited, giving me the chance to accept or deny.

The exhaustion had me taking his offer, and he tugged me to my feet carefully. Once on my feet, he turned his back, the reason clear.

I pulled my shirt off, the action so instinctual I didn't even think about it at first. Once the fabric fell to the floor, however, that fucking shaking started again. It came on fast, hitting me so hard that I couldn't seem to get my fingers to work on the button of my jeans. Hell, my hands felt so cold it was like they'd fallen asleep, turning numb and useless.

"It's okay." Yazmor's words came out in a whisper before he set his hands over mine, helping.

He helped undo the button, then crouched as he pulled the jeans down my legs. It wasn't sexy, not in the least. This wasn't like when Hale stripped me, when he was so desperate for me that he yanked the clothing away. It wasn't Tyrus who teased me, making each touch making me burn more. It wasn't Gorrin, either, who had ripped my clothes from me.

Instead, Yazmor did it like he would if he undressed something small and precious, as though nudity meant nothing to him.

Then again, he'd always treated me that way, hadn't he? He'd seen me naked when I'd first been in the Chasm and he hadn't given it a second thought.

Considering that helped focus my mind somewhere other than the memory of what I'd just gone through, helped to hold that back even as it battered at the edges of my consciousness.

Yazmor took off my bra and underwear with the same lack of interest he'd had thus far, which was the only reason I held it together.

Well, sort of held it together. I still shook like a baby deer standing for the first time.

"In you go." Yazmor grasped my upper arm in his hand, reminding me of just how large those hands were. Yazmor never seemed large most of the time, but every once in a while, I was forced to recognize that he was still male, still larger than I was.

The heat made me flinch when I set my foot into it.

"Too hot?" Yazmor reached past me for the cold water handle, but I stopped him.

"It's fine." I fully stepped over the edge of the tub, wincing as the water stung my other foot as well.

"Your skin's turning red." Yazmor's voice came out oddly uncertain.

I used his grip on me for balance as I sank down, that stinging from the heat moving up my body each place it touched. I didn't stop until I was submerged to the tops of my shoulders.

While the bath wasn't huge like the one at my place, it was plenty deep. A small layer of bubbles floated on top, making me wonder if Yazmor had brought the bubble bath or if Tyrus had already had it. It smelled of strawberries and sunshine.

"It's too hot…" Yazmor repeated.

I let the back of my head rest against the edge of the tub, my eyes drifting closed. "I like it like this. It feels like it's burning away everything."

My honesty had to come from the heat, as if it not only eased my muscle but loosened my tongue as well. Otherwise, I'd never admit such a thing. Sure, clearly I wasn't firing on all cylinders at the moment, but that didn't mean I wanted to come right out and say that.

It reminded me of the old saying — *better to remain quiet and let people think you're a fool rather than open your mouth and remove all doubt.*

Between Yazmor and the hot water, I found it more difficult to remain quiet.

"Why am I okay with you?" I asked, the darkness behind my closed eyelids making it feel safer to ask.

Yazmor didn't pretend he didn't understand what I meant. "I'm not like the others. You know I'm not like them, so you don't fear me in the same way."

"They make fun of you sometimes, saying you're not interested in sex."

"Is that really a conversation you want to have right now?"

I gave myself a moment to consider his question. He wasn't wrong, really. After the memory of what had happened, any discussion of sex felt dangerous. Somehow, though, Yazmor felt removed from that. Not to mention that it was a question I'd wanted to ask for a while, and the interest held my attention from things I didn't want to think about.

I sighed and let all the things spinning around in my head pour from my lips. "I want to understand you better, and that distracts me."

"Okay, but sit up. I want to get your hair washed."

I did as he asked, the water deep enough that hunching forward slightly allowed the water to still hide almost everything.

"Tip your head back." He poured water through my hair when I did so, careful enough that none got on my face. Next, his fingers moved through the strands, rubbing the scalp, and a lavender scent filled the room as he worked the shampoo through. "My world, my species wasn't much like yours, like many of the others. You saw it—you should understand how different we were."

"Hubis' cycle was different, but they sure as fuck had those kinds of feelings…" Those words alone threatened to remind me of what I'd experienced, but I swallowed to keep in control.

Yazmor's hands paused for a moment, then he let out a soft sigh. "Those drives have been part of most cycles, but not all. For mine, we lacked a sexual drive. Reproduction was done asexually."

Jayce Carter

"So you aren't interested at all?" I struggled to understand what he meant, to make sense of something that felt like such an innate part of life to me.

"I wouldn't say that, not exactly. I have taken this form, which means I experience the same physical reactions to touch as anyone else. It means things will still feel good. I just lack an actual drive, an instinctual desire for sexual contact. I've never really felt any inclination to explore it before."

He poured more water to get rid of the shampoo, repeating the motion a few times. "So the reason you're more comfortable around me right now is probably because you know I'm unlikely to want the things that are frightening at the moment."

"And you don't want them? Ever?"

"You sound disappointed."

"I thought we were getting closer. I guess I can't imagine not taking that step with someone I 1—" I clamped my lips together before *that* word came out. Clearly the magic of Yazmor's hands had managed to completely dismantle my defenses.

He chuckled, the soft sound implying he heard what I'd almost said. "If someone asked me that before I met you, I would have said no. I would have said I had no interest and never would. Now, I'm not quite so certain of that."

"But if you don't have that drive, then why would you? I'd never want you to do something just for my benefit—"

"I don't mean it like that. I mean that I've considered trying with you. I may not have the same drive you do, but that doesn't mean I wouldn't enjoy it, it doesn't mean I don't think about seeing you in that way."

I let silence eat up the space after that comment as I considered it. He didn't sound forced, didn't sound as if he were thinking about doing something he hated. Instead, his tone held curiosity.

I pressed that conversation away, though. It wasn't like anything would happen right now — I was in no state for that — so I went on to something else. "Why would Hubis make me go through that?"

"Hubis came from a very troubled cycle. They split the world into different parts that all behaved wildly differently, and when they interacted? Chaos. I have a good guess of what you went through, and I can only extrapolate his reasoning based on what I know of him. He probably wanted you to understand why he destroyed everything from before, why order matters to him so much."

"That sort of thing still happens now. How does putting me through that show he's any different than whoever was in charge during his cycle? Does he think violence is gone? That people are all loving and gentle to one another now?"

Yazmor didn't respond right away, and it took so long that I opened my eyes to check if he was even still there. He sat on the edge of the tub, but he didn't look at me. Instead, he leaned forward, his elbows on his knees, his back bowed forward, his gaze locked on the other wall. "He didn't show you something random, just some glimpse of the old world."

"Were those his memories?"

Yazmor shook his head, his profile looking shockingly serious. "No. He wanted you to understand what made him what he is, the final straw that drove him to do what he's done."

"He's fucking crazy—that's the reason for what he's done."

Yazmor pulled his lips into a lopsided, sad smile. "We're all a little crazy. Anyone who manages to survive any amount of time loses their sanity or they wouldn't still be here. Who would want to see things come and go? Who would choose to live, knowing the pain that exists? Sane people never last long—it's the crazy who inherit the world. That's true of me, of you and of Hubis. Still, I suspect he showed you what he did to try to explain himself, to make you see and understand."

"Don't you defend him, not after…"

Yazmor twisted to look at me. "Don't get me wrong—I'm not defending him. He made a mistake by choosing this path, because he all but ensured his own destruction. Hale, Tyrus and Gorrin won't let this go, won't ignore this. Even if they weren't sure about facing him before, he just pulled them in for the long game."

"Just them?"

"No, not just them. There was a time when I worried about you seeing too much of me, but you've seen it all, now. There's no reason to hide anything now. Clint hurt you, and I didn't let that stand, either."

I frowned as his words hit me, and when they made sense, my eyes widened. "That was you? I heard the place was leveled, that everyone there was slaughtered."

"Tyrus called me to his place while you were still unconscious. You were so small and so hurt. He couldn't leave you, but he knew I could handle the problem on my own. He only needed to show me you, and that was it. They screamed so loudly, like some choir signaling their guilt, but it didn't matter. Their begging couldn't sway me, nothing could. If I did that to them, I can assure you that Hubis will *not* get off easily. His reasons for putting you through that doesn't change that he did, and they won't save him. I have no issues with mercy, don't break things just for fun or pleasure, but he forfeited any mercy I had with his own actions." Yazmor reached toward me, moving slow as if giving me the chance to object.

I didn't, though. In fact, I leaned in closer until his palm cupped my cheek and his bright violet eyes stared right into mine.

"You've seen what I truly am, what I'm capable of. I rarely see a reason to use my power, to unleash what I'm capable of, but for you? I will burn God and present the ashes to you as a gift."

And that might be the sweetest thing I'd ever heard.

* * * *

Gorrin

Myers didn't look all that thrilled to see me, but I didn't care about that. He was a tool, as he'd always been. He was insufferable at times, but also capable of efficiency.

In short?

He had proven himself useful, not only to me but later to Loch. While I kept myself hidden from most of the Chasm — word traveled faster than I wanted it to around here — I knew Myers to be trustworthy.

He had no desire to rule himself, which meant he enjoyed remaining power adjacent. If he told anyone about my presence, it would only risk him and his position. He had no true loyalty to Loch or me, but his own self-interest aligned with ours, which was the most a person could ask for in the Chasm.

"This is our current footing." Myers spread the papers over the large table in the office, the familiar sight of them causing an ache in my chest.

How long had I done this with him? How many times had we stood at this very table with information that looked just like this, reviewing how many souls we had gained and lost over the past week?

So many that we both fell back into the familiar motions without missing a single step.

Loch was still in charge. She was Lord here—not me. However, after hearing from Tyrus about what had happened with Hubis, I had found myself anxious. I'd heard she'd been fearful with Hale and Tyrus, which made me suspect my physical presence wouldn't aid her at all.

Instead, all I could do was try to take over tasks for her, to ease her in whatever way I could. That meant handling the issues that came up so Myers could leave her be.

I didn't mind the details—in fact, it gave me something to focus on beyond what Loch had suffered or what was still in store for us.

Hubis was dangerous, and not just because of his power. He saw the world in his own way and listened to no one. He was unmovable in his opinions—I had never once seen him change his mind or take the advice of anyone. He was single-minded in his focus when he had a task he felt needed to get done.

It meant should he realize what we planned, if he caught wind of any of it, we would all be in danger.

I couldn't fight Loch on her desire to remove him, either. I couldn't argue against it. Of course, there was a difference in thinking something should happen and believing it could happen.

"You're distracted," Myers said. "That's unusual for you. It seems like time away has not done you any favors."

"In case you haven't noticed, I have a lot on my plate at the moment. Besides, trying to complete these tasks without being seen or having access to the power I had before makes it challenging."

"Why not regain your old position?" he asked as if it were the obvious solution.

Which, no doubt to him, it was. To Myers, if I had ruled here for so long, why not take back that position?

Especially because I could see the strain in his face from dealing with Loch. He'd lived for a long time here, as a demon so unchanging, without showing any signs of the passing years. A few months of putting up with Loch and he seemed to have aged decades.

Loch's ability to do that was endearing in a way it truly shouldn't have been.

"That isn't going to happen," I said, trying not to snap at him over it. "I have no desire to take over again, and I wouldn't harm Loch to achieve it."

"She lacks the same attention to detail you have."

I peered down at the paper, then tapped on one. "It seems as if she has done fine. There is a similar number of souls as before, growth in line with what we had before."

"There have been skirmishes with the souls owned by the other Lords. Things are far more chaotic because the souls she owns do not fear nor respect her."

"That takes time to happen. You have watched how many Demon Lords take over? It is always an adjustment. The damned always press their luck and test the new Lord. That happens even in the most ideal transfer of power, and this one came out of nowhere. It would be foolish to think it wouldn't take some time to work out the details. Even with that, she's settled in well."

Meyers dropped his gaze, the lines etched in his face screaming that he didn't agree. Which was fine. I had never required those below me to agree with me, only to obey. Their thoughts and opinions were of no concern to me so long as they did as they were told.

I hadn't told Meyers our plan, of course. I didn't trust him that far. The wrong word breathed to the wrong person and the entire house of cards we had built would tumble down. Instead, I had only explained my return, which he had taken as yet another sign of my obsession with Loch.

Which...wasn't entirely wrong, and rather convenient. It gave me reason for returning and helping.

"I need an accurate count of those we have at our disposal."

"Why?"

"They may become necessary," I hedged.

Meyers offered me a sharp look but didn't ask, only nodding in response. "I'll have that for you within four days."

I nodded to tell him that was acceptable. Given the state Loch seemed to be in, it would take us at least that long to get ourselves ready. We needed to set up safeguards in the Chasm so things ran smoothly without the Lords, that way no one noted the absence.

When we entered the Path, we would be unable to transport anywhere else. Even Yazmor and I, who had never sold our souls and thus weren't forbidden from the Plains, would be locked into the Path once we entered it.

It meant we all had to prepare before we could leave.

Meyers stood up straight after peering at the papers and nodding. "I'll go get started on the things we've discussed."

After a wave of my hand to dismiss him, he turned on his heel and headed for the door. Just as he reached it, it opened ahead of him.

And standing there in the doorway was the one face I truly wanted to see. Even with the dark circles under her eyes, the exhaustion hanging on her, Loch was unfailingly lovely to me.

Meyers acknowledged her with a short, quick nod, then slid past her to leave. He had no idea what had happened — no one outside of the Lords did — but one look at her said she wasn't in any mood to deal with Meyers. He must have picked up on it because he didn't so much as attempt to speak to her.

I didn't move even when Meyers closed the door behind him, shutting Loch and I in together.

It was strange to look at her looking unharmed. The way she dragged her feet, the slumping of her shoulders — it reminded me of the time she had come to me after getting hurt.

Except her body carried no signs of injuries. I almost wished it had. Physical wounds could heal. Mental wounds were a far more difficult thing to resolve.

"Hey," she said, her voice soft as she acknowledged me.

"I apologize if I overstepped my bounds." I waved at the papers covering the table. "I had nothing else to do, so thought I could pass the time taking care of smaller tasks."

She smiled, though it didn't reach her eyes. Instead, it felt forced, as though she knew smiling was the proper response even if she didn't feel it. "You never can just admit you were trying to help me, can you?"

Her words caused a warmth in my chest, feeling as if they created a bridge between us, one that made me feel as if we were close. She had always felt so far away, something I wanted but knew better than to touch. Now she knew the truth about me, and the idea that we knew each other well eased some tension inside me.

Of course, she wasn't wrong about me, so instead of admitting anything, I reached for facts. "Meyers will have a full accounting of the souls you have bound to you in four days. I have already spoken to the other Lords, and they are gathering the same."

"Why do we need that?"

"We don't know what will help but going into a war without knowing our own strength would be asking for disaster. There is no way to plan unless we know what we have at our disposal."

"This isn't a war."

"Isn't it? I hope that we can get the upper hand on Hubis by taking him by surprise, but that is far from guaranteed. Should we fail there, it is vital that we know what we can fight with."

Loch came farther into the room, each step showing just how tired she seemed. She went to the couch and all but collapsed onto it.

"I thought you would have recovered longer at Tyrus'," I said. "It has only been two days."

"I don't like people hovering over me." She leaned back in the corner of the couch, slouching down, looking a few moments from passing out. "I couldn't even move without *someone* asking me what I needed. It made it impossible to relax at all."

"Should I leave, then?"

Loch looked up, meeting my gaze, then shook her head. "No. I don't really want to be alone, either." She let out a soft snort. "Isn't that funny? I don't want people hovering and I don't want to be alone, either. I guess I'm a little fucked-up, huh?"

Her self-deprecating humor put me on edge, made me hold my temper so I didn't snap at her. The last thing she needed was my lecturing her. Instead, I went over to the couch and took a seat on the other side of it, leaving plenty of room between us. "It's not uncommon to feel conflicted."

"I wanted to come back to my own space. No matter how welcoming Tyrus is, that's *his* place. I couldn't relax." She offered me a smile that could have almost seemed shy. "Maybe that's why I don't mind you here, because you belong here, too."

"This reminds me of when you came back injured before."

"After you healed me, I found you on the couch, asleep. It was weird to see you like that, because you always had your guard up. Do you not sleep because you're an angel?"

I nodded. "Angels only require sleep when we're injured or use too much power. I could have healed you far more easily if I weren't in the Chasm, if I wasn't in a demon form."

"But you did it anyway, even knowing it would exhaust you?"

"How could I not? Even back then, no matter how you frustrated me and fought me, I wanted you safe and happy. It was the very least I could do."

She sighed and shifted slightly until her head leaned on the armrest of the couch, her body curled up. "I thought I could do this. I thought I could face Hubis, and I was so sure I'd come out on top. Now, though?" Her words trailed off, as if she had no idea how to finish the statement.

"You can still do it." The certainty of my own words shocked me. Hadn't I just been thinking that we had no real shot? That Hubis was too powerful for us to have any hope of winning? Yet when I considered her failing, some part of me refused to accept that. Even if I couldn't picture us winning, I also couldn't imagine Loch failing.

Failing meant death, and I could not accept that.

When she didn't respond, I looked over at her, wondering if I'd pushed things too far. I found Loch there, asleep, as if exhaustion had hit her so hard that she'd all but collapsed on the spot.

I didn't fight the smile that tugged at my lips. Some part of me liked that she felt comfortable enough to fall asleep mid-conversation with me. I went into the bedroom, careful to make no noise, and took a blanket from the bed. I set it over her, my movements cautious so as not to rouse her.

She didn't move at all, but a line between her eyebrows said she slept fitfully. I wished I could take that from her, that I could carry all her worries and fears for her, but I knew better than most that wasn't possible.

We all had to carry our own burdens, our own pain. All I could do was remain by her side and help her stand when she stumbled.

And that was more than I ever thought I could get.

Chapter Seven

Loch

I peered at the uneven path before me, the rocks darker in color than any around them. "I always figured a road to Heaven would be gold bricks or made of diamonds or something."

"Not Heaven," Gorrin said from my left.

Would that ever get old? It felt like a shitty dad joke that I just couldn't let go of. Each time I said it and one of the Lords responded with that same bored, not-even-annoyed-anymore response, my stomach fluttered a bit.

And I'd fucking take what pleasure I could.

An entire week had passed since Hubis' little lesson. I'd slept a lot, as if my mind had wearied rather than my body. I'd tried to remind myself that what I'd seen had been nothing more than a movie, something someone else had experienced but not me. Those things hadn't broken my bones, hadn't cut into my skin, hadn't abused me. I'd only see what someone else had survived.

That trauma wasn't *mine* to carry.

Of course, telling myself that didn't make my body or mind believe it. Some of my jumpiness had abated, but I still struggled with touch. When I'd stumbled on the way to the Path, Hale had caught my arm to keep me from slamming my face into the ground.

And I'd reacted by yanking away, the action landing me on my ass while Hale had lifted his hands and rushed out an awkward apology.

Still, I *was* better than right after. I could talk with the Lords now, could handle being in close quarters with them. So long as everyone kept their hands to themselves, I was fine.

As much as that could be called fine, I guess.

I'd gone through a lot in my life, had suffered enough traumas to know how shit like that took time. It was like a slice to my brain, one that would heal slowly. I couldn't put everything on hold just to deal with that, however.

Besides, I enjoyed the distractions. I preferred focusing on getting to the Plains, on dealing with Hubis rather than stewing about that memory.

I could do something about Hubis—I couldn't do shit about what I'd experienced. The entire world where that had happened, both the victim and the attackers were all gone. The memory was just an echo.

An echo that still plays on repeat in my head when I close my eyes.

The worst part about it? The way the Lords treated me, the caution in their words, the distance between us. Just when I'd felt as if we'd figured something out between us, the floor had dropped out and we'd plunged into some new, deep water.

I took a deep breath as I looked at the way ahead. Yazmor carried a backpack with a single book inside it, the only one Tyrus had found that contained information about the Path. It held stories, but they were all second-hand and about as trustworthy as writing on bathroom walls.

Still, we could only hope that something inside them might give us an edge.

"Ready?" Yazmor asked, offering me a side-look and a smirk that said he was having far more fun than he should have. Then again, Yazmor had seen so much, there wasn't a lot that was new for him. This was one of the rare places he'd never been.

He, just like Gorrin, could pass to the Plains on their own, without having to go through all this. Since Yazmor was a remnant, since he had never sold his soul, the Plains didn't keep him out. Still, our odds of survival were far better if we traveled together, and those odds were dismal to start with.

The Path was carved out of the wall of the Chasm, a walkway that climbed up, twisting along, closed in on both sides by the rockface.

Instead of answering, I took one step, over the break between the gray rock of the Chasm and the black of the Path. Passing through it *felt* like when an elevator first started to move, when things shifted around me and I had to regain my balance. No one could find this path by accident and wander on in without realizing. That shift served as a warning, and it screamed in my head to turn back.

I stumbled, grasping the face of the wall to my left to stay upright. That feeling in my skull was far too similar to a command, to the sensation of when Gorrin had ordered me do something and I'd tried to resist. It was Hubis warning souls not to venture any farther.

Hubis didn't own my soul, though, so he could fuck off with that. I curled my fingers on the rock face and used the grip to pull me forward another step. One after another, I forced myself onward, the pain intensifying, feeling like molten lava sloshing through my brain.

That didn't matter, though. I couldn't let it stop me. We *knew* others had made it past here, so I could, too.

I lurched forward, and after another few steps, the pain disappeared so fast, it was like it hadn't been there. I clung to the wall, panting hard as I tried to regain my breath.

I turned to find the Lords just behind me, telling me that they'd followed even as they'd seen me struggle. They'd watched my pain, watched me nearly collapse, but they hadn't given up.

Instead, they'd trudge right into those flames, following me no matter what.

It made me laugh as I turned and sat on the steep walkway, giving myself a moment to recover.

They made it through the place where that warning was, until all five of us safely got to the other side. None of them looked any better than I did.

"The fuck are you laughing at?" Hale asked, the receding pain no doubt responsible for his sharp words, given how careful he'd been around me lately. "I know you don't mind a bit of roughness, but fuck, that was way more than I'm into."

"I was just thinking—the saying is always, 'I'd follow you into hell.' I never figured I'd find people willing to follow me into Heaven."

"Trust me — the Chasm is easy compared to where we're headed," Gorrin said.

"Fair enough." I got to my feet, ignoring the way my head ached and my legs already felt like jelly. The Path wound up through a narrow crack in the walls, then turned, hiding the rest from view. According to Yazmor, we knew beyond that turn, beyond what we could see, but the Path existed outside of the Chasm or the Plains. It was a tunnel that connected the two, meaning we had no idea what we might find.

I peered at the Lords, a smile threatening to spread across my lips. I fought it because if they saw it, they'd never let it go without me admitting the reason.

And I really didn't want to have to say what I thought.

Heaven or Hell — there's no one else I'd want with me right now.

* * * *

So this is the hurry up and wait, right?

I'd taken those first fateful, terrifying steps onto the Path expecting nonstop action. It had felt like the gunshot at the start of the race.

Reality fell short, as it often did. It felt like getting a super-hot guy into bed only to have him poke my left labia for a minute before asking if I came. A lot of buildup for nothing.

Worse? All these steps and uphill walking made me wish I could gain and lose weight, because I would have one sweet ass by the end of it. Unfortunately, being dead and all, my body was what it was. I couldn't get bigger tits or a tighter ass no matter how hard I worked.

"To the left is a wall, and to the right? A slightly darker wall," Yazmor said, somehow managing to keep his cheery tone.

Which was impressive, given if he kept that up, he'd have to finish the walk with a blade in his side.

Hale didn't seem to enjoy the commentary.

Actually...if Yazmor did end up with a blade in him, I really couldn't discount any of the men as the one to do it. Hale would be most proud and admit it, but Gorrin and Tyrus were both more than willing to do it.

"Are we there yet?" I asked, ensuring my voice sounded *exactly* like a kid in the backseat on a long car trip.

"I never expected myself to wish for some horror from beyond to attack us," Gorrin muttered.

"Can't you just fly there, wings?" Hale asked.

"Can't you?" Gorrin shot back.

"We *all* have decorative-only wings, so let's not go down that path," I reminded them. "None of us need to deal with wing envy."

"I hope we don't need all five of us when we arrive in the Plains," Tyrus said as he took a spot beside me, his voice low so he spoke only to me. "I have a feeling we might lose one or two on the trip."

"Well, at least if that happens, whoever kills them will get their power. That's what matters, right?"

Tyrus didn't smile, his gaze forward, but a twitch of his cheek made me chuckle. "Still," Tyrus pressed. "We should probably stop soon."

"How long have we been going? My cell stopped working as soon as we got on the Path."

Tyrus lifted his wrist to peer at the watch there. "About six hours, if my watch is still working correctly. We're nearing the area where the Path opens—once we reach there, we should set up for a break. Who knows what we'll find after that, but we would be better ready to face it once rested."

The idea of setting up some little campground seemed ridiculous. I got a sudden image of Tyrus making smores and Hale struggling to set up a tent and Yazmor chasing butterflies like some twisted little family.

Still, I couldn't argue that he was right. My body was exhausted, both from the tension of our trip and the actual climbing. Some areas of the Path were just a sharp grade and others had actual stairs. The worst were the areas with jagged rocks at steps, and one slip had me nearly on my face.

Thankfully, Gorrin had been close enough to catch me, which had meant thus far, no one had actually bled yet.

I'd like to keep that going, like one of those counters at jobs that list how many days had passed since the last accident.

"You're right," I acknowledged as we neared the top of the Path.

Yazmor walked at the front like some overly excited tour guide, with Hale behind him. I had walked next, but now stood beside Tyrus, who had been behind me. Last came Gorrin, bringing up the rear. I appreciated him at the back because Yazmor would have complained about not being able to see anything and Hale would have just made comments about my ass.

I tried to stay calm as we neared that opening and the unknown that rested beyond.

It was strange, since between the four Lords, they knew what seemed like everything. Gorrin came from the Plains, Yazmor came from before this world had even been formed, and Tyrus and Hale had spent plenty of time in the Chasm and Earth to have a handle on most things.

So the five of us walking into something *none* of us knew shit about had me anxious, no matter how hard I tried to hide it.

No one had mentioned it, probably because they were just being nice. I'd bet they knew exactly how nervous this all made me.

Still, I refused to be the frightened one. I was an equal to these men, or so I kept telling myself. It was hard to believe it, to accept it, but I had pretended enough times in my life to manage it well enough.

We reached the top of the Path, the place where the walls on either side of us disappeared, and never had I realized just how much I appreciated a large open space.

At least, I thought that until I got a look at it.

The place made the Chasm downright cheery.

It stretched out in every direction, with the walkway appearing like the stairs into an attic, where they came up at the center. The ground was rough and covered in rocks, with trees and other plants that broke up the space. Fog covered the ground in a thick blanket, obscuring anything too far away like some horror movie setting a mood.

The Path remained, with even the fog remaining off it, and twisted through the trees until I couldn't see where it went.

Still, this wasn't as bad as I'd expected. When we'd talked about the Path, I'd expected horrors at every turn, beasts and creatures of nightmares snapping at our heels without pause.

Which was why this place confused the fuck out of me. It was creepy, sure, but it didn't appear all that dangerous from what I could see.

This place had driven people mad from what I understood, but I'd yet to see anything that could do that.

Either the others were little bitches, or we had yet to glimpse the true darkness of the Path. I had a feeling it was the latter.

Tyrus peered around before speaking up. "Let's make camp here."

Hale turned back, his expression holding all sorts of 'fuck that.' "Why? We won't get anywhere if we stop all the time. We *just* got to the real shit here — we should push on."

Yazmor reached down and plucked something from the ground, then held up the strange plant. It was gray, as if all color had leached from it. It wasn't a flower, but instead looked like a rose stem with large thorns and only the center of the flower without petals. "This place seems pretty nice for a break. We could have a picnic!"

Gorrin spoke from behind me, close enough that I took a few steps forward. "Stopping can leave us open to attack. We should be cautious about letting our guard down."

Their bickering went on, the lines drawn right at the center. It reminded me of the Chasm, of the fact that because there were an even number of Lords, nothing ever got done. They never could agree and there was never a tie breaker.

At least, *normally* there wasn't, but now it seemed my job. The aching in my calves answered it for me. "Let's rest here."

Gorrin and Hale both gave me sharp looks, as if they didn't appreciate my intervening against them. However, after they moved their gazes over me, they seemed to agree.

Gorrin sighed and nodded. "Very well. The Path is dangerous and will drain our powers faster than anywhere else. It wouldn't hurt to take a small break before venturing on."

Could he tell I was tired?

Probably, the observant bastard.

We hadn't brought tents — they were too large and not worth the effort to pack or bring. Anything that was going to attack us wouldn't be stopped by a little bit of tent fabric, after all. If anything, they'd just make us into a tasty burrito.

Instead, each of our packs had a sleeping bag hooked to it.

Gorrin looked around, his gaze careful as if studying everything he could find. He narrowed his eyes until only small slits of gold peered out, then shook his head. "Okay. We can set up here. Do not move more than a few feet from the Path. This place changes around us, and if you lose sight of the walkway, you may never find your way back. So set up sleeping bags touching the Path." He dropped his pack, then took a step away from us.

"Where are you going?" I nearly shouted the question, an unexpected fear seizing me at the idea of him going out there alone.

He frowned as he looked back at me, as if thrown by my reaction. "It gets very cold here. We should start a fire."

"Won't that advertise our location?" Hale asked. "Rule number one in stealth — no fucking fires."

"Hubis can't see into the Path, and the only things here will be able to smell us well before the smoke of a fire let them know. The coldness here isn't just a nuisance. It steals power, draining us faster. A fire will help keep us from exhausting ourselves as quickly."

"Didn't you just say to stay on the walkway?" I pressed.

"*You* need to. As an angel, this place doesn't work to keep me out of the Plains. It means I'm not as affected as you are by the environment. This place won't try to trick me, won't hide things from me. If you look around, there is little usable wood just off the Path, because those who have come before have taken that. It means that to start a fire, I need to venture farther away. I'll be back shortly—don't worry."

But I *was* worried. I didn't normally stress that much, but for some reason the idea of letting him out of my sight made my chest tight. It was probably because I'd just gotten him back.

Some part of me thought if he left like this, he'd slip away again.

Gorrin stared at me, the gold of his eyes solid in a way that let me gain my bearings again. After a long moment, I nodded to tell him it was okay, that I'd gathered myself.

He returned my nod before turning and heading out, off the Path. I watched his back until it disappeared into the fog and trees, until I lost sight of him as if he'd never been there at all.

"We should get out the sleeping bags," Tyrus said, his voice breaking into the moment and reminding me not to let my mind wander.

There was too much at stake for that.

"Yeah. You're right."

And that was how we started the world's weirdest campout.

Chapter Eight

I groaned as I stretched my feet out, trying to ease the painful cramping in my calves. Thank fuck the rest of the way appeared mostly flat. I'd gotten more than my share of climbing at this point.

"Hurting?" Hale asked.

"As it turns out, I should have spent more time on the stair climber at the gym." I laughed off his worry as I continued to stretch out the sore muscles.

Hale sat on the Path just beside my sleeping bag. He patted his lap. "Bring 'em here."

"Do what now?" I lifted an eyebrow at his request. Not only was I so *not* ready for anything that Hale might want, but Yazmor and Tyrus sat up the way just a bit, arguing about…

Well, I had no idea. I'd found it was better not to ask such things, especially because they could find something to fight about no matter what.

"I ain't making a move on you, but we've got what might be a long fucking trip ahead of us. Your muscles'll feel a hell of a lot better if I work the knots out for you."

I swallowed hard, ashamed of my hesitation. I'd done *far* more with Hale in the past—what was a little massage in comparison? Not even a sexy shirt-off-on-the-bed sort of massage, but just on my calves.

He dropped his voice as if wanting to make sure it didn't carry. "You can trust me, Loch. You're about the only one who can. Won't do a thing but help with your muscles."

I wanted to say no, but something in his tone made that impossible. I didn't want to hurt him, to risk hurting anything between us. Logically, I knew he wasn't those creatures from the memory, knew that if he'd wanted to harm me, he'd had more than a few chances to do so.

So I gathered my courage and shifted, using my pack like a rest to lean my back against as I stretched my legs across his lap.

"Good girl," he said softly before rolling my pants up to my knees. He removed my shoes and socks, each touch careful and slow.

And the first press of his fingers to my calf muscle made me let out a surprisingly loud gasp. I hadn't realized they hurt *that* much.

Down the Path, both Yazmor and Tyrus swung their gazes toward me, their expressions having gone serious as if that noise was all it took to break them out of their petty fight. It only took a quick glance at me for them to realize the reason and just as quickly, they returned to their argument.

"See?" Hale said with a lopsided grin that made him look young.

"See what? It hurts worse."

"At first, sure, but it'll feel way better afterward."

"Men just love to make promises like that, don't they?" Even as I spoke, I knew he was right. He'd hardly started, and each touch hurt, but even I could tell the muscles had started to unknot and ease.

And yet, my hesitation weighed on me. After a moment, I whispered out a soft, '*I'm sorry,*' that I wasn't even sure he heard.

"No reason to be sorry. You should know by now that I ain't the type to get mad over nothing."

"Yeah, but it isn't fair to take my shit out on you."

He snorted softly, his gaze on my legs rather than my face. "That's what people do. We get our armor on and when people get too close, they get themselves cut on it. Fuck knows I've cut you a few times myself doing the same shit."

His words eased some of that shame inside me. I recalled the first time I'd caught sight of his scars, when he'd yelled at me and kept me from seeing them. I recalled the way he'd all but growled at me like a feral dog to keep me away from his wounds.

Before I had to respond, Hale dug his fingers into an especially tender area. I gritted my teeth to keep silent as he worked that knot.

"Breathe through it," he said, but didn't lighten his touch at all. Then again, that was so Hale. He didn't soften himself, not even for me. Instead, he had always looked at me as if I could take it, as if I didn't need him to lessen shit for me.

Soon enough, that pain eased, letting me pull in a deep breath.

"Better, right?"

"You're just a sadist."

"Maybe, but that fact you like me says more about you than me, doesn't it?"

The easy, familiar back and forth had me smiling beside myself. It was the first time in a while I felt like things could go back to how they'd been before. In the days since that memory, I'd struggled so much to find my place again. It had felt as if what I'd thought was stable had been yanked out from beneath me.

I'd worried I'd never feel like this again, never be able to smile and laugh with the men in my life again, but for the first time, I felt like maybe it wasn't as far gone a conclusion as I'd thought.

"I like to see you smile," Hale admitted, his touches having turned gentler. Or maybe I'd just gotten used to it? Maybe it was like his attitude — it wasn't different, but I understood him better, so it didn't bother me as it once had.

"Really? Most people say it's a sign I'm about to do something dumb."

"Well, that ain't exactly wrong, but I like the stupid shit you do. It means life isn't ever boring when you're around." He peered around us as if to prove the point. "I mean, we're in some fucking nightmare Path on the way to break into the Plains. Never would have figured this was anywhere in my future."

"We'll see if you're so happy when we get torn apart here."

"Long as I'm next to you when it happens, well, there are worse ways to go."

I used my heel to kick him in the thigh lightly as a punishment. "Don't say that. You should value your life more."

"Oh, I value it plenty, but I'm also a man who knows what things are worth. Spent a lot of years on my own, looking for a place to belong, for something worth wanting, and now that I've found that? Well, I got no plans on letting it go no matter how dangerous shit gets."

His words came out so serious that I dropped my gaze, unable to look at him, not wanting him to see the way they hit me. I thought back to when I'd met Hale, when he'd shoved me against a wall and had said he planned to fuck me. He'd sure as hell affected parts of me with that – parts a lot farther south than my heart – and I would have never thought him capable of making me feel this sort of warmth.

His laugh made it worse, but he moved on to grasp my foot in his large, strong hand. He pressed his thumb into my insole, and this time the sound I made wasn't pain at all.

I slapped my hand over my mouth to silence it, afraid to put something out there I wasn't ready for.

"Stop worrying so much," Hale said as he worked on my foot. "I'm not about to jump on you just because you moan a little. Why don't you take it easy until Gorrin gets a fire going and just let me work? Close your eyes and relax."

I was about to tell him there was no way I could relax when he touched me like that, but the moment I opened my mouth, a wide yawn escaped me.

Hale lifted his eyebrow as if to mock me, his hands never stopping their magic.

And since I couldn't really argue with him – and I didn't want to – I gave in and closed my eyes. It didn't take long before his touch eased me enough that I drifted off to the first peaceful sleep I'd had in a while.

* * * *

I woke with a gasp, a dream echoing in my head.

No, not a dream, a memory that isn't even my own.

No matter how much I knew it wasn't *me* who had experienced it, I still struggled with the after-effects. It made me feel oddly connected to whoever had, to the person who had lived through that. They'd not only had to overcome the actual event, the memories, but also physically heal. It reminded me of their broken body, the way they'd pulled themselves through the dirt and grass, stumbling the few times they got to their feet.

Sleep wouldn't come again, so I forced myself to my feet. I saw no sign of Gorrin, but a fire crackled just a few feet away, telling me he'd returned at some point. Hale and Tyrus slept, one at each end of the Path, like guards to ensure nothing could get past them.

The only one awake was Yazmor, who sat across the fire from me. His gaze was down, locked on something in his hands. When I took a step closer, I realized he had the book we'd brought open in his lap, and he scanned through the writing.

I sat beside him, the action enough for him to look over at me. "Done sleeping?"

"Seems that way."

"Nightmares?"

I nodded, then gestured at the book. "Find anything useful?"

Yazmor tilted the book my way, but the writing inside wasn't a language I recognized. "This was written by an old Demon Lord who sent people to the Path. Most never came back, but a few did."

"I thought anyone who came back was mad?"

"Oh, it seems like they were, but he still wrote down what he could figure out from them. After he did that, he had them killed."

"So much for a reward for a job well done…"

Yazmor tapped on the page. "They were uncontrollable, violent and swinging between rage and despair. It seems they were even able to ignore commands."

"I didn't think that was possible. Did it break the bond between them or something?"

"I don't think so. The Demon Lord, Hector, could sense that bond. It was like whatever they experienced here was so bad that it fractured their minds. You know that pain when you try to deny an order?"

I shuddered. "Oh, boy, do I remember that."

"Well, I'd guess they still felt it, it was just that their mind was so fragmented and broken that it didn't affect them the same way. Hector had no real choice but to kill whatever came back."

"You don't remember this? Weren't you there?"

Yazmor flashed me a smile. "I remember Hector. He came a few before Tyrus. He was taken out by a lover if I recall correctly."

"I can't imagine a Lord letting their guard down like that."

He tilted his head, and I immediately got his point. *I did that to Gorrin, didn't I?* Still, he didn't mention that, instead continuing with the story. "Hector fell for a damned name Jordan. He showered him with everything he could have ever wanted—except power. I think Jordan was playing the game from the start, waiting for his chance, and eventually he managed it. After Hector fell asleep, Jordan buried a knife in Hector's temple. Of course, damned don't handle that much power well, so he only made it a few weeks before someone else took his position. I wonder what sort of reunion that would have been…"

Probably a lot like Gorrin and mine, right?

I waved my hand to get him to focus. "We were talking about you remembering these tests he did."

"Right. Well, Hector kept things to himself. No one else except those closest to him knew anything about it. In fact, these are written *by* him, which means he was the one doing the interviews and recording the results himself. We're lucky that Tyrus had his old books still."

"Is there anything useful in them? Anything that tells us what we'll find in here?"

"Sort of. You've got to remember that the person who said all this was completely mad, so the things they said don't make a lot of sense."

"Which explains why you're the perfect one to read it." I gave him a smirk at the joke.

Yazmor laughed, no sign of anger at the mockery. "Exactly. I'm not all there either, so I speak crazy person."

"Can you read some to me?"

Yazmor nodded and ran his finger across the strange writing, his voice soft. "This is talking about the story one of the damned told him when they came back. This person has been gone for a week and was found eating dirt just outside of the city. It reads, 'Klyne said that mist covers the ground, and when he left the Path, it made it so he couldn't find his way back. He said the silence got to him, that it was so quiet, he thought he was completely alone. He wandered through the mist for what felt like weeks. I asked what he ate or drank to survive, and he said he ate fruit off the trees, and that small ponds held fresh water along the way.'"

"So there's food here?"

"Maybe," Yazmor said. "Or maybe the damned was chewing on rocks and didn't know the difference. You can't take anything written here as the truth — it's only how he saw it, and that view was twisted the longer he stayed here. A lot of what Hector wrote revolves around the landscape. Because the damned left the Path early, he mostly wandered."

"How did he go crazy then?"

"People can lose their minds from being lost. I once couldn't find my way out of one of those huge malls and after a few hours, I about went crazy."

"Yeah, but it's a really short walk for you," I pointed out.

Yazmor leaned over, bumping me with his shoulder. "Getting lost wasn't the end of it. See, here — 'Klyne says something started following him. It was in the fog, and at first, he just heard clicking and rustling. When he slept, he said it brushed against him, waking him, but when he tried to figure out what it was, it would pull back. The longer he remained lost, the bolder it grew. Klyne said it grabbed his foot once and tried to yank him, that it started to go for him even when awake. He swore that it stalked him no matter where he went, that it continued to grab him, that the more he fought, the more vicious it became.'"

"How did he get back, then? If he was lost and had something attacking him, how did he escape it and return to the Chasm?"

Yazmor scanned the page, running his finger across the words there. "It seems that when Klyne wished to return, when he gave up, he turned around and found the walkway leading down to the Chasm. The damage was done and he was no longer himself. When he was brought to the cells that Hector had, Klyne was lucid rarely. He woke sure that the thing in the fog was still after him. He attacked almost everyone he saw, believing they were in league with the creature from the fog. No matter what anyone did or explained, nothing could convince him it was gone. They waited about two weeks, but after he managed to kill four guards, Hector decided he was too dangerous to keep alive. They'd gotten everything they could from him, anyway."

When Yazmor went quiet, only the crackling of the fire filled that space. I weighed what he had said, but I struggled to believe it. That was likely just self-serving delusion.

The idea of some creature in the fog was by far the least shocking or outrageous thing that had happened thus far. I mean, we'd walked up some weird winding route carved into the mountains of hell, then found a Path that would disappear if a person left it, and, oh yeah, I was doing this all with two demons, an angel and some weird tree-being who existed from an old version of the universe.

The idea that the fog might hide some creature was a far more normal thing than anything else that had happened so far.

"Do you think he's right?" I asked.

Yazmor turned his gaze out to the darkness, to the fog that shifted like ocean waves. He stared as if he could see into it, and I'd learned to put nothing past him. "I know he's right."

"How?"

"I can sense it. I don't know what it is, but it's there. It's watching us, like it's trying to figure us out."

"What is it?"

"No idea. I can tell you it isn't something I've run across before. It's not from Earth or the Chasm or the Plains. It's bound to this place."

"Can we talk to it?"

"I don't think so. It's like it isn't quite real, or maybe it's better to explain that it isn't quite sentient. It isn't stupid, it isn't an animal, it seems to be able to think and reason, but it isn't a full being, either. It's almost like an echo, a program running directions it's had for a long time, something driven by the will of someone else."

I blew out a breath, putting my hands up to the fire to warm my palms. "So it's like a guard dog Hubis put here?"

"That's probably the best way to explain it, but I don't think Hubis made it, at least not on purpose. This place...I think it was made to protect the Plains, but I don't think Hubis made it consciously. I think he tried to sever the Plains from Earth and the Chasm, but nothing in this universe can exist in a void. It will always be connected to the space around it. The Path was shaped by that desire, and the thing here was the same."

"Great, so we should expect to get stalked by some weird manifestation of God's paranoia. Just when I didn't think this could get any worse."

Yazmor turned to look at me, the violet of his eyes reminding me of the creature I'd seen in the Lost Caves, the glimpse of what Yazmor really was.

"Why did you keep your eyes like that?" I asked, regretting the question the moment it left me. I quickly tried to fix the mistake. "I'm not saying you shouldn't have, or like there's anything wrong with them. In fact, I really like them. They're different and unique and they fit you. It's just, you changed the rest of how you looked to fit in, but no one has eyes like those." I paused and pulled in a shaky breath when I realized I'd entirely forgotten to breathe during my tirade. After that, I leveled a glare at him. "You could have stopped me from just rambling, you know?"

Yazmor laughed softly and shrugged. "I like when you ramble. I follow along with it pretty easily. Maybe my crazy plays well with yours. And I'm not insulted by your question — it's a pretty good one. I've always kept these eyes. I usually take on the form of the dominant type of life for each cycle, but somehow, changing my eyes felt like losing myself. If I look in a mirror, I want to see *me* still, and the eyes do that."

"You said you usually take on the dominant type of life, so that means not always?"

"That's right. Some cycles are boring, and who wouldn't want to pass time as an iguana or a dodo?"

"I guess I should count myself lucky you decided to go human this time. Though, I think you'd have done well as a cat."

"Just a cat? I think I'm more of a tiger."

I shook my head. "Nope — you're a house cat. Lazy, impossible to predict, doesn't give a fuck what others want or expect from you."

"I guess I can't argue with that. In fact, if it wasn't so hard to change my form, I'd think about trying that out now. I'd get to just laze about in your room, getting head rubs whenever I want, knocking things off shelves. Sounds like a pretty good life now that you mention it..."

I elbowed him in the side. "Don't you get any ideas about that. I like you in this form, thank you very much."

"Fine, fine. Can I still laze about in your room and get head pats?" Yazmor twisted until his head rested in my lap and he was stretched out by the fire, the book still in his hands.

It made him look so young and innocent. He wasn't, not by a long shot, but knowing that didn't stop me from smiling and running my fingers through his slightly messy violet hair. When he did things like this, I could almost forget everything I knew about him and pretend we were both just young, dumb kids falling in love for the first time.

What would that have been like for us? Would I have blushed at his clumsy attempts to seduce me? Would he have been eager as he hid his nerves with unearned arrogance?

As quickly as I wondered, I had to laugh. That wasn't a far cry from how we were, was it?

"Well, if we can't sleep, why don't I keep reading this?" He didn't wait for me to answer before he held the book up to see the words and started to read it out loud to me.

His voice remained soft, probably so he didn't bother the others who still slept.

At least, I thought they did. It was likely that they'd woken when I'd stood — I doubted they'd have slept through that — but they'd probably just pretended to be asleep again until I settled in.

Still, I pretended it was just the two of us telling bedtime stories, that we got this sort of simple fun that normal couples got. We weren't Demon Lords, weren't trying to take on God, weren't stuck in some weird fucking between where something in the fog wanted to *eat* us.

Nope, we were just two stupid kids telling each other stories by a campfire.

The universe would force us to wake up soon enough—might as well enjoy the fantasy while we could. Besides, I couldn't exactly deny just how much I enjoyed running my fingers through Yazmor's violet hair or the quirk of his lips at the touch, the way he arched into it, begging for more.

Fuck knew I'd spent sleepless nights in a lot worse ways in the past.

Chapter Nine

Gorrin

I couldn't pay attention to anything specifically. The conversations behind me, the steps of Loch and the Lords, they only pulled the smallest bit of my focus.

Instead, I allowed my gaze to dart over the horizon as I listened for any sign of attack. I couldn't shake the feeling that something followed us.

I couldn't hear it, hadn't seen it, but that didn't stop me from feeling it moving about in the fog.

"Keep thinking that hard and you'll burst a blood vessel." Loch fell into step beside me, her hands tucked into the front pocket of her large hoodie sweater.

"I can't help it." I stopped myself before I said anything more. There was no good reason to worry her, to tell her what I knew. Between the five of us, we had enough manpower to deal with any threats, thus informing her that we had something following us through the fog wouldn't make us any safer. "Being here makes me uneasy," I hedged. "This place might not react to me as it does to you, but something inside me tells me I should not be here."

"And here I thought you were listening for the creature in the fog."

I turned toward her, my eyes narrowed to slits. "There is no way that was just a lucky guess."

"Yazmor and I read from the book he brought, written about a damned who came here. It talked about something in the fog, and Yazmor said he could sense it, too. Given the way you've been staring off, I figured you could, too."

"Don't you think that is vital information you should have shared?"

"Maybe we should start having a breakfast meeting to go over all the new stuff." She paused, then shook her head. "Or maybe not. Hale would just talk about whatever dirty dream he had and Yazmor would tell us facts no one cares about."

I nearly laughed at how correct she was with that guess. In fact, her words had me imagining that exact thing. She truly did seem to understand the four of us, which was a rather impressive feat.

I doubted any person had really understood any of us, let alone all of us.

"That is a risk we might have to take. At the very least, please tell *me* anything you find in that book. I know little about this place and every bit of information could end up being the difference between survival and death here. Was there anything else useful?"

She shook her head, the action causing the green of her hair to fall into her face. "Nothing much. The book talked about a specific damned who was interviewed when they came back."

She went on, telling me about Hector and the experiments he'd been holding in secret.

I could hardly blame him for keeping them secret. If I'd known, I'd have probably orchestrated his immediate removal and helped put someone more easily controlled in his place. While Demon Lords had never directly killed one another because it would throw off the balance between us too much, I had never been above orchestrating for one to fall if they caused problems.

I had created my position in the Chasm to bring order to it, to try to make it a better place. The last thing I wanted was to see it delve into chaos due to poor leadership, and I had always been willing to do what needed to be done to stop that.

I doubted Loch would feel comfortable with that fact, so I kept it to myself. "Hector had always been rather eccentric. It doesn't surprise me that he'd do that, though him keeping it quiet does."

"I figured you knew everything."

"I try, but I am only one man."

"Angel."

I turned my head to look down at her, finding her smirking as if her response was the best joke she'd ever made. That sort of joy from her both drew me in and pushed me away. I'd never met someone so able to embrace life—even the bad parts of it.

Looking around proved that point. We were somewhere extraordinarily dangerous, headed for a battle we had little chance of surviving, after Loch had suffered terribly over and over again, but she still managed to find things to laugh about.

"Why are you looking at me like that?" She reached up and touched her face as if checking for something.

I shook my head to try to clear the expression away. The last thing I wanted was to make her uncomfortable. "I was just thinking that your ability to find joy impresses me. I have rarely felt any true joy in my life."

Her lips tipped down. "Never?"

"I've done things I've enjoyed, but true joy? Being happy just because I am happy?" I pressed my lips together as I thought back on my very long life, at all the things I'd experienced. I recalled the pleasant times, rare though they'd seemed. Brief flings I'd had with others, moments where good food or weather or sheer chance had put me in a good mood had of course happened.

That hadn't been real joy, however. I'd never even realized there was a difference until I'd met Loch, until I'd seen a person who honestly found joy in living, even when she had no good reason to.

"Not really," I admitted. "I always saw life as a job. I was created for a reason, to aid Hubis in keeping order. Anything beyond that felt superfluous. It seemed like unnecessary distractions. Instead, I focused my attention on what I needed to do rather than what I saw as temporary pleasures."

"Why'd you take a place in the Chasm?"

The question was hardly unexpected. Anyone would want to understand that, want to know why a person would give up their place in the Plains and relegate them to the darkness of the Chasm. Still, I didn't relish admitting it. "I just saw the chaos of the Chasm, the souls trapped there, and it felt wrong. To throw away some souls for something so arbitrary did not sit well with me."

"And Hubis was just like, 'okay, cool, have fun?' He doesn't seem nearly that go with the flow."

"It was not so long a conversation. Hubis does not seek advice from others. He gives orders and expects obedience—nothing else. I told him what I planned to do, and he said nothing in return. The lack of response is the closest to approval one can expect from him. I doubt he was happy with the choice—the other angels certainly weren't—but I stood by it. When I took on a demon form so I could own souls, it made it impossible for me to return to the Plains like that."

"So you didn't go back there in all those years?"

"No. It wasn't until you destroyed my demon form, when I reverted back to my angel form, that I returned to the Plains."

"And Hubis welcomed you back?"

"If by welcomed you mean he put me to work immediately, then yes, he welcomed me back. I would guess that he saw my return as proof I had learned my lesson and returned to the fold. I doubt he can fathom the idea that I might see things differently from him, that I might still side against him. Hubis doesn't truly understand other people. He doesn't know why they do the things they do because he never thinks in those terms. Hubis has never understood humans. He's never even tried."

"Well, he *isn't* human, so that isn't really so shocking, is it?"

I shook my head at her misunderstanding. "I am not human, but that doesn't mean I can't understand how humans think or predict their behavior. Hubis doesn't see other living beings as real. Maybe that comes from having created them, a sense that they're lesser because of that. Hubis has always seen humans as something necessary to populate a world, but he's given no time or attention to getting to know any of them. Even in the Plains, he speaks to no one."

"It's probably hard to be the only one of your kind. It has to be lonely."

"Your ability to see the good in those who do not deserve it knows no bounds, does it? Even after all he has done, you still make excuses for him?" My gaze shifted over to Yazmor, who walked behind us, picking up a rock, studying it, then throwing it aside. The next seemed to meet his approval because he placed it into his pocket. "And not all remnants behave in such a way."

Her eyes widened and when she spoke back, her voice was low. "You know…"

"About Yazmor? Of course. Anyone who didn't recognize him for what he is was a fool."

"Gee, thanks."

Her pouting warmed me. "You are still young, so you can be excused for not identifying him. For the rest of us, one look at the way he acts would make it clear enough. Kylie was a different matter. She changed her looks enough to hide, and she adapted to those around her to fit in."

"Did you know her before?"

"I knew of her would be a fairer statement. She came to the Chasm and the Plains in the past, and there had been times where Hubis dispatched me or other angels for tasks that made little sense at first. Eventually, I realized they were for her benefit, but he always swore us to secrecy. He told us she could never know of our help or presence."

"What's between them? Kylie refused to tell me."

"That I can't tell you. I have no idea — whatever it was came from their world. As far as I know, they've never spoken or faced one another in the time I've existed."

She pursed her lips, and I could nearly see the thoughts churning inside her. She really was interesting, the way what she thought played across her face, the way she worked through all the details to try to form an understanding of the situation.

I had hated that trait of hers when I'd first met her, had feared that it would lead to her demise, and yet now I could appreciate it. It was that drive that made her do as she pleased, the one that had her willing to take on the impossible. Now I understood it better. I could appreciate it for what it was — her power to do as no one else had managed. It made me wonder how far my little fish could take it, just how far she could swim upstream simply because she was the only one who would dare to try.

It was almost humbling to think that this girl, whom I had at first written off as unimportant, as foolish and naïve and weak, could have gotten further than any other had.

In fact, just looking at her made me tilt my head. She was here, between the four of us — men built by the world into vicious weapons — and she didn't seem to fit at all. While we were all different, in many ways the Lords had always been similar. We saw the world in a very strict way, as something to be overcome and conquered.

We had spent our lives bathed in blood, never afraid to do whatever dirty work would get us what we needed. We were all large, all terrifying in our own ways.

Then there was Loch. She walked between us, heads shorter and so much smaller. If I were looking at the situation from the outside, I would have worried for her safety between the four of us, yet she had never truly feared us as she should have. She seemed like a light in the middle of our darkness, hope where we only saw despair.

It was strange to think that while I would have written her off so many times, she was the driving force behind this all. She had overcome us — the worst of the worst — time and time again.

She tucked her hands farther into her sweater and hunched her shoulders, a sure sign that the bitter cold was getting to her. I fought the sudden, strange urge to put my arm around her, to pull her against my side and share my own warmth with her. It hit me so quickly, as so many things with her did, that I had to blink slowly to think about it.

She woke instincts inside of me that had always been there but slumbered.

Something farther down the way caught my attention, dragging me from my thoughts, from the comfortable quiet between us. Something dark and low to the dark shifted just off the Path. It twisted, moving in the fog so I struggled to tell what it was.

Well, beyond the fact that it was whatever I had sensed in the fog, the thing stalking us.

We approached it, and it remained there, just outside of view. Loch didn't notice it, her gaze forward, her thoughts likely taken up by our conversation. She never had been great at sensing dangers around her — as made obvious by her comfort with us.

I set a hand on her waist and pulled her gently to my other side, the one away from the thing in the fog. As I did so, it slid more into view, a single tentacle reaching for where she had been.

Loch looked at me, her brows furrowed. I gestured to our left, away from the creature. "Can you see the mountain out there?"

She squinted, trying to see where I pointed, but shook her head.

"Perhaps the fog will clear. It is a lovely sight." It really wasn't, but it kept Loch from noticing the creature, gave her a reason for my actions.

So as she stared off in the opposite direction, I risked one last glance as the creature pulled away, as it retreated back into the dense fog.

I had a feeling this was not the last time we'd have to deal with that thing, and I doubted it would make it so easy the next time...

* * * *

Loch

"Did you know that ears never stop growing?"

I rubbed my hands against my eyes, so over random fact hour with Yazmor, especially because it had now lasted *well* over an hour. If anything, it seemed worse than usual.

Yazmor always liked to supply information no one cared about or wanted, but this level of annoyance was new.

Which for me to say meant something, since he'd once left me to fend off a kinky pharmacist by myself because he'd wanted pussy — and not even the kind I could understand and respect a man for ignoring me to get.

Or, fuck, maybe my nerves were fraying from this endless walking, from the way we never seemed to make any progress no matter how far we went. That was bound to annoy a person.

"And what's the record for a person being quiet?" The snarky words escaped me without me even intending them to.

Yazmor paused, staring off as if considering it. "Probably the oldest mute person, I'd think. When we get back, I could find out for you."

His overly nice tone grated on me, even more so because I knew he'd do exactly that. If I didn't stop him, he'd spend hours upon our return — if we made it back — researching mute people to find the one who had lived the longest.

"Please, for the love of dick, don't do that."

"But you asked —"

"I was joking!" I snapped those last words out as almost a yell.

The moment the statement left me, an uncomfortable guilt gnawed at me. It wasn't Yazmor's fault that he could be an annoying companion. He couldn't help it, and it normally didn't bother me.

What the hell was wrong with me?

I opened my mouth to apologize, but Yazmor's surprisingly cold voice stopped me. "Very well. I think I'll move up closer to the front to watch for risks." He didn't wait for me to respond, his steps quickening to put distance between us.

I watched his back, that guilt pulling at me, then ran my hand through my hair.

"He's in a mood." Tyrus took the now vacant spot beside me. He didn't wear his suit jacket, and that threw me. In the Chasm, he was always dressed in a suit, but it seemed he'd realized that it wasn't as comfortable for all the walking we were doing.

He still was better dressed than me on my best day, of course. He had slacks on with a tucked in black shirt, tie, and suit vest. Without the jacket, I could see that the vest had a very light embroidered design, also done in black so they were almost impossible to notice.

"I think the stress is getting to me," I explained. "It's just all the walking without knowing what is going to happen, without knowing where exactly we're headed."

"Then don't focus on the ultimate goal. Instead, think only on the next step. If you narrow your focus, you'll find it easier to deal with the unknown."

"Is that how you do it?"

"Not usually. I prefer to actually know. When that isn't possible, though, I learn what I can to make the best choice, then focus only on the steps I need to make. I have no control over the unknowable, over things outside of my sphere of influence, so I might as well spend my attention on the things I *can* control."

I snorted softly, then gave him a tense smile when he looked toward me. "That's just so *you* advice."

"It's good advice."

"Probably," I admitted as we walked together. A glance out at the endless fog made me shiver. "I feel almost like we're on some treadmill, like we're not actually moving at all. I almost feel like if I turned around, even though we left it two days ago, that I'll see the stairs down to the Chasm behind us."

"The Path seems to be made to confuse people, to turn them around and make them doubt themselves. Still, people lose their way on Earth all the time — it isn't quite so scary."

"Yeah, well, on Earth those people don't get stalked by some weird creature in the fog."

"Have you never heard of bears and wolves? Earth has more than its fair share of predators."

I thought about that and didn't fight my smirk. It wasn't bears or wolves I considered chasing some poor lost hiker through the woods. Instead, it was the men.

"That smile makes me certain you are thinking something you shouldn't," Tyrus said, his eyes narrowed in suspicion at me.

"Tyrus and Hale and Gorrin, oh my," I whispered.

He just stared at me for a moment before a rare chuckle escaped him, as if I'd both surprised and charmed him.

A snap to our left broke the moment. As soon as it happened, the sound so strange because of the horrid silence that had filled our trip thus far, everyone moved.

Tyrus shoved me behind him, tucking him against his back in a move that annoyed me as much as it made me swoon. At the same time, the others moved closer, as if closing ranks around me.

To which I kicked Tyrus' calf. "You know, I'm a Lord, too," I muttered against his strong back.

He froze, as if just realizing what he'd done, but didn't release me.

"I have no intention to harm her."

I didn't recognize the voice at all. It was soft, clearly a woman, but the accent of it made it seem like she struggled with the language.

"That's just because you haven't talked to her yet," Hale said. "Trust me, that feeling changes."

At which I point I gave Hale a kick of his own.

An almost lyrical laugh answered the action, and I had a moment of *what the fuck* when I thought it came from Hale. Quickly, I realized that made no sense.

"I didn't think there was anyone in the Path," Gorrin said.

"There aren't many, but there are a few of us."

"Why?"

"Because when there is no way back and no way forward, people are forced to live their life between."

Right, because that doesn't sound fucking crazy…

"You all look tired. I have a camp just ahead, and I rarely have any company. Why don't you all join me?"

"Like fuck," Hale said with all the tact he normally used.

Still, he wasn't wrong.

I jabbed my finger into Tyrus' side, and he responded with a sigh before releasing me. It gave me the freedom to shift to the side to see the woman, though Tyrus didn't give me room to move past him.

She appeared young, with large green eyes that managed to mix innocence and danger all together. Long hair so pale it appeared white went to her lower back, impossibly straight and somehow clean. In some ways, she reminded me of Azael.

Well, minus all the whole evil killing thing.

I narrowed my eyes. *Maybe minus that, maybe not…*

"Following random chicks in the fog is how people get drugged and robbed," I said. "It works with men, but I don't have a dick to urge me to take that risk."

The woman smiled, her lips pale, no sign of makeup on her. She seemed oddly fitting in a simple white dress and barefoot, like an ethereal spirit that could lead any man to his doom.

"The Path is treacherous for those who don't know the way. I've been here a long time, so I can offer you some guidance."

"Why would you do that?" Tyrus asked.

She shifted her gaze to Gorrin, a meaningful look there. "Call it a favor for old times' sakes."

Gorrin let out a soft curse, so quiet I almost doubted I heard it. "Koller? Is it really you?"

The woman smiled brightly. "I didn't know if you'd recognize me."

"What are you doing here?"

She shrugged, then gestured farther down. "That is a story to be told when sitting. Just down the path you'll see a fire. Follow it."

"We can't leave the Path," Tyrus said.

"It is not far off—close enough to still see it. Trust me, you will want to stop. I owe at least that much to Gorrin, after all." She didn't wait for anyone to say anything else before turning and wandering out, into the fog and tree line.

Gorrin turned toward me, the others doing the same until we looked like a team having some huddle-up.

"So," Hale said. "Who's the crazy barefoot chick in the fog?"

"Koller. She was an angel."

"Was?" I peered in the direction she'd gone even if I couldn't see her anymore. "What does was mean?"

"She was cast out of the Plains."

"Like you?"

He shook his head. "I wasn't cast out. I opted to take a different form to rule in the Chasm. Koller did something unforgivable and Hubis removed her angel nature, turning her human, then cast her to Earth. Last I heard, she was there. I have no idea how she got here."

"Why does she feel like she owes you something?" Tyrus asked.

"Because I was the one who fought to ensure she wasn't simply destroyed."

His story made my heart beat faster. Why? I wasn't really a jealous type.

I knew Hale had fucked damn near everything that walked and Tyrus had had more than his fair share of partners. Why was it then that the idea of Gorrin having been romantically involved with someone in the past made me want to hiss at Koller and bare my teeth?

"Were you..." I asked before I could stop myself.

Gorrin said nothing back, which answered that, didn't it?

Tyrus cleared his throat. "Well, why don't we start out ahead? You two can catch up in a few minutes." With that, he headed off, Yazmor and Hale in tow.

It left Gorrin and I behind.

"We weren't like that," Gorrin said, his gaze down.

I took in a deep breath, relief swamping me.

"However, I wanted to be."

And there goes that relief...

"So why didn't it happen?" I forced myself to ask.

Gorrin didn't move or fidget as I would have under that level of scrutiny. His voice was soft when he answered, as though he didn't want to tell the story. In fact, I'd bet he'd rather face that fog monster than talk about this. "Koller was always reckless and far too enamored with humanity. She never understood her place, that she was to keep order in the Plains. Instead, she was too soft on humans, spent too much of her time on Earth." He let out a long sigh. "Eventually, she fell in love with a human on Earth. Even knowing it was forbidden, that such a union had no future, she did as she pleased."

"Hubis kicked her out because of that?"

Gorrin shook his head. "If it was only that, he wouldn't have intervened. He would have allowed her the time to realize it was a bad idea, to watch the human age and eventually die. The problem came when she attempted to usurp the order of things. She tried to take his soul herself, to free him from being bound to Hubis or anyone else. Angels cannot have souls bound to them though, not without taking on a demon form as I did. Her actions destroyed the human and nearly her as well. When Hubis found out, he wanted to kill her. I pled for her life, and only because of Hubis' fondness of me, did he agree to exile as a punishment."

Which meant that while Gorrin had cared for Koller, it had gone unrequited.

"I was never what she wanted," Gorrin whispered. "And because of that, I could only watch as she made choices that destroyed her. When she was made a human, I cut ties with her, knowing that my presence would only remind her of what she'd lost."

He didn't need to add the rest — that he'd felt the same way watching me in the Chasm, having to stand by while I made choices he feared would lead to my demise.

He'd watched one person he loved destroy themselves, and he'd fought against me so hard to ensure it didn't happen a second time.

I set my hand on his chest for balance, then went to my toes to brush my lips against his. My thoughts felt too jumbled for me to be certain what I meant with that kiss, but one thing was for sure — I better understood why he'd acted as he had.

He didn't just accept the sweet gesture, though. Instead, he wrapped an arm behind me, pulling me flush against his chest, and made my kiss seem like kindergarteners playing doctor for the first time. He slipped his tongue past my lips, delving into the heat of my mouth, to tease me in a way that made me wonder if we could get away with having sex right here on the Path.

That would be a pretty good claim if Koller saw that, right?

The pettiness might have shamed me if I were a better person.

Gorrin, forever the responsible one, broke the kiss. His panting breath warmed my still damp lips and his honey-colored eyes bore into me as he stared down. "We should get going."

"Are we going to see her?"

He nodded. "Koller can be reckless and naïve, but she wouldn't cause us harm on purpose. If she's here, she could have information that would benefit us."

I gripped his shirt tightly in my fist, not giving a fuck that I'd wrinkled it. I just needed to hold fast, to cling to him, and the way Gorrin held me said the same.

It felt strange for us, out of character for the independent people we were, but that didn't stop the way I wanted to never let him go. Even if it was stupid — and it was — I wanted to go right past Koller, to ignore any help she wanted to hold out to us.

As those feelings swamped me, I shook my head and shoved away from Gorrin.

What the fuck was wrong with me?

I peered over at Gorrin, who seemed every bit as perplexed by his behavior as I did.

I had a sinking feeling that whatever was happening would only get worse…

Chapter Ten

Wow, look at that – I still hate her.

Maybe I would never grow past being an awkward thirteen-year-old glaring at another pretty girl who my boyfriend looked at.

Which was so not the look I preferred for myself. Still…

Koller used to be an *angel.* She was similar to Gorrin in ways I could never be, had a shared history and background with him I never would. She understood him in a way I could never.

It meant that when she looked as innocent and sweet as she had before, I wondered if I could stab her *just a little.*

Not enough to kill her, just enough to make the point to stay away from Gorrin. A good scar could work as a wonderful reminder for people who struggled to learn things…

Knock it off, you fucking psycho.

I sighed as I took a seat on one of the rocks that rounded the large campfire we'd found just off the Path. There were enough spots for each of us, making me wonder if she'd set this up for us or it was just coincidence.

What *wasn't* a coincidence, I was sure, was how the spot left for Gorrin ended up right next to her.

Instead of making a scene — and boy did I want to — I held my hands up, palms toward the fire to try to chase away the chill.

"You're downright snarling," Hale whispered to me. "If you kill her, I'll bury the body." His lifted eyebrow made me unsure if I should laugh at the joke or decline the offer.

Or accept the offer. That's an option too. Fuck knows I don't want to dig a hole.

"Are you going to explain why you are here, now?" Gorrin turned a sharp eye on Koller, a sure sign that despite their past, he didn't fully trust her.

She sighed as she dragged one of her toes through the sand. "Life as a human was far from easy. I thought that when I died I would go back to the Plains. I wouldn't be an angel, but I could at least go back to where I belonged. Unfortunately, I hadn't understood how lasting my punishment was. When I died, I woke in the Chasm."

"You sold your soul?"

She shook her head. "No. I never would do that — I knew that wasn't worth it. Because Hubis took my angel form, because he made me human and cast me out, I was denied entry to the Plains for all time. Worse, in the Chasm, I had no protection, no power, nothing. I was outside the order there, bound to no one."

Gorrin frowned. "If you were in the Chasm, wouldn't you have eventually seen me there? Why did you not seek me out? I would have protected you."

And there is that stabbing pain in my chest again...

My brain supplied the image of perfect Koller all cuddled up with Gorrin, desperate for him to protect her. Is that what he wanted? Was that what he'd craved from me?

Because I wasn't ever going to be that sort of woman.

"You had done enough for me. Besides, all you could have done was kept me safe in the Chasm, made that place more comfortable as long as you were there. I didn't want that—I wanted to go *home*."

"Surely you understood that wasn't possible."

Koller peered around the fire, her gaze moving over the other Lords and myself. "Coming from you, who seems to be leading all the Demon Lords through the Path and to the Plains? Are you really in any position to tell me what's possible and what isn't?"

Gorrin pressed his lips together as though he didn't want to admit she was right but also couldn't argue with her.

"So you followed the Path to try to make your way to the Plains?" I asked, wanting her to continue the story rather than the little trip down memory lane with Gorrin.

Koller looked directly at me, and boy did she give me an expression the others didn't get. I understood it for what it was, though—jealousy. I knew because I recognized it from my own feelings. "Yes. I've spent—" She furrowed her brows as if trying to figure something out, before shaking her head. "I don't know how long, honestly, but I've spent a very long time here, in the Path."

"I thought everyone who spent time here went crazy," Yazmor said, the first time he'd spoken up since our little spat. "And I am an expert when it comes to insanity."

"This place twists people," Koller explained. "It is pervasive and subtle and never-ending. It works like the dripping of water—just keeps going until it wears away the stone beneath. The longer people are here, the more affected they become."

"Affected by what?" Gorrin asked.

"You must feel it already. Choices that don't feel like your own, feelings that make no sense to you. You feel and behave in ways you can't understand."

I thought back to the way I'd clung to Gorrin, the way I'd snapped at Yazmor.

We *were* acting strangely, weren't we? Not so much as to say it wasn't natural, that it was easy to blame on stress or the situation, but we weren't being normal.

"Why isn't it affecting you, then?"

"It is. That's the reason I'm still here."

"You want to explain that? Because I don't speak crazy so fluently," I snapped.

Koller smiled, but it lacked warmth or humor. "I came here to escape my punishment, to traverse the Path and return to my home, to the Plains, but as I spent more time here...I started to doubt if I belonged there. I thought...there's something wrong with me, something broken, something that caused me to behave the way I had that had cast me out."

She dropped her gaze to her hands as she wrung them together. "If there is truly something wrong with me, what right do I have to try to return, to overrule the most high? I wandered here, through the fog, learning the ways of the Path, too afraid to truly escape. If I make it through here, if I return, what if I'm cast out again? Right now, I still have the hope of a return, but if I made it and lost it again? If I had to confront that I don't belong, that I can never return? Would that not be so much worse?" Her hands moved against each other, starting with a slight scratching until drops of blood escaped and fell to the dirt.

Gorrin caught her hands, pulling them apart gently. Koller focused then on the damage, on what she'd done by gouging her nails into her own skin.

So much for thinking she's sane.

Still, her words stayed with me. That fear, that disbelief. I thought about how I'd clung to Gorrin, how I'd been afraid that Koller would take him despite me having no good reason to think that at all.

At least feeling so out of control made a little more sense.

"Do you know how to get to the Plains?" Tyrus asked, his no-nonsense tone the same as always able to get right to the heart of the matter.

Koller shook her head, the action causing her long pale hair to move. "Not exactly. I've spent a long time looking around, and the Path doesn't twist around me. Possibly because I was an angel, possibly because I don't feel I'm worthy of the Plains. I've learned a lot, but that answer still evades me. All I know for certain is that the Path will not lead you there."

Hale leaned in, resting his elbow on his knee. "Everything I've heard says the Path is the only safe fucking place here."

She nodded. "There is some truth to that, at least at first. The dangers here avoid the Path. The Guardian—

the creature that guards the fog — will attack on the Path if people remain here too long, but it is far safer."

"Then why tell us to leave it? That seems the opposite of a good idea. It's like telling someone to jump into shark-infested water," I said.

Koller looked at me again, blinking slowly, her eyes an unbelievably beautiful green that made me nearly fall in love with her crazy ass. "That is a more apt description than you realize. The Path is a raft, but a raft is only a temporary haven. Eventually, a person will die from exposure or hunger or thirst, or perhaps be knocked into the dangerous waters if they refuse to move. The only salvation is to face the sharks and swim for shore."

She looked at me, but it almost felt as though she looked past me, and it was then I knew that she was fucking nuts. What she said might be true, but it didn't change that this place has broken a part of her, that her psyche had deep cracks running through it.

"Others have followed the Path, have stuck to it, and they have all perished. If you wish to do what no one else has, you must behave as no one else dares. You must do what they have not." After that, she blinked again, some animation returning to her expression as if waking from a trance. "Other tips for surviving the Path — one, trust no one. Anyone you meet here belongs to the Path. The damned and demons who have survived are no longer the people they once were. Two, eat and drink as you like — the items here won't harm you. Three, remember who created this place and why they did it. Four, fight against your own darkest nature, because that is what ultimately tears people apart here."

She rose, graceful as though her every move was a dance. "And yes, I include myself in those you should not trust."

"Then why should we listen to your rules?"

Her gaze flirted over to Gorrin, quickly looking away as if embarrassed. "I wish you to make it through. I may not deserve to taste Paradise again, but Gorrin does. Still, we all have our own motives, things we want, things we will do anything to get. I am no exception to that. Even now, this place whispers to me, tells me to take what I want and damn the costs. So, no, you should trust only that every person here will do whatever they must to get whatever they most want." She took a few steps backward, toward the fog as if to leave.

"Wait," Gorrin rushed out. "Why are you going? Wouldn't you be safer with us?"

She smiled, the look showing nothing of the innocent girl she'd appeared as before. "Yes, I would, but you would not be. Go ahead and rest before you leave. This place? It drains us terribly, and if you aren't careful, it'll overcome you that way alone."

No one spoke when she waved and turned, all but skipping into the fog until I couldn't even spot her silhouette.

"Well, that's fucking unnerving," I muttered.

"That girl has her hot-to-crazy measure all off," Hale responded. "She's upped her crazy *way* too high."

I turned a glare on him, not caring for anyone to talk about Koller as hot, not with the jealousy still burning inside my chest.

Hale smirked as if he fed off my annoyance. "Don't give me that look, Loch. You've got both your hot and crazy levels maxed."

"Somehow, that doesn't make me feel any better." I crossed my arms and hunched closer to the fire.

Hale didn't appear sorry in the least, though, as he stretched his feet out toward the flames.

The conversation slowly died down until all five of us stared at the red and oranges that danced in front of us, the unknowns and dangers surrounding us, waiting for a chance to jump in and fuck up our day.

Guardian, the thing in the fog, the other people here—all crazy from what it seemed—the changes in our personalities, the question of how the hell to get out of it, it all hung above us like a beast watching for a chance to strike.

But there was nothing we could do about it right then, so instead, we set out our things to rest again.

Maybe everything would look better in the morning, right? That's what people said.

Except, I doubted anything would look different, not so long as we woke up here, on the Path.

* * * *

Hale

Fuck walking.

Fuck this stupid bullshit.

Fuck *everything*.

My eyes drifted over to a certain green-haired disaster and my hands curled as if I could already feel her.

Well, fuck her at least.

"Don't stare like that."

I turned a bored look on Tyrus. "Don't you ever get tired of bitching? Seems like it'd get old sooner or later. Fuck knows it's old to me now."

Tyrus didn't wilt under my look, but then again, he never had. It was one of the things I both liked and hated the most about him. It didn't matter how hard I pushed at him, how ugly I got, he never reacted at all.

I wasn't used to being ignored, but I had to admit, it made me offer him at least a little respect.

"She's still hesitant around us. If you make her more fearful, we will *all* suffer."

"She isn't afraid of me—she's just trapped in her own head. She'll be fine." Even as I said that, a part of my brain screamed in response that it wasn't true.

Or rather, that it might not be.

Still, if there was one thing I was good at, it was pretending shit was however I wanted it to be until I made my way through it. I'd lived my whole fucking life underestimated. If I took shit the way the world handed it to me, I'd have curled up and died a long fucking time ago.

So even though a part of me worried about Loch rebounding, another part of me refused to believe she might not. That was an unacceptable outcome.

Loch sighed and rolled her shoulder as if it ached. It probably did—these backpacks were no jokes. We might be stronger and faster than humans by a far cry, but even our bodies complained when we did too much or stressed them too long. Still, we'd needed to bring food and water. There seemed to be fruit on the trees, and we passed water sources, but we had no idea when those might disappear.

"Watch yourself," Tyrus said as though he could see my thoughts when I took a step toward Loch.

"You watch your own ass," I snapped back. "I'll watch hers."

He made a soft sound that screamed he didn't like me—and fuck did I understand that—but I left him behind and headed for Loch. Spending all day with a bunch of men wasn't my idea of a good time. Too much testosterone, too many dicks. I'd take Loch's company over that any fucking day.

Loch stood a few steps off the Path, close enough to keep sight of it and not risk getting lost. After rolling her shoulder again, she reached down for her toes.

Which gave me *all* sorts of ideas. Somehow, it felt like years since I'd last gotten to really touch her. I wanted to strip her down and reacquaint myself with every luscious inch of her body, to trace every curve with my tongue, to leave marks to ensure she *never* forgot about me.

The need beat inside my head so loudly it almost hurt.

Did she feel the same? Was this all a game to her? Did she just want to keep me close? To trick me? To see what she could get from me?

Loch twisted to look over her shoulder at me, her eyebrow lifted as if to ask me what the fuck I was doing right behind her.

"Want to take a walk?" As soon as I said that, I cursed at myself.

Take a walk? When the fuck had I turned into an idiot? We'd been walking for what felt like days already, so what sort of bullshit excuse was that?

If I could have kicked my own ass, I probably fucking would have…

Loch chuckled but didn't call me out for my stupidity. "Sure."

143

We headed off at an angle, remaining close enough to the Path to not lose sight of it but far enough to feel like we had some privacy.

"This feels like some shitty class camping trip," Loch said as she tucked her hands into the large pocket at the front of her sweater. "We're all wandering around and none of us really want to be here."

"Not wanting to be here has been your whole afterlife, hasn't it? Figured you'd be used to that."

"Yeah, but before I at least had a comfy bed."

"You want to try my sleeping bag? Might be comfier."

She snorted softly, as though she saw right through my clumsy flirting.

If that could even be called flirting, since I was totally serious about her ending up in bed with me.

Loch curled in on herself slightly, which made me realize—yeah, the cold fucking sucked here. It was pervasive and relentless. The only time that sharp edge of it disappeared was when I sat next to a fire. The moment I wandered from that small sphere of heat, it was as if that chill stole every bit of warmth from my body.

Without thinking, I wrapped my arm around Loch's shoulders and pulled her tighter against my side.

She didn't fight it, which eased part of that frustration inside of me, the one that screamed for more.

"We shouldn't go too far," she said.

"Why? Miss the other guys already?"

She tilted her head up to look at me. "You normally don't care about things like that."

"Maybe I just don't like being strung along." I tightened my fingers on her arm without thinking about it. "Maybe I start wondering if this is all some game from you and you're just laughing at us all?" My own words made some part of me question myself.

What the hell was I saying?

Yet, I couldn't argue with it, either.

Loch was fucking Tyrus, Gorrin and—well, she wasn't fucking Yazmor as far as I knew, since I couldn't picture him having sex. Still, there was something between them, something more than friendship.

Which, from the outside looking in, felt a lot like her using me. Was she laughing at me behind my back for being such an idiot?

A sharp pain in my side made me look down to realize she'd elbowed me. It cleared the anger from my head a bit, enough to realize she was speaking and hear her words.

"You're hurting me, you asshole."

I pulled my arm back, the release enough for me to see that, yeah, I'd dug my fingers into her arm *hard*. I blinked slowly as she rubbed at the spot, cursing myself for my actions.

"Sorry," I muttered, unsure what else to say. What the hell had come over me?

Whatever it was, I still felt it. This gnawing, angry part of me snarled inside me at the idea of anyone near me. It whispered that Loch was just like all the others, just as willing to fuck me over the moment it was useful to her.

"What the fuck is wrong with you?"

"No idea what you're talking about." I jerked my gaze to the side, unable to stand the weight of her eyes on me.

Loch wasn't a lightweight who folded at the first harsh word or sharp look, even from a man like me. She took a step closer to me, putting herself between me and the distance so I had to look at her or admit defeat by looking away again.

"What?" I snapped.

"You're not acting like yourself."

"No idea what you're talking about."

She narrowed her eyes as she stared at me, and despite the fact I had to look down at her, despite how fucking little she was compared to me, despite that unnamed anger inside me, I knew one thing for fucking sure…

This girl would always have the upper hand with me.

Loch

Why is Hale acting like this? I asked myself the question again and again but came to no real understanding.

I recalled Koller's words, how she said the place would twist people. Was this an example of that happening?

Hale was often rough, sure, and he was always at least a little angry. He wasn't usually angry with *me*, though. He had a strange tension inside him, as if he blamed me for something that I couldn't understand.

Was it me? Was this actually my problem? Maybe we weren't as close as I'd thought?

I pushed aside that doubt and took another step closer to him. Sure, he scared me. I recalled what had happened in that memory, and somehow, he reminded me of that time, especially with how aggressively he moved and spoke.

But I refused to let that fear rule me. Those things *weren't* the man in front of me. I knew every surly inch and bad trait of Hale.

I'm not afraid of Hale.

As far as pep talks went, that was a pretty shitty one, but I forced myself to set my hand on his chest. I leaned closer, seeking a kiss, needing that connection. I wanted to feel him against me, to know that we were still together, that our connection hadn't broken. I wanted to bridge the distance that had sprang up between us. I felt oddly alone and adrift, so I wanted a tether that connected me to Hale.

Hale reacted in a rush. He leaned down and kissed me with an aggression that had me crying out in surprise. He grasped my thighs and lifted me against him, clinging to me as if he would drown if he didn't have every part of me immediately.

He overwhelmed me with his touch, with his domineering kiss. It felt as if he branded me with his touch, as if he left marks behind to claim me. It was possessive and terrifying.

It scared me as much as I wanted more. I wanted to lose myself in his passion, to be the person I was before, but I couldn't quite release the fear.

I pushed his chest, needing space to gather myself. He was just too much, and it forced that too familiar panic sweep through me. He clung to me tighter, and my back struck something hard, the breath in my lungs escaping in a rush.

A tree? He'd pinned me to the tree, which freed his hands. He ran one up my side, then dipped beneath my shirt. The touch of his fingers against my bare skin broke the leash I'd had on my fear.

I pushed harder at his chest, trying to break his lips from mine.

"Are you just toying with me?" he asked, his voice different than I was used to, colder than I'd heard it before. "Are you just getting closer to me so you can betray me? Just playing games until you can stab me in the back?" His words were angry, but it was the pain soaked in them that really rang through.

I squeezed my eyes closed, the panic so strong that I froze. I couldn't even consider actually fighting back.

And just like that, he was gone. My legs gave out and I toppled to the ground, confusion swamping me along with that same panic. At first, I struggled only to draw air into my lungs, anything more complicated than that impossible.

"Are you out of your mind?"

The voice made me open my eyes, and the reason Hale wasn't there anymore became clear. Hale was sprawled out on the ground with Tyrus standing between him and me.

Hale frowned, as though he didn't know how to answer the question. "I wasn't going to hurt her."

"Do your eyes not work? She was *terrified*. She was fighting against you."

A deep line appeared in Hale's forehead before he peered past Tyrus and at me. Whatever he saw in my face must have gotten through, because he paled and dropped his gaze.

I gripped the tree I'd been leaning against to help me to my feet, ignoring how unsteady my legs felt, how unsteady *all* of me felt.

I went to speak, though what I would say I still didn't know.

Except, I didn't get the chance to be as surprised as everyone else by what I would say. Instead, a deafening crack filled the air and the ground beneath me disappeared. I fell into the darkness, unable to tell what way was up or down, every bit of light going out until I struck something hard.

Well, this was at least one way to get out of that uncomfortable conversation…

Chapter Eleven

The eerie silence and total blackness got to me. I closed my eyes then opened them again, trying to make out any difference, but there didn't seem to be one.

Basically?

I couldn't see shit.

It was like I'd fallen so far down into a hole that light had no way to reach me.

A groan made me twist as if to find the source of the sound.

"Loch?"

Tyrus' voice could have made me sob in relief.

I'm not all alone.

Getting trapped in the dark sucked but getting trapped alone in the dark would have been so much worse.

"I'm here," I rushed out, crawling toward his voice.

"Are you hurt?"

"I don't think so." I ran into something, and it grabbed me. I jerked backward in surprise, my adrenaline spiking.

"It's just me." This time, Tyrus' voice came from just in front of me, telling me what I'd run into. I relaxed at the realization, his touch letting me know I really wasn't alone.

Then it hit me—where was Hale?

"Hale?" I called out into the dark, fear drenching the words.

"I'm here, too." His answer was tense.

Had he gotten hurt?

I swallowed down the question, too afraid to ask.

"What happened?" I asked instead.

"We fell," Hale answered as if that were obvious.

I glared in the direction of his voice, not caring that he couldn't see it.

"How can we have fallen far enough that we can no longer see the top and yet not have gotten hurt?" Tyrus ran his hand gently over my arm as if soothing me while thinking out loud. "We must not have simply fallen a long way. This area must be separated from the rest in a different way, and the darkness must be a trait of this space."

I jerked up as I considered something, then patted at my pants. I found what I was looking for and pulled my cell from my pocket. I'd left the phone off since, as it turned out, there was no service in the Path. It worked in the Chasm, but the Path was too far.

I pressed the power button and waited until the screen lit up. I twisted the phone around, but nothing changed.

"What the fuck?" I whispered to myself. I could see the light of the screen, but it was like it didn't spread out from the screen at all.

"It's like the air absorbs all the light," Tyrus said. "You should shut that off so the battery doesn't run down."

"But it's better than nothing," I said, fearful of losing that tiny source of light in the blackness around me.

A hand sat on top of mine, squeezing gently. "You should turn it off. You're not alone here, but the phone may prove useful later."

He was right, which annoyed me all the more. Still, I did as he said, forcing myself to hold the button on the side and power down the phone. It plunged us back into the darkness, and I tried to ignore the way my heart sped, the way I searched through the black around me as if my eyes might adjust and find *something* out there.

I could see no details, though. No matter how long I sat in the darkness, I couldn't see a damned thing.

"We can't just sit here forever," Hale said.

"You don't get to have an opinion," Tyrus said, the venom in his voice obvious.

So much for them getting along anymore...

"We'll deal with that shit later," Hale pressed. "For right now, we need to work together. In case you haven't noticed, it's even fucking colder in here. The longer we wait here, the better the chance that we won't have the power or energy to get out."

When he said that, for the first time, I noticed how right he was. It had been cold before, but it was nothing compared to right now. The chill seeped past my clothes, past my skin, down to my bones.

I shivered in response, but even that didn't help.

Tyrus moved, and I couldn't stop myself from grabbing onto him, a fear that if I let go of him for even a moment, we'd end up separated and I'd be lost in this darkness alone.

He shifted his hand and laced his fingers with mine, helping to pull me to my feet. "Don't worry. I'm not going anywhere."

Sure, I was embarrassed as fuck at my pathetic display, but shame was a far cry better than the sheer panic if I lost him.

"Because we can't see, we need to remain together."

I took a deep breath, trying to clear the cobwebs from my head.

You are a Demon Lord. Get your shit together! You took down a Demon Lord, faced off against an angel, and aren't afraid to get naked with some of the most dangerous men around. You will not be defeated by a little darkness!

My little pep talk helped, reminding me of exactly what a bad bitch I really was.

Or so I thought until my foot caught something on the ground—a fucking pebble that was out to get me—and I pitched forward. Tyrus didn't let go of my hand, though, just as he'd promised, and it kept me from hitting the ground.

So much for being a badass, huh?

"Is this some sort of trap?" I asked to smother the embarrassment.

"Maybe," Tyrus acknowledged. "Maybe it's a way to separate people from the Path? If a person were alone, this sort of darkness and quiet could easily drive them insane."

I thought back to what I knew from the book we'd brought. "I don't think people normally travel the Path in groups. Every person I found in the records was on their own."

"People willing to risk this, who take on such a dangerous task, are unlikely to be ones to travel with others."

"Lucky us," Hale muttered, though his voice made me frown. He was farther away than he'd been the last time.

"Don't get lost," I called out to him.

"I won't. Your feet are like fucking horse hooves, and I could hear the steps a mile off."

"Rude, especially when I'm trying to help you. Besides, I can tell you're farther away. It's possible that the silence here is messing with sounds. Come here." I held my hand out, before realizing he couldn't see that. "You should hold my hand, too."

"I'm not a fucking kid who's going to get lost." He didn't seem to come any closer.

"Don't touch her," Tyrus snarled, his voice coming out even more dangerous in the dark.

"Wasn't fucking planning on it."

"Stop it, you two," I chided them. "We'll deal with this bullshit after we get out, but you *both* know that we're safer together. If we get separated, we'll waste time and energy trying to find one another. So get over here, Hale, and stop arguing with me."

He made an unhappy sound, but his footsteps said he'd given in.

"No," Tyrus snapped and pulled me behind him, placing himself between me and Hale—at least, I thought so given the sound of steps. "He won't touch you, not after what just happened. I won't allow it."

"Last I checked, I didn't ask you for permission." If we had been anywhere else, I'd have shoved Tyrus away for his overbearing attitude. As it turned out, my feelings were less important than my fear of being alone in the darkness. "If we get separated, we're *all* screwed. So unless someone was kinky enough to bring a rope or a leash, I'm pretty sure holding hands is all we've got."

"Then he'll hold *my* hand. I'm not about to let him touch you, not after what he just pulled."

I couldn't really argue with Tyrus about it. I wanted to, some part of me willing to scold Hale but disliking the idea of anyone else doing it. I guess that was one of those, 'I can pick on him but no one else can,' sort of things.

Still, the idea of Tyrus and Hale holding hands was unfailingly adorable. "Damn this darkness," I muttered.

"What, you want to see us holding hands?" Hale snapped, his voice coming from closer, telling me they'd probably already done it and also telling me Hale was *not* a fan of it.

"What? You would think so little of me that you think I'd want to see that to laugh? Of course not. I'm sad I can't take a picture to blackmail you two later." I didn't fight my laugh at that, grateful for the distraction that took away some of my fear.

Or it was better to say that it helped me deal with that fear, that it took up enough room inside me to shove the fear into a corner where I could pretend it didn't exist.

"We could skip, you know?"

"Loch…" Tyrus warned. "You are enjoying this far too much. In case you forgot, he *attacked* you. This isn't funny."

"It's a little funny. This is when I miss Yazmor — he'd find it funny."

"I doubt that. In fact, if Yazmor had been the one to intervene, I suspect Hale would be missing a few organs."

I tried to picture Yazmor that angry, but I struggled to do so. Then I recalled the glimpses I'd caught before, how he'd destroyed the men who had tortured me. I gulped at the memory, at realizing Yazmor hid more than his fair share of violence and darkness beneath that charming smile.

"I didn't attack her," Hale said, though the softness of his voice made me think he didn't quite believe that. "I wouldn't have hurt her."

"You scared her — that was enough."

"Ain't that up to her to decide, not you?"

"I hate to agree with Hale right now, but he's right."

Tyrus tightened his hand around mine. "He lacks self-discipline. That is the most dangerous thing for a person, to be unable to control themselves. I don't care how this place affects him, don't care the reasons he had for behaving that way, it only goes to show you are not safe around him."

I waited for Hale to argue, to tell Tyrus to fuck off as he usually did. It surprised me when Hale responded with only silence.

In fact, if he *had* argued, I might have lectured him more. When he seemed to give in, though, I found myself defending him.

"This place is affecting us all — we know that. It's difficult, makes us question ourselves, and it's so subtle we don't even notice it. It's not Hale's fault."

"Yeah, it is my fault," Hale said softly. "He's not wrong. I fucked up and I scared you and he's not wrong about me being dangerous to you."

I opened my mouth to tell him to shut up, to make things all better, but Hale's voice stopped me.

"It's fine. Let's focus on what matter right now — getting out of this fucking darkness. The rest of it can wait."

It wasn't his words that silenced my protests. Instead, it was his tone, the devastation there. I let the conversation go because we were all too close to it. There was no way to see it objectively here, no way to not react with emotions.

So I let the darkness and silence smother all the questions, all the fears, everything that hung between us.

We only needed to focus on getting out of here and trust that we could fix all the broken pieces between us.

* * * *

Tyrus

Loch's soft snoring made me smile, and because of the darkness, I didn't bother to resist it.

The fact she could sleep so soundly pleased me. It soothed me in a way, made me feel as if I could experience some level of that same peace. After wandering for a while, I had suggested we rest. We'd made no progress so far as I could tell and exhausting ourselves wouldn't help at all. It hadn't taken long after sitting before Loch had all but passed out.

I had never slept well, always thinking, always planning, always looking for enemies and ways to outsmart them. Loch closing her eyes and making herself so vulnerable around men such as Hale and myself humbled me.

And pissed me off, especially when I considered what I'd walked up on earlier.

The sight of Hale pinning Loch, her frantic shoving, the panicked sounds that had left her, those things would likely never leave me. If we had been anywhere else, if it had been anyone but Hale, I'd have likely never let them take another breath.

In fact, if we hadn't fallen right then, I might have done it anyway.

"Your growling will wake her up if you don't knock it off." Hale's voice was low to not bother Loch, and I nearly told him I wasn't growling.

Except a strange sensation in my throat made me realize he'd spoken the truth. I cut the sound off, forcing myself to calm down.

Loch was stretched out, her head in my lap, her hand gripping the fabric of my slacks as if afraid, even in her sleep, to let go. Hale sat behind me, his back against mine since we'd yet to find a wall to lean against. It seemed like we existed in a space without walls, without anything but the ground beneath us.

"I don't fucking know what came over me," Hale whispered. "In my head, I kept thinking she was fucking with me, that she was just using me, that she was going to stab me in the back. I was so angry and I couldn't think straight and I wanted some proof that she wasn't like that."

"You should know better. Loch isn't the kind to betray people—she's too honest. Even if she wanted to do so, you would be able to spot it well before she managed, because she's too honest to slip such a ruse by you."

"I fucking know that. At least, I think I do. But there's this whisper in my brain telling me you're all going to betray me, that you're all going to use me and, it screams that I need to react, that I need to do something first. It tells me to keep you all at a distance."

I rubbed my eyes, frustrated not only with Hale but with myself.

Mostly because as much as I hated it, I understood *exactly* what he meant.

I felt that discontent as well, this gnawing feeling inside me that made me hesitate in a way I rarely did.

Unlike Hale, it didn't make me react as he had.

"You have to learn to think through that," I said. "If this is really a result of the influence the Path has on us, it will only get worse the longer we are here. Loch may forgive you, but I assure you I will not should you harm her. The only option is to check yourself, to think through your own thoughts and feelings and counter the ones you know to be false. What you cannot do is take those feelings out on Loch—especially not after what she has already gone through."

Hale let out a long sigh, the action causing his back to press harder against me. "I fucking know that. Even as it happened, I knew it. I just didn't realize I wasn't thinking right. Now that I know it, now that I can spot it, it won't happen again."

"It better not."

A short break in the conversation happened, and just then, Loch rolled to her side, her cheek pressed against my thigh as she used my lap like her own personal pillow. Her breath warmed me through my slacks, and I told myself in no uncertain terms to *not* react.

My cock was not invited to this particular party. I had a feeling Loch waking up to an erection poking her in the cheek would not be reacted to well.

"Do you really think we can do this?"

I frowned at Hale's question, surprised at it. Hale rarely showed a lack of confidence, didn't let people see him flinch. Whether it was this place or what had happened with Loch, something had shaken him enough to be honest.

And a not-so-small part of me filed it away, wanting to use that weakness against him. I could plant seeds of doubt, make him question himself more, ensure I walked circles around him as he struggled to find his footing.

Except, the moment the thought hit me, I shoved it away. That was no different than what Hale had done — to do so would only be giving into the suspicion that the Path had filled me with.

I refused to be played by anything, to be manipulated by anything, even this place.

"I don't know," I told him honestly.

"So why come? Why are you here if you don't even think we can do this? You never struck me as the type to throw your life away for nothing. You ain't the white-knight martyr type."

"No, I'm not. I wouldn't lay down my life for much."

"Much? Means there are some things you would die for. Never figured you'd say that. You always seemed way too heartless to care about anything that much."

I looked down at Loch, even though I couldn't see her. "Loch would do this whether or not I agreed, whether or not I would come. The likelihood of succeeding wouldn't change her opinion or her course."

"So? Didn't mean you had to tag alone."

"I knew that I'd rather travel this path with her, no matter how it ended, then remain behind alone." I offered up the truth as a way to counter that fear in my head, as a way to tell the Path to fuck off with its attempts to manipulate me.

Hale could do as he wished with that. It wasn't as if he didn't already know how deeply my feelings for Loch ran.

"And you?" I asked, turning the tables on him. "Why are you here?"

"Same reason, I guess. I'll follow that fucking girl wherever she goes—don't matter how dangerous, how fucking stupid, if she goes, I'm following." After he spoke, he let out a loud bark of laughter that made Loch huff and nuzzle closer to me, as if annoyed her sleep was disturbed. "How fucking pathetic are we? Been at one another's throats for decades, and here we are, pussy-whipped by the same little girl."

I laughed along with him at the absurdity of it, at how not wrong he was. "I am unsure if that says something negative about us or complimentary toward her." I leaned more against him, trying to ease the ache in my back. "I never would have thought that you and I would end up competing over the same woman."

"I ain't competing. She's mine."

"And I do not plan to let her go so easily."

"Guess that leaves it up to her."

I ran my fingers through Loch's hair, able to imagine the green of the strands, the soft curls that rested there. I could see, in my head, the tattoos on her cheeks, the tiny wings that dotted her face.

I'd hated them at first, the idea of her face being marked as confusing as the rest of her. Who would do that? Who would tattoo their own face?

The symbols there meant more as time had gone on, but it was funny now that I couldn't imagine her without them. I couldn't even consider how she would look without those things that I had so disliked at first, the flash hair, the tattoos, the reckless streak and the foul mouth.

All the things I'd struggled with at first now drew me, as if they'd transformed into yet another thing that made her the perfect partner for me.

"What if she never chooses? What if she decides she can't choose? Would you be able to accept such an arrangement?" I asked, unsure of my own answer to that question.

Could I share her? Assuming we made it through this all alive, assuming we survived everything against us, could I make a life where Loch loved others and not just me?

Could I put aside my own ego? Could I trust the others as I did her? What would that mean as far as a future? How could it possibly work out with the four of us having been enemies for so long?

I couldn't picture Loch ever being happy that way, forever pulled between men who couldn't stand one another. She cared too much about us to stomach that.

"I don't know," Hale answered, taking so long I had nearly forgotten my question. "I don't fucking know if I could deal with that, if I could accept it. Of course, I also don't think I could walk away from her, so I guess it doesn't fucking matter, does it?"

I pressed my lips together as I considered the truth of his words, words that mirrored my own feelings.

I didn't know that sharing was really feasible, but neither did I think I could every walk away from her? What did that mean for a future?

Did we even really have one?

Chapter Twelve

Loch

Lips pressed against my throat, and I moaned at the sensation. I'd felt so cold before, unable to warm up no matter what I did, but the kiss managed it just fine.

In fact, a heat combusted inside me at the stroking of those talented lips, and I tipped my head back to offer more — to offer *everything*.

Some small part of me knew it wasn't real, but I didn't give a damn. That part of me could STFU while I enjoyed myself. Even if it was a dream, I wanted this. I wanted to feel like my old self, to lose everything to passion, to feel the touch of another and crave more.

So I gave myself over to it — real or not, I didn't give a fuck.

Hands roamed over me, stroking across my chilled skin, warming each place they touched. I arched into it, wanting more, especially when they missed all the places I really wanted them to touch.

Even in my dreams, my lovers were fucking teases, it seemed. I was sure that said something bad about me.

Something warm and hot and hard brushed my lips, and I responded by mouthing softly at it. I dragged my tongue across it, wishing I had my wits about me enough for more. I wanted to take it into my mouth, to drag that masculine scent into my lungs and let it saturate me.

"Loch." The sound of someone calling my name dragged me deeper into the fantasy. I imagined them whispering my name into my ear, of them groaning it softly.

"Loch!" That time I couldn't even pretend the voice was teasing and seductive. If anything, it sounded panicked.

I blinked, opening my eyes, startled for a moment to still see nothing.

Oh, right, the darkness…

I sat up, immediately thrown by an inability to figure out my surroundings. Without sight, I felt adrift and dizzy.

Worse, my heart raced, my skin somehow both chilled and flushed at the same time. My body felt electrified, and my cheeks heated as I recalled my dream.

Wow, I must be a lot hornier than I realized. I didn't usually have sex dreams like some teenage boy. Worse, as reality came back to me, I realized I'd been lying in Tyrus' lap.

Which meant his voice must have been the one calling out to me.

"Fuck," I muttered softly as it all fit. "Sorry about that."

"It's fine." Even though Tyrus said that, his voice came out tense.

Which made me think about when I'd first woken up. I recalled the firmness against my lips, the way I'd touched it with my tongue.

All that came together to mean...I'd been molesting Tyrus in my sleep.

Just wonderful.

As if I couldn't have made this shit any more awkward just by the dream alone.

Of course, knowing that didn't seem to settle my own body down at all. Not even the mortifying shame could douse my lust at all. If anything, it made me want to keep going. I missed the warmth, the security, the moments there where I'd felt good for the first time in far too long.

"I won't do anything to you," Tyrus said as if to reassure me. "You don't have to worry."

"I'm not." My words came out strong, and it helped me realize, I told the truth. I wasn't worried that Tyrus would hurt me.

"Your voice is shaking." This time it wasn't Tyrus but Hale who spoke. Somehow I'd almost forgotten he was there because of the darkness and my lust-muddled brain.

"I'm not afraid you'll do anything—either of you," I repeated, then forced myself to say the next part. "I'm afraid you won't."

Twin inhalations—sharp and loud—came as a response.

If I wasn't about a moment from begging, I would have laughed. These two men, who had brought countless to their knees, who had survived the worst of the Chasm—who *were* the worst of the Chasm—had

166

still been surprised and rendered speechless by little ol' me.

It gave me a boost of confidence, a reminder that they weren't just anyone. They were *mine.*

And I was through being afraid of them, of this, of myself. I might not be sure of much, but I was sure of what I wanted at least.

"Please," I asked.

"This can't be a good idea." Tyrus spoke slowly, as if trying to make me come to my senses. "After what you went through, this can't possibly be good for you."

"Don't I get to decide that?"

"It's dark. You can't even see either of us. How do you know that you won't panic?"

I owed it to him to at least consider that. "I can't say I won't, but I couldn't say that no matter what. No matter how much time passes or what happened, trauma sneaks back up. Will I panic? Maybe. But I can't let that fear stop me from doing what I want. Please, I feel cold, like I'm frozen all the way down inside me. I just want to feel warm…"

And I was sure he understood that I didn't just mean the temperature in this fucking place. I meant so much more, a chill so much deeper than that, one only these men could save me from.

"Who do you want?" Tyrus asked, and I could tell he struggled to ask. I had no doubt he wanted to send Hale away, to claim me for himself, but he still gave me the choice.

And knowing him, he'd follow whatever I wanted.

But the answer was so obvious, it was almost laughable.

"I want you *both.*"

And the groans that came through the darkness back told me that they didn't mind that answer one bit.

A hand touched my wrist and pulled me forward. I didn't know whose it was at first, not until I felt the soft cotton of a button up shirt.

Tyrus. Hale wouldn't be caught dead in such clothing.

Familiar lips met mine, the kiss soft and coaxing and slow enough to let me think about it, to let me pull away if I wanted to.

It was like Tyrus wanted to be the counter to Hale.

I didn't need that, though. Or maybe I did, and maybe those gentle touches of his had relaxed me enough that panic was the last thing in my mind.

A hand touched my back, and when I realized it didn't belong to Tyrus, I hesitated.

The idea of having them both at once was one thing, but reality was always different. It was like when it had seemed like a great idea to do a juice fast until I actually gave it a try. Just like then, I wondered if my body would hold out for this...

"You want to stop?" Hale asked, his voice surprisingly uncertain. In fact, it was that uncertainty that drew me in, that made me want to keep going. If he'd been all arrogance, I might have reconsidered. Instead, him being just as nervous as I was gave me strength, made me feel in control.

I twisted, grasping in the darkness until I found the leather of his jacket. I tugged him closer, my lips missing their mark and touching his jawline, first. He had no stubble—it was nice having bodies that didn't change because there weren't any five-o'clock shadows unless a person died with it. I moved my kisses from his jaw to his lips.

He returned the kiss slowly, something so unlike him.

In fact, they were *both* unlike themselves. I recalled the first time I'd slept with Tyrus, when he'd changed into his demon form because he'd been driven to the brink of his control and shoved well past it.

Hale was always aggressive, always acted without thinking. He was the type to throw himself into his feelings without thinking it through at all, to deal with consequences later, after doing exactly as he pleased.

Yet they both held back for me, to make me comfortable, and that melted me in a way nothing else could have. It made me feel safe with them, kept any fear of mine at bay.

Hale groaned when I traced his lips with my tongue. "You are fucking hell on my control," he whispered, but even then, he didn't yank at me.

The darkness made every touch so much more, electrifying them, leaving a tingle in the wake of each touch. Tyrus' lips found my neck, teasing over my racing pulse while I kissed Hale.

Hands roamed over my clothing at first, leaving fire in their wake and a burning need for more. They warmed me, chasing away the chill that had sank into me since I'd arrived in the Path.

It seemed impossible to feel cold between these two men.

A hand slid beneath my sweater, and it was amazing how quickly I could tell the difference between Hale and Tyrus just from touch alone now.

Tyrus was sure. He went slowly, but without real hesitation. His touch was harder, more planned, and when he ran his thumb over my nipple through my bra, I gasped.

Hale, on the other side, acted more carefully. He would move his hand then wait, driven by instinct and need but held back by fear. Not that it mattered, because when he cupped my other breast, I pulled my shoulders back to press myself against his hands more.

"Is this what you wanted?" A heated playfulness filled Tyrus' voice.

I nodded, not caring that they couldn't see it. They were high or stupid if they believed I could still actually form words or hold any sort of conversation at this point.

Hale grasped my sweater and pulled it off, taking the shirt underneath with it. He reached behind me, unhooked my bra then worked that off as well. I shivered when the cold air hit my skin, but I didn't have time to complain. Instead, strong hands shifted me until my back pressed against a warm, solid chest.

They'd turned me so I sat in Tyrus' lap, and he wrapped his arms around me from behind, his palms covering my breasts.

"I can keep you warm this way," Tyrus whispered, and fuck did his whispers do sinful things to me. If he'd spoken in his normal voice, it would have been hot — most of what he said turned me on, after all — but when he said it with that breathy voice right into my ear, it was like it connected directly to my clit.

He lifted his voice slightly when he spoke again, just after he ran his tongue along the shell of my ear. "You want to make up for what you did, Hale? Well, I believe this may be your time to seek her forgiveness."

"And just how're you suggesting I do that?" Hale asked, though a tension in his words said he had a pretty good idea.

"Like any bad boy does — on his knees."

Well fuck. They're going to kill me if they keep going like this.

I'd died once already by getting shot. This was a *far* better way to go.

Hale chuckled softly, the sound telling me he wasn't doing this because Tyrus said it, but that he'd do it just the same. I could almost hear his response in my head—*I'll get on my knees for Loch, but not for any other fucking person.*

Hale flicked open the button of my jeans then pulled down the zipper. He grasped the waist and tugged them down my legs, taking the underwear with them. It left me naked in Tyrus' lap, but their warm bodies kept me from shivering.

Well, from the cold, at least. Fuck knew I had goosebumps and trembled from their touches.

Tyrus teased my nipples, kneading my breasts in his large, strong hands. The calluses on his fingers scraped against my sensitive skin, and when he nipped my earlobe, I wrapped one of my arms up to grasp the back of his neck and hold on to him.

"Good girl," Tyrus whispered to me. "Give yourself over to us—trust us."

I nodded as if he asked me instead of telling me.

A rustling against stone occurred a moment before Hale ran his palms along my thighs, spreading my legs by grasping my knees and pressing them outward.

If there'd been any light, I would have been uneasy so exposed, but the darkness hid me, let me just feel without any of those normal doubts taking over.

Hale pressed his lips to the inside of my thigh, drawing a line of kisses up from my knee, stopping just short of where I really wanted him.

Instead, he pulled back, then repeated the action starting at the opposite knee.

"Don't tease me," I snapped.

He chuckled, his hot breath spilling against my bare skin. "You that needy, Loch?"

"She is always a greedy little demon." Tyrus closed his fingers around one of my nipples, the sharp pain blanking my mind or any response I might have had.

Each time they touched me, it all melted together. It washed me away, making it so I didn't care about anything beyond this. Never would I have figured *these* two, especially, could actually work together.

Maybe the darkness made that easier, too. Maybe without seeing one another, they could more easily accept this all, to ignore their hatred of one another in favor of some pleasure.

And I sure as fuck benefited from that.

Hale kept going with his torturous kisses, if anything slowing down even more. It wound me up, made me anticipate each place his lips met my skin, and by the time he neared my drenched cunt, I had started to lift my hips as if to force him where I wanted.

"Leave it to Hale to behave like a brat even when he apologizes," Tyrus said. "He is young still and would benefit from some training. I would suggest you not allow a mutt like him free rein."

Tyrus' words woke a part of me that startled me — a needy, hungry part that wanted to take. I reached out without thinking about it and ran my fingers through Hale's hair, then drew that hand into a fist. I yanked him the last few inches to where I needed him most.

And the almost feral sound he let out was a thing of fucking beauty. He didn't fight my hold despite Hale fighting *everything*. Instead, he obeyed the unspoken demand and dove in, delving his eager tongue into my pussy.

He fucked me with his tongue, the ball of his tongue ring still so unexpected and different that I cried out. He knew exactly how to use it, and when he licked through my folds, he alternated between using the tip of his tongue and the flat, to drag that hard ball against me.

"How does that feel?" Tyrus asked, his touches to my breasts rougher than before, as if he were as caught up in the moment as Hale and me.

Though I didn't need to guess about that. His hard cock pressed against me, trapped between his body and mine, kept away only due to the thin fabric of his slacks.

I angled my hips to give Hale more access and used my grip in his hair to keep him close.

Not that he tried to escape. In fact, he tilted his head to focus on my clit, then brought his other hand up to bury one of his agile fingers into my pussy. It wasn't like when he fucked me, when my body struggled to accept every thick inch of him. It wasn't nearly as overwhelming, but that didn't stop it from driving me closer to a terrifying release.

He curled that finger, stroking along the front wall of my cunt, seeking until he found a spot that made me jerk in surprise. A hot breath against me said he laughed at my reaction, and I tightened my hand in his hair in warning.

Hale groaned again, then doubled his efforts. He latched his lips around my clit and sucked hard, alternating between that and rubbing the metal ball of his tongue ring against my swollen nub.

Tension continued to draw inside me, my orgasm creeping closer, that blissful moment of pleasure right there. I leaned against Tyrus, tilting my head to expose the side of my neck, giving myself over to them and their touch.

I wanted to feel all of them, to lose myself in the two of them.

And what drove me even more was how they both focused on me. I thought back to so many unsatisfying encounters I'd had before. How often had my partner been ham-handed and rushed things and not given a damn if I enjoyed it or not?

They'd treated me like an object, like a sex toy for them to fuck then throw away afterward. Hell, I'd bet a few of them still thought the female orgasm was faked, like the moon landing.

That wasn't anything like the way Hale and Tyrus touched me. They hadn't involved their dicks at all, focused instead on my pleasure, as if that pleased them as much as anything else. They teased me, toyed with me, but it didn't make me feel used. Instead, they made me feel cherished.

And who the fuck would have thought men like this would cherish *anything*?

"Come for us, Little Demon," Tyrus said before latching his lips to my neck and sucking hard enough to leave a mark. It stung, but the claiming gesture excited me all the more.

Hale nipped my clit, the sensation so strong that I couldn't possibly decide if it was pleasure or pain.

I didn't need to decide, though, because my body knew exactly what it thought. All my muscles tightened, so the movement of Hale's finger inside me felt even stronger, especially because he didn't stop.

Fuck, *neither* of them stopped. If anything, the way I twisted egged them on. Hale sucked harder at my clit, his finger plunging into me no matter how my body squeezed around him. It made it so even the knuckles of his fingers teased me, so I could feel every bit of him. I came so hard, lost in that darkness, that it felt as if I'd never recover, that my body wasn't my own.

Tyrus stopped sucking on my neck just as I started to come down from that high, when the waves broke over me and I felt as if I could draw air again.

"Another," he whispered, the word having no meaning until an even sharper pain on the curve between my neck and my shoulder hit me.

He bit me?

I could yell at him later about that, but right then? I gasped as another orgasm took me over, my body not having recovered from the first, dragging me under until it felt as if I were dying.

And through it all—and fuck knew I lost count of how many times they made me come—I never pulled away. They left no room for fear, for questions, for doubt. Instead, it was just us, the passion between us, the need.

Even when I felt as if I might die from it, that it might be more than my little body could handle, I didn't resist. I gave myself over to them, to their care, to the pleasure they forced from me.

If I was going to die again, this was one hell of a way to go, and if someone was going to end me, I was pretty sure I'd happily let these two men do it.

* * * *

Yazmor

My skin *hurt*. It felt pulled too tight, as if it could no longer fit my true form. It felt thin, as though it might split at any moment.

"Where could they have gone?" Gorrin asked, a panic in his voice that was entirely at odds with the man I'd known for so long. I'd watched him face nearly impossible odds in the past, but never had he so much as blinked in response.

Then again, Loch was chaos incarnate. She managed to upend every individual she came into contact with, throwing their actions and life into disarray.

She has certainly done that to me.

"She's this way," I said as we walked through the fog, having left the Path.

"How do you know?"

"I sense her."

Gorrin narrowed his eyes at me. "And how is it you can do that?"

"My species were apex predators. Tracking one little demon isn't that hard." *Especially her.* Somehow, I was always aware of her, like we had a connection between us no matter how far away we went. It ran through the world, something outside of time and space, something that bound us together.

"Why would they wander off?"

"Maybe they saw a butterfly."

Gorrin rubbed at the bridge of his nose. "They aren't you. They wouldn't do something so foolish."

I thought back to the time we'd been scheduled for a meeting, so long ago that Hale and Tyrus had yet to become Demon Lords. I'd missed it because a green butterfly had fluttered past me, and I'd been unable to resist chasing it.

"How often do you see green butterflies?"

"That doesn't explain how you ended up in the bounce house of an eight-year-old's birthday party."

"No one else showed up. It would have been rude to not stay." I looked over at Gorrin with a smirk. "And as I recall, *you* had a piece of cake as well when you found me."

He let out a sigh and shook his head.

Which pricked at my nerves. I recalled Loch's harsh tone from before, when she'd snapped at me, wanting me to be quiet.

People had done that for a long time with me, so much so that I thought myself past caring. I *wasn't* human. I had no reason to feel hurt or bothered when they pointed that out, when they made it clear I did not fit in.

It was like a dog getting upset when others pointed out he wasn't a bird.

So why was it that the behavior I had grown so used to suddenly bothered me?

I couldn't answer, which darkened my mood all the more.

Still, no matter my unresolved feelings, when Gorrin and I had realized that we no longer saw any signs of Loch, Hale and Tyrus, that took priority. Even if I couldn't quite place my feelings, that didn't mean I could ignore a missing Loch.

I doubted I could ever wash my hands of her. That bond between us was far too strong to break over something so trivial.

Is there anything more than that bond, though?

I thought back to how she'd looked at me when she saw what I really was, when she'd glimpsed the world I'd come from. She'd said she didn't care, that whatever I had been, whatever I was, didn't change the way she felt about me, but people lied.

She believed her words, but people lied to themselves more than to anyone else.

People told themselves whatever made them feel secure in the world and in themselves. They told themselves they were good people even when their actions said the opposite. They told themselves that they could succeed, even when history and reality said differently.

And Loch told herself she could accept me because she wanted it to be true.

Belief did not change reality, and I had lived long enough to know I'd fit in nowhere. I had barely fit in to my own world, so what hope did I have in those that came afterward?

"You're quieter than usual," Gorrin said.

"Elephants are the only mammal on Earth that can't jump." At Gorrin's confused look, I went on. "I thought we were offering random facts."

"You are impossible. People make statements as a way to bring up a topic."

"Then you should have just said so instead of making vague statements."

"Fine. If you want me to be direct, I'll oblige you. Why are you acting strangely? I have never seen you pout. Normally, if you're angry — which is rare — it ends with blood, so seeing you behave like this is disconcerting. Beings with the power you hold shouldn't behave like sullen, angsty teenagers."

Ouch. Still, I couldn't deny his words. I was behaving differently than usual, and I couldn't pinpoint the reason. Perhaps it was like I'd told Loch in the past, that a person could be too close to a situation to see it clearly, to gain a full understanding of the picture.

Did that mean Gorrin might be able to discern the reason for my unease?

I didn't enjoy the idea of exposing my shortcomings or weaknesses, yet perhaps it was like a wound. A terrible slice to one's back needed treatment, and it was not an injury a person could treat alone. There was a risk to allowing another access, but it was, sometimes, a necessary risk.

Was this the same? A necessary risk?

"I feel unsettled." I looked ahead as I spoke, opening and closing my hands as though that might ease the tension inside me. "It feels as if my skin is too small, as if my true form is pacing inside me and reaching out. Things that did not bother me before irk me. I feel an annoyance at my attempts to fit in and more so at those attempts failing. I am not human—why should I be held to human standards?"

Gorrin didn't answer at first, but after a long moment, his voice came out slow and careful. "You remember Koller saying this place twists people? It exposes people's deepest fears and magnifies them."

"My fear is not fitting in? That doesn't make any sense. I've never fit in, and it's never bothered me before."

"And if you were here a decade ago, I bet you wouldn't feel this way. You're different since you met Loch, though."

"Am I?" I didn't ask that as a way to be a smart-ass. I feared I could no longer clearly see myself.

"You haven't shown interest in many individuals before. What if the Path is magnifying your fears about her accepting you? You may not care if anyone else accepts you, but perhaps your fear revolves around hiding your true nature, about how Loch might react if she saw it?"

I frowned, not responding to his words right away. They felt uncomfortable, which in my experience, meant they likely had some truth to them.

Of course, the idea that something as insignificant as this tiny strip of space known as the Path could manipulate me in this way, could affect me, chafed. It felt beneath me.

I was too old and far too smart to fall to such tricks, yet when I rubbed my shoulder, trying to ease the aching in my skin, I couldn't deny it.

When I could neither agree with nor dismiss his statement, I decided to set it aside. I could think about it later, let it simmer, gain more information before I made a decision.

"Loch's just ahead," I said to change the topic, that electrical sensation on my skin drawing me nearer to her. I scented no blood, no signs of violence, nothing to imply she'd been harmed.

Gorrin and I passed by a few more trees, then came to a stop.

A darkness filled the space before us as though bathed in a deep shadow. I could see into that darkness, peering through it into the secrets it hid.

The sight before me might have made me trip over my own feet if I had to walk much farther.

Every inch of Loch's skin was on display, with small bruises that had obviously been a result of either bites or rather aggressive sucking on her skin. Where this may have set me off, her expression kept me still.

Her eyes were closed, her face relaxed and peaceful. She had her head in Tyrus' lap, her arms wrapped around his waist. Behind her laid Hale, his arm thrown

Jayce Carter

over her, his head in Tyrus' lap as well. The whole thing appeared uncomfortably cozy...

Tyrus narrowed his eyes but didn't focus on us, as though he sensed us but couldn't actually see us.

Gorrin rushed forward, and before I could stop him, he stepped into the shadow. He froze immediately, his gaze darting around.

They must not be able to see anything inside.

I approached the shadow but didn't pass through it, not wishing to end up trapped as well.

"Yazmor?" Gorrin called out, his voice distorted.

So it isn't just light but sound that is affected inside that.

"Gorrin?" Tyrus responded, his hand going to Loch and Hale's shoulders to wake them.

"Well isn't this a fun reunion?" Loch muttered, sleep drenching the words.

And boy didn't her voice soothe me? No matter how awkward things might get between us, it seemed hearing her could calm me.

"Can you hear me?" I called into that darkness.

Gorrin turned toward me, answering me with his actions before he had to respond. He held a hand out toward me, but when he took a few steps my way, he didn't seem to actually move closer.

That meant the shadow also distorted space. No wonder they hadn't escaped it, yet.

"Don't try to come toward me," I said. "It won't work. Go the opposite way so you're with the others. Give me a minute to work out a way for you to escape."

Gorrin nodded, then turned his back to me. He called out for the others, and it was almost amusing to watch them all fumble about in a game of Marco Polo in the darkness.

Well, Gorrin did at least. Hale guided Gorrin with his voice while Tyrus worked to dress Loch, covering up all her lovely skin. No doubt if Loch knew I could see her like that, she'd be embarrassed. It made it feel as though I'd glimpsed something not meant for me.

It increased that discomfort inside of me, the feeling that I would forever be on the outside looking in. Stranger, it made me want to touch her. My fingers itched to run across her skin, to find each mark there, to…

I wasn't sure any further than that, the desire new and strange and uncomfortable.

I picked up a long, dead branch from the ground. If I could reach that through, it could serve as a guide for them to make their way out of the darkness.

Or not… The moment I attempted to put the branch through the shadow edge, the branch turned to dust, as if disintegrated by the barrier.

Inside, Gorrin had managed his way to the others, and Loch had finished dressing. It meant all I needed was to find a way out for them.

I grabbed a rock and tried to toss it in, but it met the same fate as the tree branch had.

Still, Gorrin had passed through it. That meant it only allowed living matter through? Or perhaps only sentient beings? I would have tossed one of the birds that woke me early in the morning through to test if any living matter worked or not, but seeing as they weren't here, I didn't have that option. *I would have killed two birds with one shadow that way…*

Which left me with one last option.

I went to the edge of the shadow, took a deep breath, then reached through it with just my hand.

182

A tingle told me I interacted with the shadow, but nothing of me turned to dust.

That was a good sign, right?

Still, my arm wasn't that long, and I feared that if I placed the majority of my body through, I'd find myself trapped there as well.

Which left me with just one choice, one that irritated the dark places inside me, the fears that the Path magnified inside me.

I pulled my hand back through, relieved to find it still in one piece.

"I'm going to reach for you, Loch," I called into the darkness. "Grab onto me and I'll pull you back through. Make sure you're all holding on to Loch as well."

All my fears about Loch accepting me, about what I really was, I somehow was forced to face them sooner than I'd planned.

Here goes nothing…

Chapter Thirteen

Loch

It was crazy just how terrifying waiting in the darkness really was. While Yazmor said he'd reach for me, I had no idea when it was happening or from where. I could do nothing but just wait, just trust in him.

And amazingly, I *did* trust him. Normally, I'd have done more myself, would have wandered forward, tried to meet him. Something inside me refused to move, though. Instead, I found myself frozen in place, one of my hands held out in front of me while the other intertwined with Tyrus'. As far as I knew, Tyrus also grasped Hale who then held on to Gorrin, like some weird, super violent kindergarten line.

I jumped when something brushed my hand, especially because it didn't feel like skin. It was smooth, hard and far firmer than anything covered in flesh should be.

And I don't mean in the way people describe cocks as being hard like stone. That was just ego-stroking for men. No, this felt like polished wood, but it moved, with something wrapping around my hand before I could yank away.

"It's just me." Yazmor's voice in the darkness should have reassured me, but boy did it not.

My brain went back to what I'd seen in the Forgotten Caves, to what he actually looked like. Had he taken that form? Why?

Because he could reach farther? I recalled just how long the limbs of the creatures from his world had been.

Even if I wanted to pull away, he didn't give me the option. It was probably for the best.

Instead, he tugged me forward, guiding me through the blackness, not hard or fast enough to make me stumble but unwavering. That primitive part of me wanted to run away. It knew that Yazmor was a predator, the type I was in no way equipped to deal with. It wanted to yank free from his grasp and rush into the darkness, no matter how foolish that would be. Even if that part of me took over, I didn't have the option, not with the way Yazmor grasped my wrist so firmly.

I closed my eyes, giving in because I didn't really have another choice. I tightened my grasp on Tyrus' hand as if that were my one lifeline.

It didn't take nearly as long as I'd expected to get out. I'd walked for what had to have been hours with Hale and Tyrus, yet it only took a few—very long—seconds until the sounds of the world came through again. It reminded me of just how quiet the blackness had been.

I opened my eyes, squinting and unable to make anything out at first. The Path wasn't all that bright to start with, but it was still a far cry from the entire pitch blackness from before. I looked over my shoulder just as I tugged Tyrus forward, as he stepped out of the strange shadow and into the light with me. He recovered faster than I did, repeating the motion until Hale and Gorrin got out as well.

My legs felt weak, seeing them all safe, realizing we'd escaped that horrid empty void.

No, I will not fall down like some fucking damsel.

Or so I told myself all of two seconds before I did just that, collapsing down to my knees in relief.

I lifted my gaze, ready to thank Yazmor, but the moment I saw him, any words I might have uttered died a slow and painful death on my tongue.

He looked nothing like the man I knew. That young face, the ever-present smile, it was all gone. Instead, he resembled the creature from the Forgotten Caves, more like a nightmare tree than a living being. His limbs were long and thin, and more branch-like things went back from his head almost like hair. He had hands with three large fingers, and his legs bent in ways nothing in my world did.

He looked like a monster, like the sort of thing a kid would draw and claim they saw out in a dark forest at night.

His eyes were the only thing I connected to, since they remained the same color as before, that same bright violet. They peered down at me, unblinking, as if waiting to see my reaction.

Calm down, I told myself, using my best guru self-soothing voice.

This was Yazmor. He might look different—a *lot* fucking different—but he wasn't. He was the same man I knew, the one who stole my coffee, who hugged me when I'd sobbed, who had washed me so carefully when I'd shattered apart after that horrible memory.

Still, I searched his face, hoping to connect *this* with the man I knew so well.

Yazmor tore his gaze from mine then shook his head, the action strange from him, before his form shimmered and shrank until he looked like he had before. Even still, he didn't look *at* me. He didn't turn back toward me, didn't reach out for me to help me up. Instead, he gestured toward the fog. "The Path is this way. We're not far off from it, so we should get back."

Yazmor didn't wait to see if we followed, just heading off with steps that seemed far too heavy for his normally jovial attitude.

It forced me to scurry to my feet, afraid of getting left behind, of losing my way in the fog.

"Was that his real form?" Tyrus asked behind me.

"So it seems," Gorrin answered.

"What, you've never fucking seen it before?" Hale clicked his tongue. "Not a surprise he wouldn't pull *that* shit out much. Fucking unnerving, that is."

I couldn't argue with their words, even as they whispered to keep Yazmor from catching any of it.

Not that he still wouldn't. Yazmor had excellent hearing I'd found.

Still, they were right. It was terrifying and so different from anything we'd ever seen. It wasn't even like a demon form, where it resembled a human. Fuck, even Hubis' real form was familiar.

Instead, Yazmor was so different it felt as if it tested the limits of my sanity—and that wasn't a very solid thing to start with. Especially with how he'd said nothing to any of us, how he behaved usually, actually coming face to face with the *real* him was bound to throw anyone for one hell of a loop.

"He's like a monster," Tyrus said. "I knew he was a remnant, but I had no idea he would appear like *that*."

Yazmor's shoulders tensed ahead of us, a change so slight I doubted anyone else would have noticed it.

Guess that answers if he can hear us…

Guilt ate at me and it had me turning a sharp look on the other men to tell them to shut the fuck up.

We *all* had ugly sides to ourselves that we preferred not to show off. In fact, Tyrus had physically kept me from looking at him when he'd changed, and Gorrin had hidden that he was even an angel! I doubted Hale hid much of anything, he just hadn't had a reason to change.

Still, were we really in any position to judge Yazmor?

The three of them dropped their gazes and quieted down, telling me they understood my point.

I turned away from them and jogged the few steps up to Yazmor, unsure what to say. I'd be lying if I told him I wasn't afraid of him, that his true form hadn't bothered me.

I really didn't want to lie to him.

"Yazmor…" I said, the name trailing off to silence when I couldn't figure out what to say next.

He didn't look at me, didn't make a stupid joke to ease the tension. Instead, he gestured at the Path which appeared just ahead of us. "We should gather our things and get moving again. That shadow was a trap and who knows what we might run into next."

With that, he ended the conversation, walking away from me as if he couldn't stand the idea of being near me for a moment longer.

And standing there, staring at his back, I didn't think the Path had ever felt *quite* this cold and lonely…

* * * *

Gorrin

I had my hands out flat toward the fire, but the chill inside me just wouldn't warm. It had worsened over the time we'd spent on the Path, as if some deep area inside me had frozen and that block of ice increased with each hour we remained, as though the fire could no longer reach the depths of me.

When it no longer worked, when I'd grown tired of a useless attempt, I rolled my shoulders and allowed my wings to appear. I curled them around me, using them to block the breeze and to trap more of the heat from the fire near me.

"Those are rather impressive," Tyrus said from across the fire.

"No more than demon forms."

"Can you really say that? If anyone saw the two of us side-by-side, I doubt we'd get the same reactions."

"That is because humans are short-sighted and easy to trick. Hubis has ensured that angels are warmly regarded, laying that groundwork from the earliest days of humanity. Likewise, he was as quick to seed fear of demon aspects. Neither of those change the innate benefits of either form." I knew my words held resentment, and I didn't bother to hide it.

Why should I? For better or worse, I was tied to Tyrus, to the other Lords, at least until the conclusion of this foolish plan. Our odds of succeeding — at least in some small way — would go up if we weren't at one another's throats and hiding secrets.

Hubis was a large enough enemy — there was no need to fight one another as well.

Tyrus peered to the side, down the way where the Path led. "I feel like we are spinning our wheels. We're walking and wearing ourselves down, but for what? We don't seem to be making any progress at all."

"Be careful. Many of the stories we've reviewed show damned saying the same things before losing their minds. The trip to madness is a shorter one than people realize."

Tyrus shook his head. "I'm not so weak-willed as to succumb to madness first in this group. In fact, I'm pretty sure I'm the furthest from it."

I considered the others, and I struggled to deny it. Compared to Hale and Yazmor — both of whom had one foot already in the padded cell — Tyrus was sure-footed. "Fair enough, but hopelessness will ruin a man faster than anything else. Perhaps Hale and Yazmor will survive this place longer than either of us if for no other reason than neither are smart enough to recognize when things are hopeless."

Tyrus chuckled at my joke even if I didn't smile, if I didn't make it clear that it was, in fact, a joke. Normally, my dry humor went right over other's heads. Because I didn't often smile or show many outward signs, people accepted my words at face value.

It took me back to Loch sitting with me, back before everything had become so much more difficult, so much more complicated. She hadn't trusted me, yet she'd *seen* me in a way few others had. She'd spend time with me, and I'd never really understood why.

I hadn't been a great conversationalist, hadn't had the ease she'd had with Yazmor, the passion she'd had with Hale, the mutual respect she'd had with Tyrus. Despite that, she'd spent time with me when she hadn't needed to.

It was strange, and as much as I wanted to ask her about it, I didn't dare. What if she tainted the memories by telling me she'd done it out of fear? That she'd done it just to get closer to me? To betray me?

No, I'd much rather accept the nice memories as the unknown than risk ruining them.

"Where is Yazmor?" I asked.

"He went ahead to scout, I believe. Or that's what he said at least. I'd guess he just wanted to avoid being around us."

My gaze moved to the other fire, to where Hale and Loch sat. We'd created more than one to help increase the amount of warmth they generated, to ensure each of us could rest as close to a source of heat as possible. "I doubt he was avoiding *all* of us."

Tyrus snorted softly. "Fair enough. Still, I can hardly blame her for her reaction."

Loch smiled at Hale, and the sight stopped me as it always did.

The woman could be deceitful and dangerous. She'd driven a blade into me — a blade *I'd* given her. She could stand her ground against impossible odds, willing to take on any risk for what she felt was right.

In short? She'd proven herself someone to not underestimate.

And yet there were times like this where she appeared entirely unguarded. She sat across from Hale, a man I would leave no one I treasured with alone, and she showed no signs of fear. Instead, she smiled so sweetly, as if truly enjoying herself.

"If anyone could accept a person for whatever they were, I think Loch would be that person."

"Just because she *can* doesn't mean she should. Perhaps some people don't deserve that kind of acceptance," Tyrus said.

I turned my gaze from Loch and Hale to Tyrus, but he didn't look at me. Instead, he stared down at his own hands.

Ah. This isn't about Yazmor.

Instead, it was about Tyrus and his own self-hatred. It seemed none of us were exempt from our own doubts, and it made me realize, I wasn't sure if I had *ever* seen his demon form.

Despite fights he'd been in, despite showing how capable and vicious he could be, he always did so in his human form. Hale had changed before, and I'd seen his in the past, but never Tyrus.

It seemed we all hid parts of ourselves we didn't care for.

"The way a person appears does not change who they are," I said.

"Is that why you hid your true self for so long?"

"That was out of necessity, not self-hatred. Do you truly believe anyone in the Chasm would follow me if they had known? Would they submit to an angel's authority? Even if I took the form of a demon there, if they had known what I was at my core, would they have ever accepted it?"

Tyrus pressed his lips together before letting out a sigh. "I suppose you're right. Was it hard to leave the

Plains?" He asked that last question softly, as if he hated to admit to his own curiosity.

"Not really. Do not mistake me, there were many times I missed it. With my demon form, I could not return anyway, and there were times where I so desperately wanted to see it again. Or, perhaps it was better to say I wished to revisit the way I had felt there, as if I belonged. The Plains is not the haven it is made out to be. In many ways, it is no different than the Chasm, just with prettier wrappings."

"My wife and children are there."

I brought my gaze up to Tyrus, surprised to hear him utter something so personal. I knew nothing of his past, nothing of how he came to sell his soul or die. The thought of him having a family struck me as strange. He always acted alone, as if untouchable by anything else. I couldn't picture him having a wife, of going home and tucking children into bed.

I had no idea what to say, and I had the feeling he didn't expect a verbal response. Instead, I allowed him to continue at his own pace.

"I wonder if I'll see them when we get there. I don't know if I'm hoping for that or not. A part of me wants to know they are well, that they're happy, that they've lived well in the Plains all this time. Another doesn't want them to see what I've become."

He let out a strained, empty laugh. "Don't get me wrong—I was far from a good person when alive. In a lot of ways, I suppose I'm the same person. Still, the years in the Chasm have pushed me further, have had me doing worse things than before. Not only that, but if they've existed in the Plains, away from me, all this time, perhaps they realized just how bad I was. If they

193

saw me, if they hated me, I don't know how I would react to that. Sometimes it's better not to know."

He didn't speak again at first, and I could have let the conversation drift away. I could have let his silence stand as the end of this talk, but I couldn't bring myself to.

Why?

My gaze shifted over to Loch once more, to the source of so much change, so many things I couldn't understand within myself. She had broken apart the familiar life I'd had before, the comfort I'd had with myself, with understanding who and what I was.

Now, that had all changed. She had opened my eyes to *more*. My life wasn't just my duty, just my work, just motions toward an end where I existed entirely by myself. She'd bridged that gap, and when she'd done it, she made me crave it from others.

No matter how pathetic that felt.

"I understand," I said, bringing my gaze to the fire before me. "I spent a very long time in the Chasm. When I returned to the Plains, I stood outside the main city, unsure what to do. I couldn't return to the Chasm, had no wish to be on Earth, but I didn't know how to return to the place I had come from, the place that had been my home for so long. No, not just the *place*, but more the people. The souls there, the angels I had spent so many days with, even Hubis. Seeing them all again, after I had spent so much time away, so much time changing, made me uneasy. Time passes and people change and the idea that we may change in ways that drive us apart is quite an unwelcome thought."

I let out a soft sigh and shook my head. "Not that I had anyone important waiting, so perhaps I don't understand fully. I made no real connections in the

Plains, had no one waiting for my return, no one who would care if I came back or not."

Tyrus moved his gaze from me over and past, to where Loch sat. Again, I found myself thankful to never have had to go up against Tyrus in a real way. He was far more observant than anyone should be, too good at picking up a person's weaknesses.

"Perhaps it was more similar to when you returned the Chasm. You may not have been gone so long, but you did have someone you had to face, after the two of you had both had time to grow."

And yes, right there, Tyrus proved again why he had gotten and held his position in the Chasm.

Worse? I had no argument, so I offered him the truth. "If you're right about that, then you should take heart—it worked out for me, and I have a feeling I did things far worse than your family could ever levy against you."

"So we're both just men at the mercy of the women in our lives?"

I snorted softly at his statement. "Maybe that's the true secret of life. No matter what you do, how hard you strive, you always end up under the thumb of someone. It makes our efforts feel a little hopeless, does it not?"

Tyrus shook his head. "Not at all. Maybe the point of life is simply to find a person whose thumb you don't mind being beneath."

And that was a philosophy for life I could actually understand and get behind.

Chapter Fourteen

Loch

"Are you just going to be an asshole this whole time?" I threw the small rock, and about the time it bounced off Yazmor's back, I had a quick thought of... *Is insulting and throwing a rock at something as powerful and unpredictable as Yazmor really smart?*

And I didn't even have to think about the answer, because no, it definitely wasn't.

However, I couldn't stand him ignoring me anymore. I had slept, eaten, woken and walked more than any person should every fucking walk, and through it all, he'd paid me no mind.

He'd refused to even meet my gaze let alone speak to me.

Being angry about it felt a *lot* better than crying, after all.

Yazmor stopped and turned toward me, his eyes narrowed in a way that almost had me taking a step back. Wow, those violet eyes of his could look scary when he wanted them to.

I steeled my nerves. I didn't back down to anyone—I wouldn't start with Yazmor. All it would do was add more distance between us, and I already hated how much had grown.

"You shouldn't throw rocks at things that can kill you," he muttered and shoved his hands into the pocket of his sweater, his shoulders hunched forward. He didn't make it into a joke, didn't smile.

It felt downright unnatural, like I was looking at a totally different person. Still, I tried to remind myself that the Path twisted people, that it affected us all, that whatever this was with Yazmor wasn't him—it was Hubis' doing.

It was like when someone got super drunk. I couldn't blame them later for what they did—we all turned into idiots when drunk, so we just took turns between being the drunk idiot and the helper friend who put up with them.

Right now, he was the drunk idiot, and I was the helper, which meant putting my feelings aside and not letting it get to me.

"Well, you shouldn't ignore things that can throw rocks then."

"I'm not ignoring you."

"Really? Because normally I can't get a moment's peace around you but now? You haven't said anything in *hours*. If I didn't see you walking, I'd check you for a pulse."

"You wanted me to shut up."

My mouth hung open for a moment. "Are you really just pouting over that? I'm sorry, okay? I lost my temper. I'm under a lot of stress and this place is affecting me, too."

He let out a soft sound, one full of frustration. "Don't apologize — it doesn't make me any happier to see you unhappy or feeling regret."

"Then don't ignore me, because that *makes* me unhappy."

Yazmor finally lifted his gaze up and looked at me for real, without that distance, without the threat from before. It was as though he'd brushed off that chip from his shoulder finally. "I don't want you unhappy, not ever."

I came closer to him, wanting to shrink the gap that had opened between us. "You've never cared what anyone says about you. Why did that affect you so much?"

"Do you really not get it? I don't care what *people* say about me, but you are not *people*. What you think of me matters, and that isn't something I've ever worried about before. This place? It feels like it whispers in my ear nonstop, this incessant sound like a buzzing insect I can't shoo away."

"What does it say?"

"That I don't belong. That I'm different. That I can never hope to be accepted for what I am. It tells me that the only way to have a place in this world, with the people of this world, is to pretend. It tells me that *you* will never truly care for me, that if you knew the real me, if you understood exactly what I was, you would flee."

"You know me — I'm not smart enough to run away, not even from you." I placed my hand on his chest, the sensation of his heart beating reassuring in a strange way. It felt like a reminder that we were connected, that we had similarities, even if we came from such different places.

He set his hand over mine, the warmth of it surprising given how cold everything else was. Then again, I recalled the almost choking heat of his world. Perhaps he ran warmer because of that? Maybe, because he struggled with keeping that part under control, I could feel it now where I hadn't before?

"You saw what I am when I pulled you from the darkness, and you flinched away."

"So what? Anything new will freak someone out. It doesn't mean I can't accept it once I get used to it. You can't throw something like that at someone then get mad when they don't catch it the first time."

He wrapped his fingers around my wrist and tugged me closer, bringing my fingers toward his mouth. A part of me recalled all those teeth in his other form, yet it didn't startle me as it had before. He had *always* seemed like he had too many teeth, after all. He pressed his lips to my fingers, the touch shockingly gentle. It was strange to feel something so caring from Yazmor.

He could be funny, terrifying, irreverent, even occasionally informative—assuming I could get past the things he said that made no sense—but he'd never been so gentle, as though he handled something precious.

"I have been rejected in my life more than you could imagine, always because I didn't fit in, because I didn't fit the mold. It hasn't ever mattered to me, though. I was happy enough on my own. You changed that, made me want to fit in, made me want to have people who accepted me. This place, it feels as if it's peeling my skin off, as if it's dug a knife tip beneath this mask of humanity I wear and is prying that camouflage free. I struggle to remember how I'm supposed to act, to even look this way. It's like my true form is prowling around inside me and scratching free."

"So let it," I said, staring up and into his face, trying to make my words come out strong, so he understood I was serious.

He laughed softly, continuing to move his lips across my fingers. "That's easy for you to say. The problem is that once seen, things can't be easily forgotten. Hippos seem like fat hairless guinea pigs. They look innocent and sweet and like the comedic relief of the large mammal world. However, the first time a person sees one attack, it will forever change their view. They can't go back to seeing them as they had before. They can't just pretend they never saw it. Likewise, if you see me fully, if I shed all of this that I've worn to fit in, you can't ever go back. You can't unsee it or unknow it later, and if it's too much? I lose the first thing I've wanted in so long…"

"You should trust me more than that," I whispered, setting my hand on his cheek. "I've accepted everything else about you—and in case you've forgotten, that includes your tendency to act badly then immediately apologize, your random trivia, you desire to play with animals that do *not* like you, and the weird gifts you give me. No matter how weird all that gets, I've accepted it. Whether you look like this or like that tree creature doesn't change who I *know* you are."

"How can you be sure that is who you know? How do you know that all those things, all the things you know about me, aren't just another part of my subterfuge? How do you know they aren't just things I do to appear harmless, to sneak beneath the defenses of others? If I hide so much of myself, how can you be sure any of it is real?"

I rubbed my thumb against his cheek, enjoying the way his heat soaked into my palm. "Because I know *you*. I've spent enough time with you to know who you really are. What you look like doesn't matter to me at all, and no matter how much you try to ignore me or run away or tell me that I won't be able to accept you, I'm sure that I know you, that I've seen who you are, and that I love who you are."

He blinked slowly, as if my words had surprised him, and it took me *way* too long to realize what it was exactly that I'd said.

I'd just uttered the unthinkable. I'd gone and blurted out something I wasn't *ever* supposed to say and certainly not to any of these men.

Yet I'd put my foot in my mouth and somehow admitted my true feelings. It went to show just how reckless I really was.

He stared down at me, his breath warming my fingers as he stood almost frighteningly still. My gaze moved from his eyes to his lips.

Normally, in the tension of a moment like this, it would lead to a kiss.

Well, usually it'd lead to a *lot* more than that since I'd never been a woman with much patience or self-control. However, Yazmor was different. I didn't want to push him, to beg for something he didn't want to participate in given our previous conversation about sex.

Before I could apologize and make some stupid joke to ease the tension between us, Yazmor used his free hand to grasp the back of my neck and pulled me forward. The action was so fast, so unexpected that I couldn't stop myself from a startled cry.

Yet no sound left me, because just as quickly, Yazmor pressed his lips to mine and swallowed the sound, stealing it from me and breathing it down.

His kiss wasn't overly practiced, yet it wasn't like Hale's, either, something wild and passionate. Instead, it felt like a test, as if he were seeing what he thought of the whole thing.

And that meant I wanted him to think he enjoyed it. I kissed him back, wanting not to feel like a clumsy teenager who might scare him off the whole thing. I sure knew how it felt to try this shit out for the first time and want to write it off when it wasn't great.

If I turned Yazmor from *possibly interested* to *not for me* just from a kiss I was pretty sure I'd hate myself forever for it.

So I went up to my toes, tilting my head, keeping the kiss sweet and soft. I teased his lips with mine, even darting my tongue out to trace his full bottom lip, to dip past just slightly as if to tempt him with what could come later.

Too quickly — much too quickly, really — I broke the kiss and looked up at him, wanting to read on his face what he thought.

Sure, my pride would take quite the blow if he seemed to hate it, but I needed to know. I nibbled on my own bottom lip as I tried to read his expression.

He smiled, though the edges seemed strained, before he brought his thumb to my where my teeth pressed into my lip, rubbing at the spot. "Don't worry so much. I enjoyed that very much."

Jayce Carter

"Really?" I cursed myself for that weak response, for my own uncertainty. Cursing it didn't change it, though.

"Really." He stroked once more before pulling his hand back. "I saw you in the darkness with Hale and Tyrus, you know."

My eyes widened at that, and I wondered just how long he'd watched. I also had to admit that I didn't really mind the idea of him having watched it... "And to think you chastised me for peeping on Wayne."

"I wasn't peeping, and in fact, you'd already finished. You were just lying there with them." He didn't go on at first, his violet eyes locked on mine. He felt so close for one, as if I could understand him if I just watched him a little more, peered just a bit closer, I'd unlock all his mysteries. "I've seen you naked before, had no reaction to it, hadn't cared about it. A body is a body to me. In fact, in my world, clothing didn't exist because we didn't need a shield from the elements, so nudity has never affected me. Seeing you there felt different, though. My hands kept curling as if I wanted to grasp something."

His voice caught me in a web, as if he were trying to understand his own feelings. How could someone who read others so easily, who predicted everyone else's motives and actions to the point of seeming to be able to see the future, be so unaware when it came to his own feelings?

"Were you jealous?"

He shook his head. "No. I didn't fault you or them, I just... I think I wanted to be there as well. I didn't think I belonged there, didn't see how I ever could be, but I still wanted it."

A smile tugged at my lips, but I fought it, not wanting him to think I was mocking him. I doubted he'd love it if I said I found that unerringly cute — guys tended to find that sort of description emasculating.

He narrowed his eyes, but it lacked the anger and distance from earlier, when I'd thrown the rock at him. That said we'd made progress, right?

"You know, there's no point in hiding your smile if you make it so obvious. If anything, that's more insulting."

I gave into the smile — what was the point in trying to resist it anymore? "Well, maybe next time you'll join in." I turned to walk away, feeling as if I'd taken control of our interaction, as if I'd gained the high ground with him and would leave him off balance.

"Maybe I will," he said.

And there went my high ground. Yazmor managed to throw me off with those three words, my brain immediately running wild with a filthy fantasy, one where I got to touch Yazmor all I wanted, where we both gave into something we wanted. My foot caught a small rock buried in the Path and I pitched forward, barely catching myself before I crashed into the ground.

A familiar chuckle echoed behind me, and the burning of my cheeks was my only companion as I walked faster to try to avoid having Yazmor see just how much he affected me.

It just wasn't fair for him to turn *me* into some blushing virgin when I was pretty sure I had *way* more experience than him.

Yazmor really was more dangerous than he looked — in all ways.

* * * *

"Truth."

"Tell me about the first time you got *super* drunk."

Gorrin sighed as if he found me—and my games—beyond tedious. "You remind me of a child in the backseat on a road trip when all the adults want is a little bit of quiet."

"That doesn't sound like the first time you got super drunk." I offered him a smirk that I'd bet came across as less adorable and more annoying than I was going for. "Come on, you agreed to play!"

"I agreed to play because your last game was eye-spy, and given *everything* out here is some shade of gray, I grew tired of that."

"Look, if *anyone* understands how deals work, it's you. You agreed to play truth or dare so long as I stopped with eye-spy. I did my part, now you fulfill your part."

He rubbed at the bridge of his nose, and I wondered if I were closer, if I could have seen his temple throbbing. It felt like it had been *far* too long since I'd last annoyed him so much, and seeing it now really made me realize that he was back.

And how fucked-up was I that bickering like this, that seeing him that annoyed with me made me this happy?

"I was still in the Plains," Gorrin offered. "I drank a wine they make there for the first time and hadn't understood just how hard it would hit me. Being an angel, liquor made for humans had never done much to me, but this wine is made specifically for angels, so it takes far less of it to intoxicate me."

"And what happened? Did you flash people? Start a fight? Steal a badger from the zoo?"

He narrowed his eyes as he stared at me. "That last one seems a bit too specific to be a random example."

"I admit to nothing, but his name was Sir Snarlyface and he was the best roommate a person could ask for. If you think a dog will scare intruders off, wait to see what a badger does. Besides, the zoo clearly didn't take good care of him if a random drunken eighteen-year-old could sneak in and steal him."

Gorrin said nothing for a while before letting out a soft laugh. "Sir Snarlyface aside, I blacked out that time. I'm not sure exactly what I did, but I woke the next day with the crystal that sits atop the palace tower clutched in my hand. Also, a few other angels snickered behind my back for a few weeks afterward, but I never dared to ask what exactly I'd done."

I tried to picture Gorrin like that, reckless and free and young. It was so different from that man I knew that it made no sense, like looking at the blue sky and someone telling me it was orange. "Well, that's a pretty good story. Did you put the crystal back?"

He shook his head. "I have no idea how I even got up there to get it. Wings don't work for flying, and there is no path up. Besides, Hubis was *not* thrilled when he discovered it missing, so instead, I hid the crystal in my room."

A strange sadness colored his features. "Before I left the Plains, before I went to the Chasm, I would sometimes take that crystal out and just stare at it, as if it had some meaning I'd yet to figure out. It wasn't a large crystal, just small and with a blue tint. Hubis never spoke about it, never explained why it was up there, but it would catch light and reflect down, visible even from ground level. I think, looking back, it was the first time I truly opposed him, when I did something outside of what he wanted me to do, when I didn't just blindly obey him. So I kept it. It is still there, hidden in my room, even after all this time."

I thought about how far Gorrin had come, how much he had grown from the angel he'd once been, the one desperate for Hubis' approval, to live up to what he thought he was supposed to be. I could almost picture him staring at that crystal, trying to understand why it meant anything to him, not fully realizing how badly he craved rebellion and freedom.

I stretched my legs out more on the sleeping bag. It was strange, because there was no day, no night, no way to mark the passage of time on the Path. We stopped to eat and rest, but I couldn't work out how long we'd been here.

It felt like just one mess after another, but I didn't feel any closer to an end than I had when we started.

A crack to my left drew my attention, and I saw the shadow of Guardian moving in the fog. It had grown bolder, showing itself more, drawing closer all the time.

I almost felt like it was testing us, seeing how close it could get before we reacted. It hadn't actually attacked yet, but I had no doubt it was coming.

"Don't worry about it," Gorrin said.

"I'm not." At his look, I shrugged. "Okay, look, I've seen enough hentai. I *know* what tentacles can do. I am equal parts worried and a little curious, I'll admit."

He choked, then hit his fist against his chest. Since he wasn't eating, he must have choked on his own saliva.

So much for an angel, huh?

"The things you say…" he muttered once he'd caught his breath again. "I used to think you said things just to unsettle me, but I've since learned you say them to everyone. I'm not sure if it's a brilliant way to keep others off balance or if you simply don't recognize how inappropriate they are."

"Probably a bit of both," I admitted, then gazed at the fog again. "It's getting closer, you know?"

"Of course I've noticed. It swipes out of the fog now. Normally, it goes for you..."

"Yeah, well, don't get too comfortable. Hentai also taught me that men aren't immune to the lure of the tentacles."

Gorrin winced, telling me he knew *exactly* what I was talking about. Given his expression held absolutely no excitement, I had to guess he didn't have any desire to try out that specific fantasy.

"Koller called it The Guardian," I said to move the conversation away from tentacle anal sex, which wasn't a topic I often had to skirt around. "Does that mean it guards the Plains?"

"That would make sense."

"You'd think it would attack us more, then? Why would it just wait around so much? From what the book said, it isn't like it can't attack us."

Gorrin pressed his lips together, and I could tell he didn't know. Fuck knew that wasn't a nice thing for anyone to admit, but I had a feeling it was worse for Gorrin. He was an angel. He came from the Plains. He knew Hubis better than anyone else. Even with all that, he didn't know exactly what The Guardian was, why it acted the way it did, or what purpose it really served.

I closed my eyes, leaning back on my hands, trying to ease the aching in my body from the long hours and little progress.

"Maybe it's made to drive people here crazy? Maybe it's not meant to actually kill people, just to make them constantly on guard, to ensure they don't sleep and can't rest until it breaks them?"

"So Hubis is a sadist?" I thought about what he'd made me endure and shuddered. "I guess that sort of checks out. I mean, look at the shit he's pulled so far."

Gorrin didn't respond, and I cracked one eye, wondering if I'd pissed him off with that. He wasn't all that loyal to Hubis anymore, but that didn't mean I couldn't flip that switch by accident.

Except, when I opened my eyes, Gorrin wasn't there.

Not just Gorrin, either. I leaped to my feet, spinning around to find myself not where I had just been. No fire, no sleeping bag, no Lords at all. Even the landscape from where I'd been was gone.

I stood in a clearing, surrounded by trees and fog, with the Path nowhere in sight.

And I was entirely alone…

Chapter Fifteen

I am a strong, independent woman who doesn't need men.
Normally that thought came to me when I was trying to open jars, reach things from tall shelves or occasionally when the batteries of my vibrator ran out *right* before I got off. All those times I cursed my luck then pulled myself together and got the job done myself.

This time, when I found myself lost out in the middle of nowhere in the Path, no idea what direction the men were in, where to go or where I'd come from, I had a feeling just slapping some new batteries in wouldn't solve this problem.

"This isn't so bad," I said out loud, thinking that hearing some conversation would make the whole thing easier.

It didn't. In fact, hearing my own voice in the otherwise silent space was downright unnerving. It reiterated just how alone I really was.

I wonder how Bubbles is… I almost laughed at the idea of my stuffed whale hanging out back in the Chasm, probably running shit in my absence. Myers handled most of the details, but even he knew better than to fuck with Bubbles.

Some things were sacred, after all.

The thoughts were pointless and random, but they seemed to keep panic at bay for a little while.

A snap to my left made me jerk my head to that side only to find the rolling fog barely hiding a glimpse of Guardian.

"What the fuck is your problem? There are *four* others you could be bothering! I'm sorry to tell you this, but you are *soooo* not my type." I kept walking through the fog with no real endpoint since I had no idea what direction to go. And, sure, complaining to a weird tentacle creature that was stalking me was pretty pointless, but when a person finds themselves all alone, they can't really be choosy about their company. "I know that I am dating some pretty fucking weird guys, but I do have a few specific requirements. A dick is one, and guess what? Tentacles don't count!"

Another sound behind me made me sigh and drop my head back. "I said I'm not interested! I'll say the same thing to you that I said to an old guy who hit on me on the bus. Keep your wiggly bits away from me!" I turn to glare at Guardian, as if *that* would make it finally realize I didn't want to play. Hell, maybe it would make it finally attack, since this waiting was the worst part!

Wait…maybe the whole tentacle sex was still the worst part. Only time would tell on that one.

When I turned, the sound hadn't come from Guardian. I took a big deep breath, relief sliding through me.

Finally.

"Took you long enough!" I shouted as I jogged toward Hale, Gorrin, Yazmor and Tyrus, who all stood a ways behind me, looking like the best desert mirage ever. "I thought I was going to wander around aimlessly forever. Wouldn't that be a shitty way to go? I'd go the rest of my life without anyone to annoy except for Guardian there." I jerked my thumb over my shoulder toward where that thing in the mist had moved.

Which was strange...because when I turned that way, I saw no movement in the fog. It either was keeping its distance or it had gone silent as if to hide.

The action made the hair on the back of my neck stand on end. Guardian had not only *not* ever seemed afraid of the men, it had stalked us all this whole time. Why would it go quiet now?

I turned back toward the men. "That's weird... Guardian seems spooked by something." I glanced up and into Hale's eyes, the blue exactly as it had always been, yet with a flatness that screamed a warning into my head.

I tried to take a step backward, the action driven by instinct alone, but Hale shot a hand out and wrapped it around my throat. It wasn't the way he normally did it, not as a weird form of kinky foreplay that *always* got me off. Instead, the hand tightened so much I couldn't draw air past it.

I peered to the side, trying to seek help from one of the others, able only to move my eyes because Hale's grasp kept my head still. The moment I got a good look at Gorrin, my fears solidified. Yazmor and Tyrus further confirmed it.

These *weren't* my men. They looked exactly the same, but an emptiness in their eyes, a flatness, reminded me of a frozen lake.

Which meant right now I was getting the like choked out of me by something that looked exactly like the men I loved.

When I'd thought about duplicates of my lovers, I'd sure come up with *far* more pleasurable ways we could pass the time. I was down for a night of debauchery with *eight* sexy men—who never fantasized about a set of twins let alone four of them?—but this was way too rough for me.

Shut up and focus!

I tried to shake away the stupidity running through my head, to remind myself that was nothing more than a defense mechanism to keep me from freaking out.

Now was probably a good time to freak out, after all.

So I brought my knee up and aimed for Hale's groin—it didn't look like I'd get to use that area the way God intended anyway. It weakened his grip, and I yanked backward, striking the ground hard enough that it rattled my thoughts for a moment.

Except when I lifted my gaze to find all four of them advancing on me, I realized I didn't have time to think, time to collect myself.

If I didn't put up a good fight, I was about to get my ass handed to me, and even if it was by *these* faces, I wasn't going to just roll over for them.

I only rolled over for *my* men.

Hale

"I'm going to spank her ass the moment I fucking find her."

"Like *that* would ever stop Loch from doing exactly as she pleases," Tyrus pointed out. "If any of us thought a good spanking would keep her line, don't you think we would have tried that?"

I lifted my lip and snarled at Tyrus, not giving a fuck about his opinion.

"Besides the fact that it wouldn't work," he went on. "This wasn't Loch just wandering off."

"So? She made me fucking worry — she should have to deal with that."

"You both are exhausting me," Gorrin pointed out from his place behind me, his tone like a father sick of the squabbling of his children.

The way he could sound so in control pissed me off all the more. I mostly accepted myself — hot-tempered and all — but sometimes seeing me so out of control made me feel lacking. How they kept their heads on straight when Loch was missing was beyond me.

"Don't you fucking care what she might be going through?"

"Of course I care," Gorrin said. "But losing my composure now won't change things, will it? If anything, it will only make it more likely that I will miss things, that I will make a mistake. Keeping a tight leash on your feelings will serve you best."

My gaze moved beyond Gorrin to Yazmor, who walked ahead, his face a mask of focus as he followed a *feeling* he had with Loch. I didn't quite understand it, didn't get why he had that connection with her, but at no time was I more thankful for it than right now.

"Loch is tough," Tyrus said, his voice softer. "After everything else she's survived, I doubt there's much even here in the Path that could hurt her too seriously. I'm sure she's fine."

I snorted at how *not* convincing his words were.

We all understood the risks. We knew just how dangerous this fucking place was and how likely it was that any person alone wouldn't last long. Loch was tough—I sure as fuck wouldn't claim otherwise—but she was still young and way too sweet. She was always trying to save other people, too concerned with their wellbeing and too reckless with her own.

Which made me want to poke Yazmor in the back to get him to move *faster*. I wanted Loch in my arms, to reassure myself she was fine. The last fucking trap we'd fallen into, at least it had happened with Tyrus, Loch and me together.

This time?

The Path had separated her out, taking her alone, plucking her from her spot. Gorrin had said she'd been there, talking to him one moment, then gone the next.

Why?

"Why is the Path targeting Loch?" I asked.

Yazmor's feet slowed, and Tyrus furrowed his brows. I got the sense it wasn't just my question that stilled them.

They probably were just as surprised that I'd be the one to bring up a good point.

Always fucking underestimating me, huh?

"The Guardian does seem most interested in her," Gorrin pointed out. "In fact, I didn't see it at all when you all were trapped in that shadow, and I haven't seen it since she disappeared this time."

"Two traps so far, both sprung around Loch," Tyrus added.

Yazmor turned back toward us, his lips pressed together. "The Path is focused on her. Why?" Even though Yazmor seemed to ask us, he went on as though we weren't there at all. "She is a Demon Lord as three of us are. Is she the weakest? Is the Path trying to focus on what it perceives as the easiest prey?"

"She took my place, so in terms of sheer power, she has to be at least equal to any of you," Gorrin said.

The words might have annoyed me any other time, but we had bigger problems right now than measuring dicks.

Besides, he was probably right... As the oldest of the Demon Lords, he'd had the most time to collect power.

"But she's more conflicted," Tyrus said. "Maybe the Path senses that and sees *that* as a weakness. Maybe it can tell that she's the least seasoned, the least vicious?"

Gorrin shook his head, his expression tense. "The Path sees her as a threat."

"Aren't we *all* threats?" I asked. "I mean, we're all fucking here to go kill Hubis, so shouldn't this place see us all as threats?"

"I'm sure it does, but who got us here? Who brought us together? Who was the only one who even *considered* this as an option? Loch might be more conflicted, more naïve, but she's also the only one who got us here," Gorrin explained. "The Path is a form of protection for the Plains, and thus for Hubis. If The Guardian works in conjunction with that, it would focus on whatever it finds the largest threat—which is Loch. If she were gone..."

"We wouldn't keep going," Yazmor finished. At my sharp look, he continued. "Loch binds us together, makes it so we have a common goal and can put our own hatred aside. Without her, that alliance would dissolve. We would have no hope of working as a team."

The words sank in, and worse? Their truth.

Sure, without Loch we'd *want* revenge, but we wouldn't work together well enough to manage it. That meant the Path was focusing on Loch to break us all, and that it wouldn't stop until it ended her.

Yazmor pulled in a quick breath, seeming to fully understand it the same moment I did. He turned and took off in a run, and I followed suit.

I wasn't about to let this fucking place have Loch, and I didn't give a damn what I had to take on to ensure that didn't happen. I'd done a lot of fucked-up shit in my life and my afterlife, but I'd do *anything* to protect Loch.

The Path had no idea just what it was up against.

Target my woman at your own peril, fuckers.

Chapter Sixteen

Loch

"The good thing is that you guys aren't *nearly* as quick as the real versions." I dodged to the left when faux-Hale swiped for me, narrowly avoiding his hand.

Thus far, I'd managed to stay out of their grasp after my first run-in. The more I moved around these four, the more obvious it became that they were really shitty copies of the real thing.

The real Lords would have handed me my ass if they'd grouped together like this. Instead, these four didn't seem to work together, all blindly grabbing for me.

Then again, I'd felt faux-Hale's strength when he'd wrapped his hand around my throat. It didn't take being good if a person had numbers and luck, and worse? The presence of non-virgin incels showed that everyone got lucky eventually.

The men didn't speak, which further showed they weren't the real ones. My men, even the quiet ones, still talked. They bitched and moaned, mostly, but it was still noise. These hadn't uttered anything.

The more they moved around, the more they went for me, the surer I became that they were little more than animals in the shape of the Lords. They reached for me on instinct, the actions showing no signs of intelligence or planning.

Thank fuck they aren't working together.

I dodged to the right when faux-Gorrin went for me, but I slammed into the side of something hard. When I twisted, I found that faux-Tyrus had guessed my direction and beat me there.

Which meant they were getting smarter…

Just fucking great. My men couldn't seem to learn new tricks but these did?

He wrapped his hand around my arm to hold me, then lifted a hand. It wasn't some slap or backhand — no, faux-Tyrus apparently wasn't the type to worry about me being female. Instead, his hand curled into a fist that sailed through the air at me.

And *wow* had I underestimated the strength this version of Tyrus had. He slammed into my cheek, the action knocking me backward into the soft ground. It rattled my brain around in my skull, making it hard to regain my thoughts, to move, to do anything. I wanted to lie there for a moment and rethink my entire life.

However, when a heavy body pinned me from above, *that* plan went out the metaphorical window.

Above me was Yazmor, the violet eyes so shockingly familiar that between the hit and the physical similarity of this Yazmor and real Yazmor, I struggled to tell them apart. Those eyes had looked at me *so many* times, had made me feel safe. Even with the messiness between us here in the Path, a part of me almost instinctually melted for him, giving into Yazmor as I had so many times, placing myself in his hands and trusting him.

Except, he didn't smile. This Yazmor didn't pull his lips into a grin that was too wide and entirely inappropriate. That shook me free of the nostalgia, reminded me that *this* wasn't my Yazmor.

I tried to roll, to knock him off, but he was so much larger than me. He hadn't ever seemed that large, but pinned beneath him like this, I recognized how deceiving that really was.

When no side-to-side motion worked, I did the next best thing. I planted my feet on the ground and lifted my hips. It was an exercise men *loved* to watch women do, as if exercise were just a show for them, but it was effective.

By doing it, I unsettled faux-Yazmor's balance, throwing him forward.

In for a penny…

I lifted my head, hissing in a sharp breath at the impact when he slammed against me. Still, it did what it needed to, and when I rocked to the side, he fell in that direction.

My head pounded, my thoughts fuzzy, telling me I had probably hurt myself as well with that little stunt. Still, it was like an animal chewing their own foot off in a trap.

Better to give up the foot than to die entirely. With him off, I rolled, scrambling in the dirt to get to my feet.

Except someone wrapped a hand around my bag, tearing the pack from me and tossing it aside. I squirmed, but the person grabbed my leg, next.

The action took me back to a place I didn't want to go but couldn't seem to avoid. I found myself back in that memory, the one Hubis had forced me to endure. The hand around my leg yanked, causing me to slide backward, the dirt scraping my knees.

Weight settled over me, knocking me to my stomach, and large, strong hands wrapped around my throat, squeezing tight. I kicked, managing only to roll over, the action placing me on my back once again.

This time, it was Gorrin over me. *Fuck.*

My brain was muddled and slow, as if a drunken hamster stumbled along in the wheel now. My thoughts drifted backward and forward, connecting all the dots.

The attack I'd experienced from Clint, the fight with Gorrin where I killed him, the memory of the attack I'd seen, the sex I'd had with Gorrin. It all mixed and melted together until it was just one big bowl of 'fuck no.' Until Gorrin's face melted into that attack, until these creatures were the same ones from that memory of the attack.

I clawed at his arms, but he wouldn't relent, would let me gasp in any air at all.

Was this it? Would I die here, in the Path, ending *everything?*

The world slowed around me, time crawling by. Was I seeing my life flash before my eyes a moment before my brain died, before the sparking electricity that ran my meat suit gave up and I turned to nothing?

What came after this life? No one knew. Maybe nothing, maybe a new world, maybe all that reincarnation shit wasn't fake, and I'd get another shot at this all.

Did I want another shot? Fuck knew I hadn't done great this time, but hell, maybe I'd learn some new tricks for the next round?

Except, faces floated by my dimming vision.

I saw Hale, back in that empty group home, all by himself, refusing to let anyone close to him. I saw Tyrus hating himself and working himself until he collapsed. I saw Gorrin, unsure who actually cared about him, or what he was supposed to be. I saw Yazmor, so desperate to fit in, to find a place where he belonged, yet so sure he never would. That was assuming the four of them could even return, but if brought down to only the four of them, the odds of that were slim.

It went beyond them, though.

I also saw Brendon, the kid I'd saved, devastated when Hale never returned to visit. I saw Jay trying to hold her family together, trying to learn to become the woman she needed to to take over, to protect everyone she cared for. I saw Kylie alone, wishing for connections to a world that wasn't hers. Koya would lose his protection in the Chasm, leaving him at the whims of whoever took over for Tyrus. Myers would probably be fine—that asshole would probably let Bubbles take over and rule from the shadows.

For the first time, it really hit me how many people would be affected if I died here. In my first life, when I'd gotten murdered, the world had just kept on spinning.

No one cared. Not even Gunnar, not even the man I'd sold my soul for. No one had mourned me, no one had looked for me. I hadn't been important enough for anyone to give a fuck about me.

That wasn't true anymore, though. For better or worse, no matter how it had happened, the world would *feel* my loss this time.

And that meant I couldn't just stay here and give in. I recalled my mom's voice in my ear, calling me Salmon with that almost endearing tone of voice.

I'd wanted so badly to not matter, to keep my head down, but that hadn't been what had happened. Instead, I'd endeared myself to this world, had made friends, allies, enemies and even lovers.

So many would suffer if I fell here.

And while I still might, I couldn't just give in. My mom had always laughed about the fact that I never gave in, that I never went with the flow, that I always did things my own way. I'd told Gorrin the same thing, refused to give in.

The Path could want to kill me, but *fuck what it wanted.* I might not win, but I sure as hell wouldn't make things easy on it. If it wanted to kill me, it would have to try a lot harder, and I'd make it bleed for every inch it took.

I curled my fingers into the dirt beside me and tossed it up and into faux-Gorrin's eyes, closing my own at the same time. Nothing worse than blow-back.

The action loosened faux-Gorrin's hands, but I didn't use that break to try to knock him free as I'd done with faux-Yazmor. *Nope.* I'd been playing too nicely before. Instead, I reached up, knocking his hands from my throat with my arms, then went for Gorrin's rapidly blinking eyes as he tried to clear the dirt from them.

I cupped the sides of his face and dug my thumbs into his eyes, the action both incredibly gross and against my every instinct.

Even if I knew it wasn't *my* Gorrin, a part of me struggled to actually hurt him.

I could struggle all I wanted, though, because I wasn't about to stop.

The evil-clone didn't make a noise—but none of them had, not so much as a pained shout, nothing more than breathing—but he did yank backward and scramble away like a wounded animal.

I took the chance to leap to my feet and take off. I couldn't out-dodge them forever, but I could run. Hell, I didn't think f-Gorrin would even manage to follow given what I'd done to his eyes.

My feet struck the ground as I ignored any complaint in my body, any sluggishness from the fight, from the exceedingly long trip thus far. Nothing mattered but putting distance between those things and me.

I'd escaped that blackness before by getting guided out by Yazmor. I hadn't actually been anywhere else, so I had to hope this was the same, that this was just a tiny pocket inside the Path and I'd find my way out if I just ran fast enough.

As I ran, even with distance between me and the doppelgangers, I noticed that there seemed to be a slight clearing in the trees that led and guided me. It wasn't as clearly defined as a trail, but still, I followed it.

The snapping of twigs behind me said I hadn't lost the others, that they followed me. Were they tracking me somehow? Fuck, the Path probably allowed them to find me, made them drawn to me no matter where I went.

Funny that I actually missed Guardian right about now.

I almost tripped, catching myself on a tree, my chest burning from exertion. Just ahead of me, that same slight clearing of the way forked into two directions.

To the left was lighter, as if the trees lessened. It would be easier to run that way. I might be able to get farther…

To the right, appeared more densely forested. It was even darker, with the fog thicker. There was something else that way, something that rested on the edges of my senses. It took a moment before I recognized what I felt.

Them.

I had a strange pull, something that told me the Lords were that way — the real ones. Then, whispered through the fog and darkness that way, a voice.

"Loch!"

I peered down that path, into the darkness there, an air of 'don't you fucking think about it.'

The mess in my brain, the mixture of everything that had happened along with the faces of the Lords, it made me pause.

What if I was wrong? What if it wasn't *them* down that way? What if it was just another trap?

Could I really rely on anyone else? Maybe it was best to just keep running? Or to turn around and fight the creatures stalking me? I was strong, after all. My fingers brushed my wrist, the mark of the dagger there.

But four of them was a far cry from a one-on-one. It was easy to be overwhelmed with those numbers.

"Where the fuck are you, Loch?" *Hale.*

I almost smiled at the anger in his voice, could see his expression in my head.

I had to choose. Would I trust myself? Trust them?

I gripped the bark of the tree once more just as the four fake Lords caught up to me. They stared at me, that same emptiness in their eyes.

It made the choice for me, and I took off down the way to the right, toward the voices. Just ahead was a strange wall of fog, and I pushed myself in that direction.

As if the things behind me knew they had the last chance, they seemed to run faster, closing the distance between us. Had they just been toying with me before? Screwing with me? Wanting me to feel the fear of being stalked, of being hopeless and helpless?

Fuck that. I wasn't helpless, no matter what anyone wanted to see me as or make me feel.

A hand grasped my arm from behind just before I reached the fog, and I twisted, swinging my elbow backward. I connected with a hard jaw but didn't bother to wait and see who it was. Instead, I yanked away and rushed through the fog, collapsing to the ground.

Someone grabbed me again, and when I turned, Gorrin's face brought me back to the creatures. Had they followed me? I swung again, connected with his eye.

Just as quick, the others surrounded me, and panic took me over. I kicked, trying to get away, cursing myself for making the wrong choice.

"What the fuck?" Hale snapped, his voice breaking the trance.

Those things hadn't spoken, had they?

Just as I convinced myself that these were *my* men, the doppelgangers broke through the fog as well, like nightmares made flesh. They looked identical to the four that surrounded me — well, other than the injuries they'd taken from me — and that made me shrink away, my brain unwilling to make sense of it all.

Thankfully, it didn't need to for long. The things dissolved before us, as if they'd never been there all, which left me on the ground with the *real* Lords above me.

And wasn't it funny just how much safer I felt with these? They were capable of doing so much more damage than the creatures before, could hurt me far worse, were significantly more twisted and devious, but just seeing them standing there…

I felt like I was finally home.

* * * *

A few hours later, I sighed and rubbed my eyes.
What a long fucking day.

Wait, no, forget that. What a long fucking life! It felt like one disaster after another, as though I just jumped from one fire to the next, never getting a real rest.

I recalled flipping tortillas on the stove when I was a kid, the way I'd grab it with my bare hands. It burned but I did it so fast it never *really* hurt me.

That felt like my whole life, except I never got a break. The heat would burn at my fingers, but I'd move from one to the next so fast that I never got a break but moved fast enough to not kill me.

And it was exhausting.

"We don't have much food left," Gorrin said as he peered into his pack.

"Sorry," I muttered, wrapping my arms around my legs as I recalled how the fake Lords had torn my pack away.

"I wasn't trying to make you feel bad." Gorrin closed his bag and set it aside, his body pressed up against mine.

Since they'd found me — or had I found them? — they'd been unwilling to let me be even a foot away from one of them. For whatever reason, the Path seemed focused on destroying me, and the last time, it had snatched me right away from Gorrin.

It meant they were being overprotective.

And it meant one of them would lose a limb when I had to go to the bathroom the next time if they didn't give me some space. I sure as fuck didn't plan to try squatting together like some weird synchronized peeing thing.

"You *should* blame me. I lost my pack which had a lot of food in it."

"You were attacked by *four* assailants. Your survival is more than enough. We will make do with what we have, or we will find other sustenance. The book and Koller both implied that the fruit from the trees is edible."

"Yeah, because eating random shit *here* is a great idea," I snapped, then sighed and rubbed at my temples. "I'm sorry — it isn't your fault. I'm just frustrated with this all. I feel like I get why people go mad here."

Gorrin wrapped his arm around my shoulders, pulling me against his side. The warmth helped ease my mind a bit, as if a reminder that I wasn't alone in this all. "Humans need purpose. It is one of the things that makes you all both dangerous and interesting. Other creatures simply do what needs to be done or whatever they wish to do when they wish to do so. Humans think further ahead than that. They need a direction. Without that, they can't find happiness or contentment. This place steals that from a person. It forces us to wander along a Path with no ending, with no hint as to when we may escape or how long that might take. That can break the minds of humans."

"But not yours?"

He shook his head. "I am not human. I was created with the understanding that my task was to aid Hubis. That was my direction, my purpose. I do not need a purpose or direction beyond that."

"But you don't follow him anymore."

Gorrin peered over at me, a fleeting glance that lasted only a split second before he looked away. "No, I don't. I found something else to follow, something that matters far more to me. This place feeds and magnifies my fears as it does anyone else's, but it doesn't risk my sanity as it does yours."

"So we're all supposed to just wander around until we starve or go mad? And you considered yourself some sort of tactician?"

Gorrin said nothing back, his fingers tightening on my shoulder as if he knew no words would reassure me. What was there to say? It felt a bit like when people knew death was coming, that there was no escape. Lying to each other was pointless. Sometimes all a person could do was be there with the other one, just face the hopeless situation together.

My gaze moved toward the forest, away from the Path that Gorrin had led us back to.

That's it…

"We need to leave the Path," I said.

He jerked his gaze to the side, his eyes narrowed. "That is a terrible idea. The Guardian is out there, and each time you have found yourself trapped, it has been off the Path. We've been fortunate to find our way back at all, even with my skills."

I twisted so I could face him, trying to make him understand. "We want to get to where no one else has, so we have to do what no one else has. That's what Koller told us. Maybe the Path itself is a trap, just a lure this place uses to keep people going, to give them hope only to destroy it over and over again. There's no telling what we might find if we leave the Path."

"Like more dangers than we can even guess —"

"But those dangers found us here! The last trap literally yanked me off the Path and away. Guardian keeps going for me, and before you know it, it's going to stop playing coy. We don't have another choice."

"Of course we do. We could return to the Chasm. If we turn back, if we want to leave, the trail back should appear."

"And have this all be for nothing? No. That's not an option."

"What are you arguing about?" Hale sat down on the same sleeping bag as me, on the other side as Gorrin.

"We're leaving the Path," I said.

"We aren't," Gorrin argued.

Tyrus approached as well, sitting in front of me. Yazmor came closer, but his eyes burned brighter, his color not pale but darker, as if his other form bled through this one. Neither spoke, but their expressions said they'd heard.

"Pretty sure the one piece of advice *everyone* has given us was to stay on the Path," Tyrus said.

"Not Koller."

"Koller is probably mad," Gorrin said. "She has been here a very long time. There is no way to know if what she said was true or if it was nothing more than her own insanity trying to draw us to our own demise. Even she said we shouldn't trust her."

I shifted, moving to my knees as though that extra bit of height would make them hear me better. "You don't get it. I've been thinking, and if this place is set up to protect the Plains, why would there be a Path to follow? Hubis doesn't want anyone to make it through, so why would he set up a safe route to do it? That wouldn't make any sense at all! Even if that was the case, we've been walking for what feels like days, probably weeks, and we've gotten nowhere. We're running low on supplies, we're injured, exhausted. We don't have a lot to lose at this point by trying it another way."

"We've left the Path," Gorrin pointed out. "Yazmor and I have left a number of times to scout and to retrieve you when you've gone missing."

"Could we not make me sound like a kid who got lost? Or like Yazmor when he wanders off? But besides that, you left with the purpose of returning. That's different. We've yet to leave the Path with the *intention* of going out there. We've tried everything else — this is all that's left."

The men fell silent, and worse, I couldn't read any of them. It made me glad I'd never tried strip poker with them because I'd have been naked in a hand or two.

Still, the fact that none fought with me said they struggled to find a good argument against my point. Was it a bad idea?

Absolutely.

But when a person had no good options, they had to pick between whatever shit they had. We'd done what we could on the Path, we'd tried that, taken it as far as we could, but that clearly wasn't working.

Which meant we had to do something different.

"Fuck," Hale muttered, his curse as close to agreement as I'd probably get.

"I don't like it," Tyrus said. "But I can't come up with a better option either."

Yazmor shrugged, a flash of his old smile making my chest tight, like seeing an old friend. "You know I adore the unknown."

I faced Gorrin, the final hold-out, and honestly the one with the most say. He knew more than anyone else about this place, about where we were headed.

He let out a sound of frustration, like a low growl. "You *will* stay close. We will walk in a line, with me up front, and you will step only where I step. There is no telling what is out there, and the farther we venture into it, the thicker the fog, the more dangerous it will become."

With his agreement, we packed what little we still had — the benefit was that the packs we still had were lighter than before.

I pulled in a deep breath, my gaze peering out into the fog, the forest, the unknown, before taking my first step, following Gorrin, off the Path.

I'm coming for you, Hubis, no matter where you hide…

Chapter Seventeen

Just act like it's no big deal.

That was the advice I used for myself when some weirdo on the subway with his dick out was having the time of his life, but now it seemed I needed to use it for Yazmor, too.

I would have preferred his dick out over this, but he hadn't asked my opinion.

Instead, Yazmor's eyes almost glowed, his skin having darkened more until it appeared more like his other form. He still was shaped like a human, but the wrapping had changed.

"I don't know what to do about him," Tyrus said from beside me.

We'd done the whole walk in a single-file thing, but that had gotten old pretty fast. After a few hours in the fog, Gorrin had lightened up when nothing else had attacked us. He still led, but we didn't have to do all this kindergarten style.

"What's there to be done?"

Tyrus pressed his lips together, his eyes narrowed. Had he ever looked quite so much like a predator before?

Maybe, when he looks at me naked, but that is a very different kind of stalking then...

"If he loses himself entirely, he'll prove a *very* dangerous adversary. If we wait too long, we may not have as much of a chance to stop him."

"Isn't that true about all of us?" I asked. "Because in case you haven't noticed, *none* of us are doing fantastic. Hale is walking farther away from everyone, won't let anyone stand behind him and is snapping worse — and to say his mood is worse considering how *friendly* he normally is, that means something. Gorrin won't give me more than a foot or two of space before he's breathing down my neck, like he's afraid of letting me out of his sight at all. And you? You're acting like nothing's wrong, but don't think I've missed out the way you keep watching *everyone* like you're just waiting for them to turn on you. You don't snap and snarl like Hale does. Instead, you seem to be one step ahead, trying to figure out what moves we'll all make so you can kill us first."

"You are imagining things." How a man as dangerous as Tyrus could manage to sound like a pouting child I didn't know and I shouldn't like, but it charmed me endlessly.

"Am I? Because I'm pretty sure you've got more food and water in your pack than anyone else has. You've been stashing sharp rocks in it as well, like you're just waiting for us to fuck you over, and you want to be ready."

His eyes widened. *Talk about underestimating me as always.*

"I'm not trying to bust your balls," I added on softly. "This place is bringing out all our worst sides, our fears. It's amplifying them all so they seem so much bigger than we are, like they're impossible to overcome."

"If you saw what I'd done, why not mention it sooner?"

"Why mention it at all? Will me telling you that I'm not going to betray you change anything? Are you going to hear that and feel all better? I know better than most people that fear doesn't work that way. It doesn't go away just because it's faced with actual facts. If fear was that easy, none of us would ever have to deal with it."

"Is that how you're able to deal with it?"

"Me?"

Tyrus didn't turn to look at me, his gaze pinned ahead. "You had a hard life before you died, suffered many things from what little I know. You were tortured by Clint. You suffered through Hubis' punishment. You were attacked by creatures who wore *our* faces. I would hardly blame you if you couldn't stand the idea of any of us anywhere near you, but you don't do that. You are braver than I would think possible, and I can't say I understand how you manage it."

I wrapped my arms around myself, the chill getting to me, the fog thicker and colder the farther from the Path that we ventured. "I remind myself that none of you did those things to me. If anything, you all have saved me, time and time again. You've never had a reason to take care of me, but you all have. It isn't always easy, but I just keep correcting myself until it sticks."

"You seem to be the only one who still has her wits about her. Why is that? Why aren't you being as affected by this place?"

"I am," I admitted softly. He did cast me a glance at that, as if he struggled to believe it. I offered him a weak smile I was sure didn't reach my eyes. "I've never felt that confident in myself."

"This coming from Salmon?" His gentle smile warmed me, and I bumped my shoulder against his.

"I've always known *what* I believed in, what I wanted, but I've never felt that confident in how to get there, in if I could. I might have taken the steps I needed to, but I never felt sure I could manage it. Being here...I'm questioning myself constantly. I'm wondering if I'm right, if I've made the right choice, if *I* can be trusted. I question you guys, but it's not about trusting *you*. It's about trusting myself, in knowing I'm right about you. Normally, I'd dig in and just keep going, consequences be damned, but I'm hesitating. I'm convincing myself that I'm wrong, that I should wait, that I should let someone else make the decision because I don't want to be wrong." Just admitting it felt like picking at a healing wound.

But the more I spoke, the more I seemed to organize my thoughts, the more obvious it became just how much this feeling had spread through me.

Tyrus caught my arm and pulled me to a stop, the action making me turn slightly to face him. He set a finger beneath my chin to lift my face to his. "You should trust yourself more, Little Demon."

And fuck, I melted at his nickname. He didn't use it all that often, but each time he did, it felt like a special bond between just the two of us. It felt endearing, as if I'd claimed some part inside of him no one else had. Tyrus was a stern man, one who didn't generally do things like sweetness, yet that name made me warm in a way that made me feel impossibly closer to him.

"Didn't I tell you that just being told the truth doesn't change fear?" I whispered.

"Then I'll tell you as many times as you need to hear it. Each time you start to doubt yourself, I will tell you yet again that you are capable and strong and while you are sometimes reckless and foolish, you have the fortitude to follow through to the end."

I blinked slowly at him as his words sank in, feeling strange. Tyrus was one of the most logical men I knew, and one of the harshest critics of my rather laissez-faire method of behavior. To hear him praise that part of me made me stop and listen in a way it wouldn't have from others.

"Don't look so surprised," he whispered. "I've told you before how much I admire that part of you. I always think things through, behave based on what is the most likely to succeed. I can appear confident in myself because I have weighed the pros and cons and determined my odds of winning. You don't do that. You decide what you want, and you go after it. That is something I am envious about. You risk so much, and that way you can keep going no matter how hopeless something seems is a rare trait in the world and one I hope you never lose." He brushed his lips to mine, the touch so gentle that it felt like we were under a star-filled sky rather than lost in the fog of the Path.

When he pulled away, he took his bag off and held it out to me.

I frowned but didn't reach for it. "What? Get tired of hauling around the heavy shit? Don't think you can unload that junk on me. I am *not* a pack mule."

Tyrus didn't pull the bag back toward him, his gaze serious. "You said just hearing something doesn't change how we feel, but that to do so, we have to counter that voice. The voice tells me to prepare, to ready myself because in the end, I stand alone and have to eliminate all threats against me."

"So why are you trying to pawn your heavy shit off on me?"

"I'm countering that voice. I'm giving up my advantage to you because I *know* I can trust you. So I'm letting you have the food and weapons I've gathered."

I peered down at his hand, noting a slight tremble there. While his face hadn't shifted, while he looked as if he were just handing me some worthless item, the shaking of his hand proved his true feelings.

Tyrus, so used to having to outthink everyone else, to remain one step ahead of them, to hide his advantage until he could use it to come out on top, was choosing to give that up. He was trusting me—and in turn, trusting the other Lords.

I took the bag, keeping my mouth shut at just *how* heavy it was, then slid the straps over my shoulders.

"The fuck is that?" Hale's voice drew my attention, and when I turned, I first didn't have a clue what he meant.

Until the moving fog—thicker and covering more the farther from the Path we traveled—lessened enough for me to make out a huge shadow ahead of us.

It was like a massive beast, a darkness that the fog made impossible to identify.

Maybe we shouldn't have ventured this far out...

Before I could freak out, I realized it wasn't moving. It felt as if it were, because of the swirling fog, but it hadn't. I walked that way, drawn forward at the chance of *anything* different. We'd wandered for so long, surrounded by just trees and dirt and fog, that something new felt like a massive prize.

It was like getting lost at sea. Anything became a prize worth paddling for.

I passed Gorrin, who seemed frozen in place, but Yazmor had also gone forward. We walked side-by-side until I could make out the strange darkness.

A house?

As much as that made no fucking sense at all, I couldn't deny it as more and more details became clear.

It appeared to be a two-story house, out in the middle of fucking nowhere, looking like something I'd find in any suburban hellscape, complete with a little white picket fence out front.

"Well that's fucking unnerving," Hale muttered as he took a spot beside me. "Never figured a picture-perfect place like that could look that fucking scary."

"A house in suburbia is simply your own personal version of hell," Tyrus answered.

"I've got to side with Hale," I added. "Why is this out here?"

"Koller said there were others here, damned and demons who have survived as we have thus far," Gorrin pointed out. "Maybe they built it?"

"If we were talking about some shitty tent or some sticks all bundled together to make shelter, sure. How would a person manage to build something like *this* though?"

Yazmor tilted his head, reminding me of a dog trying to understand a noise. "It was made from the Path. This place is a pocket, just like the Forgotten Caves. It's formed out of the minds here."

"I thought it was made by Hubis."

"The place is made by Hubis and his feelings, his subconscious mind, but once inside it, it is impacted by anything else here. Enough time and parts of it can be shaped into new forms, such as this one."

"So someone is living there?" I paused, then tacked on, "Living being a very generous term."

Yazmor leaned forward and inhaled deeply. Was he sniffing the air? *Well, isn't that unsettling?* After closing his eyes as if savoring the scent, he shook his head. "It seems empty. I only scent the four of you and Guardian."

And wasn't it weird that I almost felt better knowing Guardian was around? As if he were my new pet that I worried about.

"Should we stay here?" Tyrus asked.

I shot him an *'are you stupid?'* look. "Have you never watched horror movies? Because when you find an abandoned house in the middle of the woods, you leave it the fuck alone. That is like, the number one rule."

"What's number two?" Yazmor asked.

"Don't have sex. Horror movies don't like easy women, so if you have sex, you're dying. Also, don't go alone anywhere and don't follow any sounds."

"Well you're fucked then," Hale said. "If to stay alive *you* have to not have sex and not do stupid shit, well, you're for sure dying."

"Well, at least I won't die a virgin, then."

"That hasn't been a risk for you in a *very* long time."

The back and forth with Hale felt oddly normal. Sure, we were in the middle of this weird-ass situation, we had no idea if we'd survive the next few hours, let alone longer, we were all quickly losing our minds, but we could still interact like our old selves.

It almost made me feel like things might be okay.

"We should stop here," Gorrin said, his tone tense as if trying to get us back on track. "This is the first time we've seen somewhere that we might actually get a good rest. We should take advantage of it." He didn't wait to see if anyone else agreed, instead striding forward as if entirely unworried.

Tyrus and Yazmor followed, equally unfazed.

"They just don't get it." Hale shook his head as though unsurprised by their upcoming deaths.

"It's because they're all too fucking old. When they were alive, they didn't even have television. Fuck, they didn't have electricity. None of them know the horror movie rules." I let out an overly dramatic sigh and shook my head. "They know not what they do."

"Should we let them deal with whatever's in there alone? We could just test out that whole no-sex rule on our own?"

"You know we can't do that. Deny it all you want, but you don't want them to die either."

He sighed and held his hand out to me, waiting until I took it and laced our fingers together. "You're too fucking soft-heated."

"Probably. Still, let's go stay in the creepy murder house."

And fuck did I hope those were *not* my last words.

* * * *

"Who would have thought a weird house in the spooky woods could be this nice inside." I had my legs stretched out as I sat in front of the fireplace, the flames roaring inside.

We'd had campfires many times, but they'd never managed to warm me up quite like this. It had to be because this focused all that heat in one direction, and it seemed as if this finally thawed some parts of me that had felt frozen this whole time.

"Worth getting murdered for?" Tyrus asked from his place in one of the chairs of the large living room. The place had furniture on the main floor, but on the second, the rooms were all empty. I'd been looking forward to the idea of sleeping on a mattress again, but it seemed that wouldn't happen.

"Depends on the type of murder. Worth it for one bullet to the head? Yep! Worth it for getting flayed alive? Ohhh, that's a harder one to decide on."

"I'm sure," Gorrin said, his tone flat. "Besides, how would you remain warm if you were flayed alive?"

Instead of calling him on his sarcasm, I just went with it. "Exactly my point. A little warmth now for no skin later? Not sure that's a good deal, and we're all about understanding a good deal, after all."

The front door opened, drawing my gaze over to where Yazmor stood in the doorway, heading out. "Yazmor?" I called out to him.

He paused, then turned his head slightly but didn't face me. "Yes?"

"Where are you going?"

"Out." He said nothing else, so I jumped to my feet to follow him.

Tyrus and Gorrin remained in place.

The moment I stepped outside, it felt as if all that warmth I'd found leached from my body. I wrapped my arms around myself to fight off the chill.

Yazmor stopped and turned back toward me, his expression unnaturally flat. "You should go back inside."

"So should you."

He shook his head, the action causing his hair to shift, a few strands catching the breeze. How could his face appear so young but his expression seem so ancient? It was a strange juxtaposition that I couldn't seem to square. "I can't settle inside. I don't belong there."

"Why not?"

He pulled his gaze from mine and looked out at the forest beyond the fence. "My world didn't have much technology. We were far more closely related to our natural surroundings. We slept where we wanted, strong enough to easily withstand the elements. We were the apex predators, so nothing bothered us. Sometimes, when I'm inside, it feels wrong."

"But it's cold out here."

"Not to me—but you are more fragile. You should go back to the heat." He paused, then let out a long breath. "Back to *them*."

"Why are you acting like this?"

"Because it is clearer and clearer to me that I am not good for you. The longer I spend here, the more I lose my grip on my mask, the surer I am that I will only hurt you in the end. They are from your world—they make more sense for you." He took a step backward, then turned and grasped the latch of the gate.

But I was tired of this tiptoeing thing we were doing. I was sick of him pulling further and further away. If I didn't do something, he'd end up out of reach.

So despite the way he took long, sure steps, seeming to pay me no attention, I chased after him. I grabbed his arm and yanked him to a stop, just outside the fence line.

Yazmor sighed but didn't turn toward me, didn't look at me. "Why are you so unreasonable?"

"I thought you liked that about me."

"I thought I did, too. You are chaos incarnate, something I can never predict or truly understand. You make things interesting that have been dull for a very long time."

"So why are you ignoring me now?"

"I am *never* ignoring you. My life would be far easier if I could."

"You running away isn't ignoring me? What is it, then?"

He turned on me then, his eyes seeming to glow in the dim light outside. "I am always watching you."

My breath caught in my chest at the intensity of his gaze as his words sank in. I thought about what he'd done to Clint, about how he had saved me with Wayne, the pharmacist, even when it hadn't seemed he'd been paying attention. There was truth to his words, that he'd always been right there to jump in, to pull me from the fire, even at times when he seemed so far away.

He seemed to realize I understood, because he cupped my cheek in his large, warm palm. "I will always watch you, but that doesn't mean I need to be close to you. Perhaps my purpose is a yard dog — something to guard his masters but not fit to live in the house."

The amount of self-hatred in his voice broke my heart. I turned my face to press my lips to his palm, wishing I could make him understand.

He pulled his hand away, a pained expression on his youthful features. "You are too foolish for your own good. No matter how much I warn you, you don't understand the danger."

"So you're just going to avoid me? You think I'll allow that?"

"I think that no matter how stubborn you are, you will eventually see reason, and I can outlast your foolish romantic notions. Besides, I don't think I can hold this form much longer. It's taking everything I have to do it, so I'm sure *everyone* will feel better if I stay a little farther away." When he pulled away again, taking a few steps backward, I found myself frozen.

I knew when to push and when to hold, and this was a time to hold. Yazmor wouldn't hear a damn thing I said right now anyway, so I might as well let him go.

He wandered into the fog until I lost sight of his silhouette, until the swirling gray out there ate every bit of him.

Still, I stood in the cold, watching where he'd gone, all that warmth I'd felt before disappearing until I shivered.

What else could I do?

I hated this feeling, the helplessness, the doubt. It ate at me, magnified by the Path, until I ran my fingers through my hair in a rough motion that probably pulled a few strands.

I hated the idea of not being able to help, but I had to believe that I could do something later, that with time we'd figure it out.

None of that helped the aching in my chest at his absence, at the gnawing feeling that the Path was stealing everything I cared about.

When I'd gotten here, I'd thought the risk would be my life, the lives of those around me. I hadn't realized that the true danger wasn't that we'd get ourselves killed.

It was that the Path would manage to strip away everything that made my life worth living.

Chapter Eighteen

Tyrus

I woke almost unbearably warm. My sleep-addled mind wondered if I'd fallen asleep too close to the fireplace.

Two rooms sat upstairs in the strange, empty house, and Gorrin and I had picked one while Loch got the other. Each room had its own fireplace, in addition to one in the living room, and we had started each to heat the entire house. There was no power, but because the Path was dim rather than dark, it didn't matter so long as we kept the windows open.

I would have rather slept beside Loch. However, she deserved a good night's sleep.

She wouldn't get that if any of us stayed in the same room as her.

Still, this warmth...

Something soft and teasing pressed to my throat, the sensation familiar. Still, it took me longer than it should have to rouse fully, to open my eyes.

And when I finally did, I found far more than I expected.

Loch straddled me, her body naked and bathed in the glow from the fire. She looked like some demon who would drag men's souls to hell. Worse? I was pretty sure that if she wanted it, I'd sell my soul all over again just to touch her.

She lifted her gaze from where her lips had lavished gentle attention to my throat until they locked on mine, and I hadn't realized just how much of a turn on eye contact could be.

There was something lovely about having her full attention while she had her lips on me. It made me want to see her down on her knees, her lips stretched around my thick cock, her eyes locked on mine as if nothing else in the world existed.

I'd known I could be possessive, but the depths of that desire surprised even me.

I groaned at the thought before I could stop myself, before I could scold my libido for running wild.

Loch is still nervous. Don't behave like an animal.

Plus, a glance to the side showed Gorrin across the room, sleeping on the floor on his back. He didn't normally sleep in the Chasm, but it seemed the Path wore even him down.

"What are you doing here, Little Demon?" I asked.

She scooted up my body, her lips teasing my jawline until she whispered into my ear. "I was lonely."

"Were you now?" I lifted my eyebrow, calling her out on her little lie. "Lonely people don't normally get naked and molest sleeping people."

She rocked her hips, but because of her shorter height, she wasn't quite lined up to rub against where I *really* wanted her. Still, it seemed the hard planes of my abs were enough for her, because she shuddered hard and repeated the motion. Because she wore nothing, I felt her heat and wetness against me. It made me grateful I'd gone to sleep naked.

I reached out and slid my hand into her hair, forcing her away from me enough to capture her gaze again. "Are you sure?"

Loch stared back at me, as it felt as if her little game broke apart. That was fine with me, because one of the things I adored most about this woman was how unfailingly honest she was. She lied, sure, but *this* part of her had never managed to hide a thing from me. Her passions and her fears and her desires had always been clear to me. I didn't want her playing a part, behaving in a way she thought she should.

If she wanted me, I doubted I'd ever turn her away, but I needed it to be *real*.

"I feel like I'm losing everything," she admitted, her voice shaky and unsure. "Everyone is suspicious of everyone else. All the things that matter to me are slipping further and further away. Hubis fucked up my head, and now the Path is doing the same, and I just feel…" Her voice trailed off, as if she didn't know exactly how to finish the thought.

She didn't need to finish it, though. I understood because I felt *exactly* the same way. The Path made me feel as though I were losing my grip on everything, on the things I'd thought so solid before.

So instead of arguing with her, I pulled her closer and took her lips in a deep kiss, then whispered over the crackling of the fire. "Okay, but I expect that you will tell me if you want to stop. If you change your mind, or if you want me to slow down, I swear to you that I will."

And that promise *mattered* to me. I lied all the time to get what I wanted, having little care about the truth when it came to my goals. This one meant more to me than any other, though. It didn't matter how far I went, how desperate I was for her, if she wanted me to stop, I would.

Loch took her bottom lip between her teeth, the fire reflecting off the whiteness, before she nodded in agreement.

Which was all I needed to hear.

Still, I held myself back from fully giving in. A part of me still worried that it would end up too much for her, that she'd panic and hate me.

And here, in the Path, where I was so unsettled, I didn't trust myself, either. I still recalled when I'd taken her that first time, when I'd lost myself to my demon side. I'd used my wings as a balance while I'd thrust into her, rough and mindless.

My demon side made me uneasy, made me struggle to accept it. I *hated* that part of myself, the lack of control, and shifting into it always felt as if I'd failed.

I ran my life on control, on managing not only everything around me, but myself as well. When I sprang those wings, when my teeth sharpened and my claws grew larger, it didn't feel like me at all.

It was a bitter reminder that I couldn't even control my own body.

So no matter how badly I wanted Loch, how much I wanted to let go of my own tightly held sense of self and give myself to the pleasure, I couldn't. I held it back and leaned up enough to kiss her, my lips playing gently across her lips.

I ran my hand up her side, starting at her knee, which was pressed into the blankets by my hip. I worked up her outer thigh, then over the flare of her hips, the curve where her waist pulled in, her ribs. All of it excited me, and each place I touched felt like the first time.

I'd seen her naked, I'd tasted all of her, but somehow it still felt fresh and new. The mole at the small of her back, the scar at her stomach from the gunshot wound that had killed her, all of it drew me in. I wanted to know more, to discover places on her that she didn't even know she wanted touched.

Eternity had seemed so long before, as if it stretched on forever, as if there would be no way to fill it, at least until I met Loch.

That had changed, now. I doubted an eternity would be enough for me with her, would give me enough time with her.

But I would never utter such a pathetic thing, so instead, I nipped her full bottom lip, drawing a soft whine from her. The sound was better to me than the most famous symphonies. I wanted to record it and put it on repeat, to lose myself in it. Loch normally held tight to everything, fighting everything, but she gave into me. She surrendered herself to her own needs and, more importantly, to me.

I slid my hand between us, swiping my thumb across her erect nipple. She shuddered above me, showing how on edge she was already.

You really do need this, don't you?

And she'd come to me for it. She could have gone to Hale, who was downstairs on the first watch shift, but instead, she'd come here. It made me want to puff out my chest, as if I'd won something.

When she broke the kiss and slid down just a bit, enough to rub her bare cunt against my erection, I was certain I'd won.

"Waking others is rude." Gorrin's sleepy voice drew my attention to where he'd rolled out his blanket across the room, and when I looked that way, glowing golden eyes met mine.

Loch also froze, the action so sudden I nearly laughed.

Or rather, I would have if my cock didn't ache quite so much, if I didn't crave her movement so badly.

Gorrin sat up, his weight rested on one of his hands as he stared at us. I certainly hadn't ever thought I'd end up naked in the same room as that man — *that angel, I suppose*. It was strange at times when life slapped me in the face with truths I had never seen coming.

Despite all my scheming, despite all the work I did to manipulate things, to get what I wanted, to foresee what others would do, Loch managed to throw that all into disarray.

"Should I leave?" Gorrin asked, an edge to his voice that showed the question was *far* from rhetorical.

Loch pressed a hand to my chest, using it to sit up and look over at him, the room lit by the dancing light cast from the flames. Again, she struck me as almost magical, as ethereal in the best and darkest of ways.

And I had never thought the sensation of someone pinning me down would be enjoyable, yet here I was, my cock hardening further when I felt like a sacrifice to her lust.

She looked down at me, the question in her pretty eyes obvious.

She wanted us both, just as she had before with Hale, but she couldn't just invite Gorrin without my permission.

Hale was one thing—we already had a love-hate relationship that swayed heavy on the hate side—but Gorrin was different. We weren't all trapped together, and I didn't know Gorrin as well. It required more trust from me.

I pulled my gaze from hers to look back over at Gorrin, weighing the options. I could say no, could tell them I wasn't comfortable with that. I knew both well enough to guess the result.

Gorrin would leave the room, head downstairs to give us privacy. I could enjoy Loch to my heart's content, letting her sweet sounds spill from this room as I had her all to myself.

But...the idea of that made me uneasy for a reason I couldn't pinpoint. My brain screamed that letting a man like Gorrin close to me at such a crucial point was foolish.

I'd tasted betrayal before, so could I make myself that vulnerable near a man like Gorrin?

I swallowed hard at the fear but pulled in a deep breath and reminded myself that I wouldn't allow the Path to win.

"You can stay," I forced myself to utter, surprised that the words didn't feel like as much of a lie as I suspected.

Maybe I was more okay with this than I thought? In fact, the way my cock twitched, as if it cheered me on, said at least that part of me wanted to keep going down that line of thought.

Gorrin nodded and rose to his feet, the action masculine and almost hypnotic. In this setting, drugged by the atmosphere and Loch's need and the light, I could admit that Gorrin was handsome.

I'd slept with men enough times — once people died and came back, things like gender stopped mattering so much. It had been quite a while, but even I could appreciate Gorrin's looks. He was strong, his body cut and beyond impressive. He moved with such certainty, as if he doubted none of this, as it didn't strike him as strange at all. The fact that he'd also worn nothing to bed meant *none* of us had to go through the hassle of disrobing.

He crossed the short distance to us, then dropped to his knees beside us. He caught Loch's chin and turned her face, kissing her with a passion I would have *never* expected from him.

In fact, it felt like seeing a part of him I wasn't meant to, something private and personal and precious and not intended for me. He was aggressive with his kiss, slipping his tongue past her lips, but he didn't touch her as if she were just a toy. Instead, he curled his hand tightly, holding her, and the whole thing made my chest tighten.

He broke the kiss and turned that gaze to me.

I was used to feeling in charge, yet I felt oddly prey like beneath that gaze. Was this how Hale had felt the last time, when Loch had ordered him about?

And why did I...enjoy it?

I couldn't even say for sure that enjoy was the correct word. It was deeper than that, more consuming.

And worse? Gorrin ran his thumb across my bottom lip, then paused and slipped it into the heat of my mouth, the action blanking any worries that had run through my head before.

I latched my lips around him and sucked, closing my eyes, tired of thinking rather than feeling, worrying rather than experiencing.

If the Path was going to end us all anyway, if things were truly as hopeless as they felt, I would give myself over to this. I deserved at least that much, didn't I?

And even if I didn't, I wouldn't throw it away.

Loch

Fuck everything else.

Or at least everything in this house…

The sensation of Gorrin's lips against mine while I rocked my hips, rubbing my clit against Tyrus' hard cock, made me wonder if we hadn't made it to Heaven already. Maybe we'd managed to cross over to the Plains and I just hadn't realized it?

They lit up my entire body, made me gasp and shudder. How was it that they could make everything that had weighed on me disappear the moment they put their hands on me?

That distance and loneliness I'd felt before couldn't stand against *this*. It was as if whatever existed between us was so much more powerful than the Path, than the magic Hubis used to twist us all.

And I felt it in the touches of Gorrin and Tyrus.

Tyrus, who feared being betrayed, who feared getting close to others without a plan to outwit them, laid beneath me, sucking on Gorrin's thumb. He did nothing to defend himself, to protect himself, instead choosing to trust us both.

Gorrin, who had clung to me, who had worried for me, kissed me with such recklessness it showed he acted rather than thought, that he gave himself over to the feelings without questioning them.

And he allowed this with Tyrus.

Not that I was a fan of the word *allowed*, since he had fuckall say over where I put my pussy, but him joining in showed he refused to allow his own clinginess, his fear of losing me to control him.

Maybe this was how we needed to get out of the Path.

Not sex, although I wouldn't have minded that route, all things considered. Rather, our connection to one another.

I'd escaped the shadow because I had them. I'd found the way out and away from those doppelgangers because I'd rushed *toward* my men. Time and time again, our connection to one another had saved me, had gotten us further than we'd ever have made it alone.

So I melted into the moment with these two men, men who had frightened me at first, who had seemed bigger than life, like stars in the dark sky I knew I could never reach. Never would I have thought I'd have them like this, that I could feel so comfortable with them, as if I'd never not had them with me.

Gorrin broke the kiss, slid his fingers from Tyrus' mouth and shifted behind me, the warmth of his chest pressing against my back. He slid his hand around me, his fingers leaving trails of heat in their wake.

He grasped my waist with one hand, while his other cupped my breast. With his grip, he helped me rock my hips, sliding me forward and back again, grinding Tyrus' cock against me.

I tipped my head back, resting it against Gorrin's shoulder. He closed his fingers on my nipple, the sharp pain surprising me enough to snap my eyes open.

"You don't want to miss a moment of this, do you?" Gorrin whispered into my ear.

I looked down, realizing what he meant.

Tyrus looked *amazing* beneath me. He rolled his hips up, as if he couldn't stand to remain still a moment longer, as if he were starving for the contact. His dark eyes reflected the light from the fire, and they were locked on me. The muscles of his abs shifted, tense from his efforts to submit, to let me do as I pleased, and for a moment, I almost laughed.

I thought about all the civilizations through time that had made sacrifices to gods and devils and demons. I'd never understood it before, but I had to admit... Tyrus would make for a fine sacrifice.

I was pretty sure I'd be willing to make a few deals and offer a few favors in exchange for *this*.

Tyrus paused, looking up at me. "I don't know if I care for that smile."

I didn't bother to hide anything—what was the point?—so I leaned in closer, Gorrin's hand slipping from my breast as I did so. Even still, Gorrin kept me rocking against Tyrus, so that fire inside me never died down.

I licked across Tyrus' bottom lip. "I was just thinking that you'd make a wonderful sacrifice to me. You know, like in the old days where they'd offer up virgins to appease the gods."

Tyrus snorted softly, though the sound broke off when Gorrin pressed me forward far enough that I lost contact with Tyrus' cock. Still, Tyrus spoke, his voice strained. "Sorry to disappoint, but I'm not a virgin."

"Well, no one's perfect." I kissed Tyrus more fully since I was closer, and something about kissing him like *this*, something about feeling in control above him turned me on in a way I hadn't expected. Hale had done as I'd wanted, but he'd never fully given himself up. He'd licked me because he'd wanted to as well, turned on by my aggressiveness.

Tyrus gave in fully, surrendering himself to me.

He grasped the nape of my neck, holding me to him as if afraid I'd get away. He deepened the kiss, and I parted my lips for him, giving him access to anything he wanted.

A quick, sharp pain in my tongue made me try to yank back, but Tyrus held fast. Copper filled my mouth, the familiar taste of blood. Tyrus didn't stop his kiss, though, and it let me figure it out.

His teeth had sharpened, a sure sign he was losing his battle with his demon form. It reminded me of when we'd slept together that first time, when he'd refused to let me see him like that, when he'd kept my gaze forward.

With him pinned beneath me, he couldn't hide anymore, so I flattened my hand against his chest and yanked back. I probably wouldn't have even considered forcing the matter at any other time, but something about being above him, about having him beneath me, made me want to see every part of him, *especially* the ones he wanted to hide.

And seeing him was worth it.

He was beautiful in such a dark and twisted way,

Where my demon form looked mostly human—just with wings, fangs and claws—Tyrus was a far different matter.

He appeared snake-like. His eyes were narrowed, and while they remained dark, the pupil was now slitted.

He had a beautiful, lethal quality to him, his skin having grown a sheen. I stroked my fingers over his chest, noting the change in texture. It was darker, and it seemed like his skin had changed into something that resembled incandescent scales. He twisted slightly, arching his back, because those leathery wings had appeared. Thankfully, they seemed to rest flat beneath him comfortably.

His face resembled his normal one enough that I'd recognize him in this form easily, but the details were different. His eyes had changed, but only his canine teeth had shifted. The rest were still flat, but now he had two long fangs, furthering his resemblance to a snake.

He stared at me, silent, as if waiting to see how I'd react. Would I turn and run? Would I cast him away?

I nearly laughed at the stupidity of that worry. If anything, this side of him excited me even more. It seemed so fitting to the man I knew.

Tyrus wasn't someone cuddly and cute. Even though he could be kind, he could treat me carefully, I wasn't stupid enough to think he wasn't every bit the cunning snake. I could think of no more fitting creature than this for him.

Still, I knew I couldn't convince him of that with words alone, so I leaned forward and ran my tongue along his left fang, teasing it to convince him that it didn't bother me. I expected him to enjoy it, but I sure didn't expect it to affect me like it did.

My pussy tightened as if to remind me that it was *still* waiting for some action.

Tyrus released a sound so similar to a growl, a sign that he enjoyed the touch as much as I did. The next sound he made was almost a hiss, though, and I didn't have time to wonder what that was caused by before Gorrin pressed a hand to my back, pushing so my back arched, my hips raising a little.

Something blunt and warm and hard teased my cunt, and it didn't take much to figure out what it was. Some things were just instinctual, and it seemed the sensation of a cock against me was one of them. I tried to shift back, to sink it into me, but Gorrin held me in place.

"Do you want him?" Gorrin asked, his voice almost loud in the silent room. He wasn't next to my ear, didn't whisper filth only to me, and it made his words come across as so much more vulgar than they were.

"*Yes*," I whined, the sound able to break through all the desire raging inside me enough to embarrass me.

Gorrin laughed softly, an odd noise from him, but he pulled back on my hips to force Tyrus' hard cock into me.

It hadn't been that long, all things considered, since I'd last had sex. Still, I whimpered at the way he stretched me. Something bumped into me, and when I twisted to figure out what it was—I didn't know much about Tyrus' demon form, so if he has a second cock or something, I felt like I should have gotten a warning about it—only to find Gorrin's hand wrapped around the base of Tyrus' shaft, guiding him into me.

My cheeks heated as the truth hit me, that reason for the noise Tyrus had let out earlier. Gorrin had been stroking Tyrus.

And fuck, I wished I'd gotten to actually watch that. That felt like a masterpiece, like a work of art I would have loved to sit back and study for a while. What a waste to miss out on it…

Yet, when Gorrin released Tyrus to pull me back in a hard yank, one that plunged the rest of Tyrus' cock deep into me, I found I couldn't regret anything too much.

I didn't need Gorrin's help before my hips began to move, sliding forward then back again, dragging the head of Tyrus' dick against every sensitive spot inside me. It was strange, having him beneath me, submitting to me, allowing me to take my pleasure from him.

It was even stranger given his current form, because by looks alone, he appeared as a monster, as something impossible to hold down. Yet he let me keep my hands on his chest, pinning him to the floor, as I fucked myself on his thick shaft. He didn't fight it, didn't try to take control back, just gave me whatever I wanted.

Gorrin ran his hand up my back, following the curve of my spine until he reached the nape of my neck. He used it to pull me upright, the change in position allowing Tyrus' cock to stroke somewhere different inside me.

"You look lovely like this, so lost to pleasure, so hungry. One of the amazing things about humans is how easily they devolve to instinct, how quickly they shed their civility to reveal the pleasure-seeking animal they are beneath it all. How do you feel, little fish, between us like this? Do you like this?"

Since my brain hardly worked, I was damn thankful Gorrin asked easy questions.

"Yes," I admitted.

"Good." Gorrin nipped at my shoulder, his teeth scraping over my skin, making me wish he'd bite harder. "You're the sort of woman who would never be satisfied by a substandard showing, but you're also the only one I would care enough to ensure you had all you could take."

He slid one of his hands down my front, trailing his fingers in the valley between my breasts, over the softness of my stomach, then traced to the side. He passed over my hip, over the side of my ass, then reached down to run his fingers over my cunt, along where Tyrus' cock spread me open. "You are drenched. I would love to take you at the same time as Tyrus, to fill you so much more."

"Yes." As soon as that word left my lips, I realized it was all I'd said lately. So much for playing hard to get.

Gorrin let out a long sigh, the breath warm against my neck. "Do not tempt me too much, because my self-control can only be pressed so far before it snaps. While I would love to sink into you, we lack the proper tools or time to prepare you."

I almost asked what he meant, but when he moved his fingers—now drenched with my own wetness—from my cunt and up to my ass, I caught up fast.

He didn't keep moving from there, though. I was used to that area being more of a passing place, the kind of spot where a partner got turned around before realizing they weren't where they'd meant to be.

Gorrin made it clear he knew *exactly* where he was when he rubbed gently at the tightness there, pressing without breaching.

Which meant he was saying he wanted to...

I froze at the thought, some of the lust inside me cooling.

"If you seriously think you're putting *that* anywhere near my ass, you don't need to worry about the Path driving you crazy—clearly you're nuts already."

Gorrin snorted before scraping his teeth over my shoulder. "Are you sure? The way you're twitching, the way you're bringing your hips back is pressing my finger harder against you. I think you are more interested than you want to admit. Just imagine it, hmm?" He brought his other hand up, sliding two of his thick fingers into my mouth, and despite the embarrassment of it, I greedily took them in just as Tyrus had before.

Gorrin wielded his words like yet another body part he could use to turn me on. "Imagine having someone here." He jerked me down roughly, forcing Tyrus' cock deeper into me. "Someone here." He pressed those fingers deeper into my mouth, mimicking thrusting to drive home his point. "And someone here." With that, he sank the thick tip of one finger into my ass. He didn't go deep, just barely breaching the tight ring of muscles there, but it sure as hell made his point.

Between the touches and his words, my mind supplied all the filthy details itself.

I pictured *exactly* what he'd implied. I swirled my tongue around Gorrin's fingers, imagining they were thicker, that it was Hale's cock, that I could tease the piercings that lined the bottom of his shaft. It wasn't the same, but I could pretend with the best of them.

At the same time, I imagined that the finger Gorrin teased my ass with was his cock. That was a *lot* harder to pretend, given that a not-so-insignificant part of my brain couldn't do the mathematical gymnastics needed to work out just how he could fit there, or better put, how I could actually enjoy it.

Still, the feeling of his finger wasn't unpleasant. Areas of my body that had never really been paid attention to lit up, responding to his touch with something that broached pleasure. It was like experiencing *just* how good oral felt the first time, when a whole damn new world opened around me.

"Not so opposed to it as you thought, are you?"

Instead of answering—I didn't want to give him that satisfaction—I nipped at the fingers he'd pressed into my mouth.

And if *anyone* could deal with my difficult, defiant side, it was Gorrin. He didn't so much as flinch, instead pressing the pads of his fingers against the top of my tongue, pinning it down, then rubbing over the top. "If that was your attempt at annoying me, you've made a mistake. In case you have forgotten, I rather enjoy your more defiant side. Or, perhaps it would be better to say I don't mind it because bringing you to heel excites me. I like when I have to work for your submission, when I have to earn every inch of it. Things that come too easily bore me, but you never have. So if you want to bite, if you want to scratch, if you want to struggle, I welcome it. You are *more* than worth the effort."

Something about that statement did what little else could.

So often in my life, that part of me, the one that wanted to do as I pleased, that saw the world as I wanted to, it had gotten me into trouble.

I'd spent my life knowing how much my personality grated on others. I'd accepted it for the most part, recognized that I'd annoy people and figured the best I could expect was to find people who were at least amused enough by me to ignore my less-desirable traits.

I hadn't thought it possible for people to actually *like* that part of me. I hadn't expected to find others who not only accepted me, but who couldn't get scared off by that.

Gorrin didn't just know about my stubborn streak, wasn't just willing to deal with it—he *liked* it. Even better, he didn't expect me to change it. He wasn't just hanging in there until he trained it out of me, or because he thought he could get me to behave as he'd wanted eventually.

It was a far cry from how he'd treated me at first. I pulled back, his finger sliding from my mouth, so I could speak. "You sure wanted to change me before..."

He nipped my ear, closed his teeth on the lobe then tugged gently. "That was before. Back then, I'd thought keeping you safe was the most important thing. I thought I could make you understand the world as I did, that if you just complied, you would see the wisdom of my words. I am a man who focuses on results—not methods. I had always thought that the only thing that truly mattered in the world was survival."

"But not anymore?"

"No, not anymore." He ran his finger along my lip as if to remind me of what we were doing, as though he thought I might forget or that the lust inside me might cool. "You made me realize that living isn't enough. Ensuring you continue to breathe matters, but it can't be the ultimate goal. If my actions break you—if they shatter the person you are—what is the point of any of it?" He dragged his tongue up the shell of my ear, his warm breath making me shiver. "*You* matter, just as you are, so if you want to struggle against me, I respect that. I will stand toe-to-toe with you, but I will never try to control or change you again."

His words were soft and honest, and they convinced me more than anything else he could have done would have. Gorrin had tried so many things over the years to bring me to heel. He'd threatened me, he'd coerced me, he'd used anything he could against me to try to make me fall in line.

It had all failed, in the end.

So why did I submit to him now? Why did I give myself over to whatever he wanted?

Because he gave me the *choice*. He acknowledged me, my feelings, my personality, and that made it so I could trust him.

When I relaxed and leaned back, it was me accepting him, my way of showing how much his words meant to me.

And Gorrin accepted that weight with ease, reminding me that no matter what, I could trust him. He was more than strong enough to carry anything I needed him to.

And he seemed more than ready to prove it.

Gorrin

Feeling Loch fully give herself over to me loosened a tightness in my chest that had worsened with my time in the Path. Sure, she and I had had sex just after my return, but that had been more about passion and anger than anything else.

Then Hubis' *'lesson'* had further complicated matters. She had seemed perpetually out of reach, and as the Path had twisted my thoughts, had made me even more worried, I'd stewed in my own head.

Would she ever accept me? Would I ever manage to cross the distance between us? Would she ever really trust me?

Those fears had taken over, growing from a shadow in my mind until they eclipsed everything else, until I couldn't draw breath properly when I wasn't touching her.

Yet all it took was *this* – her leaning against me, her surrendering herself into my care – to wipe those fears away.

Sure, they would come back – I was far too practical to think that having sex would fix all my problems – but for now, I could release it to focus on this moment.

I withdrew my finger from Loch's ass, unable to hide a groan as I imagined sinking my cock into her. Her reaction suggested she'd never tried anal – or perhaps it was better to say she'd never tried it with any sort of satisfaction – and the thought of being her first excited me far more than it should have. I wanted her to trust me, to give me a part of herself that she'd given to no one else.

It was selfish and stupid, but knowing that didn't stop me from wanting it.

Still, I'd been serious that now was not the time. The wetness I'd gathered from her dripping pussy had worked well enough to aid a single finger, but it wouldn't be nearly enough for her to take my cock. I wouldn't dare risk hurting her, not for something as trivial as me getting off.

Of course, I didn't *need* that either.

The sight of Tyrus stretched out beneath Loch was something I would have never imagined to be as enticing as it was. Tyrus had pissed me off enough times, had proven himself a more than capable adversary time and time again.

I *never* would have thought we would end up like this. The warmth of his leg pressed against the inside of my knee, since I straddled his legs behind Loch.

His body was impressive, especially given I had never truly seen it before. He always wore his suits, always looked presentable and untouchable. I never would have thought to see him so undone, so unguarded.

He breathed heavily, his muscles twitching, his wings shifting as if it took everything he had to remain still.

And wasn't that a testament to his self-control? That he could offer himself up to Loch, that he could let her use him as she pleased?

Could I ever do that?

I wanted to say yes, to claim there was nothing Tyrus was capable of that I could not do just as well if not better, but I doubted it. I didn't think my patience ran so deep that I wouldn't grab her, lift my hips, and take her just as hard as I wanted when driven to the mindless place Tyrus was.

As proof of my own shortcomings there, I had reached my limit when it came to waiting.

I grasped Loch's hips and pulled her back, smiling at the way Tyrus and her made nearly identical sounds of disappointment.

Not that it was going to dissuade me in the least.

"Since having your ass tonight is not possible, I wish to fill you in another way," I whispered as I pulled her into my lap, though I still rested on my knees. It only took a moment of shifting her before I forced my shaft into her waiting cunt, before her tight warmth enveloped every inch of me.

And I didn't hide my groan at the feeling, wanting her to know *exactly* how much I enjoyed it.

I peered over her shoulder, down at Tyrus whose eyes reflected the dancing flames, who looked ready to pounce and fight over her.

"I wouldn't mind a few rounds with you," I said, "but I don't think that is needed." I reached up and hooked two fingers past her lips again, using the grasp to open her mouth like a peace offering. "I believe you'll find this more than satisfactory, won't you?"

Tyrus dropped his gaze from my eyes to Loch's mouth, and the way his body tensed said he was *more* than willing to accept that idea.

He rolled to the side and hopped to his feet in a motion so fluid as to be impressive. He wrapped his hand around his cock, stroking himself slowly as his gaze moved over Loch.

Then again, she was in my lap, filled by my cock. Would Tyrus take that well? There was, as always, a chance that foolish things such as jealousy could cause a problem that might ruin the moment.

Except, the dark of Tyrus' eyes filled with even more lust, as though he found the situation more arousing than he would have ever expected.

Though I understood that—there was something undeniably primal about watching this, as if we had cast aside all those rules society had taught us and embraced our animalistic sides instead.

I grasped Loch's hips, keeping her from moving too much, choosing to pull her only a short distance from me before yanking her back, trying to get deeper inside her.

Tyrus came closer, looming over both of us. At any other time, I would have found this position unacceptable. I knelt on the ground, and Tyrus basked us in his shadow, silhouetted in darkness from the fire behind him. It was a vulnerable place, and I would have never thought I'd willingly remain like this, that I could trust Tyrus.

Was it Loch? Did she distract me with her body? Had she created some bond between the other Lords and me? Did I simply trust Tyrus now?

I had no answer, so instead, I focused on the sensation of Loch's tight, hot cunt wrapped around my cock.

Tyrus came closer until he grasped Loch's chin, his touch surprisingly gentle. He used the grip to make her lean forward, then traced her lips with the head of his cock.

Loch parted her lips, but didn't struggle, didn't try to get more or less.

Well, other than darting her tongue out, that edge of mischievousness that she would never rid herself of. Even when Loch submitted, that troublesome side of her would likely never disappear.

The change between them as they switched positions was fascinating, the way Tyrus had gone from giving to taking, from beneath her to above. Perhaps they worked so well together because the two of them could trade back and forth, because they were equal in power and stubbornness.

"Do you feel better?" Tyrus asked, his voice deeper and rougher than usual.

Loch nodded, her eyes drugged by the moment.

The corner of one side of his mouth tipped up, the expression so subtle it would have been difficult for anyone who didn't know him well to see it. Somehow, seeing Tyrus sweet and caring was strange, something I never expected to witness, but it also fit him in a strange way.

"Open for me, Little Demon."

Loch did so without hesitation, and Tyrus immediately slid past her lips. There was a softness in his expression, such a dichotomy compared to the act between us.

I understood that, though. Did Loch not do the same for me? She seemed to allow everyone she met to expose a part of themselves that they'd always hidden away.

Loch placed a hand on Tyrus' hips for balance — which was fair given how I moved her, chasing my own pleasure. She didn't take Tyrus deep, instead seeming to focus on the head, teasing him, moving between pressing kisses over his length and wrapping her lips around him.

The sight made me worry I would not last much longer. She made for such a lovely, wanton sight between us. I wanted to see more of this.

I wanted to see her naked and spread out for *all* of us. I wanted to see her riding Tyrus with her hand around the front of his throat. I wanted to see her on her knees between two of us, trying to please us both. I craved seeing Hale between her thighs, licking her until she cried and begged for a rest.

In short? I wanted to see it *all*.

I grasped her free hand and brought it down between her thighs. "Let me see you come, Loch. I need to feel you tighten around me, to see you lose yourself to this moment entirely, to watch you drown in the pleasure."

Her hand started to move, despite the fact that I couldn't see it. Then again, Loch was the sort of woman who knew damn well how to please herself—yet another thing I adored about her.

She gasped, and when she opened her mouth wider, as if she couldn't breathe, Tyrus took the chance to sink deeper into her mouth. His wings surrounded us, making me feel almost small in comparison. It was a strange feeling, but not one I minded. I had never been so close to a demon in this way...

I reached out and brushed a hand over the edge of his wings, surprised to find the leather warm. The wing twitched beneath my touch, and Tyrus let out a startled sound, something between a yelp and groan.

Then again, given how uncomfortable he seemed with this form, it hardly surprised me that he wouldn't know exactly how *sensitive* wings were.

Angels didn't mind toying with them, but Tyrus had far too many hang-ups to have ever explored.

Which gave me an idea, one I would have written off years before as perhaps the most foolish thing I could ever do. Yet, in this moment, I couldn't stop myself.

I wrapped my free hand around his wing and tugged softly. I brought it away from the floor, the tip of it a sharpened claw, reminding me of a bat's wing.

Feathers made certain activities more difficult, but the leather and scales of demon wings had an advantage. I showed that benefit when it shifted the tip of that wing up and ran my tongue over the clawed end, then pressed my lips to the edge. I sucked at it, leaving rough kisses along that neglected space.

I didn't have to ask if he enjoyed it, because Tyrus answered by grasping Loch's chin, sinking deeper into her mouth, and shuddering hard. The movement of her throat said she swallowed.

And whether it was that sight, or the way Loch tensed around me with her own release, or what I did to Tyrus' wing, I didn't know and truly didn't care. Instead, I allowed my own release to tumble through me, taking the clawed tip of Tyrus' wing past my lips, to suck harder at that lethal, dangerous part of him.

The sensation of filling Loch with my seed felt as life changing as it had before. I couldn't have children, but that didn't stop some strange instinct inside of me from *needing* to spill inside of her, from wanting to claim her, to cover her in my scent.

In fact, it made me want to see her covered in our cum, to have her claimed so fully that no one would ever think to take her away.

If anyone tried to get between Loch and us, they would never get the chance to make another mistake for the rest of their very *short* lives. The four of us had done so many terrible things, but those would seem like nothing compared to what we would do if *anything* tried to take this woman from us.

Chapter Nineteen

Loch

"I miss the murder house."

"And to think you were *so* sure that it would end up killing you," Gorrin said.

"Yeah, well, I got to take a *bath.* As it turns out, my price isn't all that high." As soon as I said that, it took me back to just how easy I really was.

I recalled waking sandwiched between Gorrin and Tyrus, my body well rested but sore and covered in more than a few bite marks. Clearly it didn't take all that much to convince me of just about anything. Thank fuck I wasn't a teenager still or any smooth-talking boy would have gotten a turn.

"We couldn't just stay there forever," Tyrus reminded me.

"It had water — *hot water* — and warmth and even a swing out front! We could have lived a very happy little life there." My words even surprised myself as I spoke, especially because I couldn't seem to stop them. "Just think about it? No Hubis, no Chasm, no enemies."

"What about The Guardian?" Hale pointed out and gestured toward the fog, the familiar tentacle showing as if it had heard us call it.

"Guardian could be the pet. Who needs a pit bull when we've got him, huh? We could make meals, live a nice, quiet life, and worry about nothing." I let out a sigh as the thought consumed me, as I wrapped it around me and sank into the fantasy.

No running. No fighting. Nothing but time with the men I cared about. I didn't have to worry about something taking them from me, about us drifting apart. We could just *be* us.

That was something that existed nowhere else. Even if we dealt with Hubis, even if we won, this wasn't over. We would *never* be free from the obligations and worries of the world. If anything, we'd only entangle us further in the mess, only take on more responsibilities if we came out on top.

I glanced over my shoulder, in the direction we'd come from. I couldn't see the house anymore, but I still stared as if I could.

No one spoke, but what was there to say? I wanted the impossible.

So I sighed and turned my back on that fantasy. It was a nice dream I could revisit at night, but for now? I had to focus my attention ahead.

"A life like that is still possible," Tyrus said.

"I don't need you to lie to me. No matter how this all goes, we won't ever be free from our obligations. We won't ever be able to just walk away from it."

"Perhaps, perhaps not. One reason I have worked so hard in my position, why I can be so ruthless, is to create a measure of order and peace. If we all continue to work, if we overcome what is before us, we can shape our future in whatever way we want." He glanced around, looking toward Gorrin and Hale with a question in his gaze. "Even if it isn't the future we might have expected."

Which took me back to the night before, back to when Gorrin had touched Tyrus, to the lust in Tyrus' eyes. None of the men got along all that well, but I continued to see sparks of something more, a sign that they no longer simply orbited me, that they had some connection between them as well.

Why did that warm me? Why did I care?

I stared down at my feet as I took one step after another, my mind working.

I pictured this all going badly, thought about what might happen if I never made it back. If this ended me, if I were gone, what would that mean for them?

In my mind, I saw them as they'd been before— isolated and alone. No, worse than before. Being alone sucked, but it was made so much worse after a person knew what it felt like to *not* be alone, after they experienced feeling wanted and accepted.

The idea of them in that state hurt so much worse than it should have.

They deserved more. Sure, they were psycho killers with little if any conscience, but they still deserved happiness.

So the idea of them finding a bond together made me feel as if, should things go badly, should I fail, they could still be okay.

"Drink." Hale held out his water bottle, the metal of it cool as he pressed it into my palm. "You don't want to get dehydrated."

I should have rolled my eyes at him — again, since that was my go-to reaction when any of the Lords tried to mother me — but I couldn't deny he was right. I *was* thirsty. It was the sort of thing I often didn't notice. Usually, I just poured more coffee on top of a subtle unwell feeling.

The water was crisp and cool, something surprising in a place like this. I would have figured everything would taste mildly like dust, as it did in the Chasm, but thus far the water we'd found was always clean tasting.

Don't look a gift horse in the mouth.

After gulping a bit, I went to put the lid back on.

Before I could, something touched my leg. I glanced down, ready to glare at whatever I'd walked into. With the trees around, the dead branches scattered in the dirt and my inability to lift my feet high enough, I constantly tripped over things.

I looked at what touched me, but it took my brain a long moment to work it out. Before it could, the thing touching my leg wrapped around me and yanked.

The air rushed from my lungs when I hit the ground, and despite the startled shouts of the men, no one had time to react.

Guardian had me...

My back hurt, the dirt scraping against it as Guardian yanked me through the fog. I grabbed for branches and trees, but everything passed me too fast for me to catch.

Pain spread through my side as I bounced off the trunk of a tree, Guardian's tentacle never loosening its grip on my leg, wrapped around at least twice and squeezing so tightly that it reminded me of watching a boa constrictor eat a mouse once.

Of course, getting eaten was probably a *much* better option than the other things tentacles could do…

And who thought I'd ever have to pick between *those* two options?

If I wasn't getting dragged through the Path by Guardian, I might have reconsidered the choices I'd made that had led me here of all places. Now wasn't the time for major life reflections.

I tried to focus, to look ahead despite the fog and the way the world bounced around me. I aimed carefully, and when we neared another tree, I shifted my weight and planted my free foot against the trunk.

Pain blossomed in my hip, a sure sign the joint did *not* love the abrupt stop. Guardian lost its grip on my leg, and I took that chance for what it was. I reached blindly around me until my fingers wrapped around a branch on the ground.

Better than nothing.

I snapped it in half as I sat up, and when Guardian came back for another swing, I brought the stick down over that tentacle and buried the sharp edge into it.

Guardian released a frantic noise of pain before retreating into the fog.

I laid back for a moment, breathing hard, my back scratched raw and the leg Guardian had yanked on useless. I couldn't even move it.

After a moment, a rustling in the fog reminded me I couldn't stay here forever. I doubted Guardian was going to take this as an *L* for long. If I didn't get myself moving, I'd end up in the same position as before, and I doubted Guardian would fall for the same trick twice.

I grasped the tree that had saved me — I should name the thing in thanks — and used it to pull myself to my feet.

When I tried to put my foot down, it refused to hold weight. Had Guardian managed to dislocate it? If I caught that bastard, I was going to chop off one of its limbs as payback.

I wasn't in a position to follow through that as I was, so instead, I grabbed a thick, relatively straight branch from the ground and used it as a cane, limping in the opposite direction to where Guardian had gone.

We'd taken so many turns that I had no hope of making my way back to the men. I had no clue where they were.

Then again, they'd managed to locate me each time I'd ended up separated, so I had to just trust that they'd find me yet again. Fuck knew they were moving better than I was.

Which meant I just needed them to find me before Guardian decided to take another swipe.

I moved slowly — far too slowly for my liking — but what did the speed matter? Since I didn't know where I was going, it wasn't like I needed to get there faster.

Sweat ran down my back, despite the chill in the air, and I gritted my teeth against the pain. I forced myself to keep going, resting more and more weight on the stick.

Fuck, I missed that bath and that house and all of it. It was a far cry better than *this*. I wished I could go back to before this, to that moment of happiness and ease I'd found.

Instead, my vision wavered in and out, telling me that I was *really* fucking close to passing out. *That's not a good sign.*

I collapsed forward, unable to hold myself up anymore, the world spinning around me.

Something moved in the fog, twigs snapping beneath it.

"Well, at least if you do anything weird, I'll be unconscious," I muttered. "But just so you know, Guardian, I have a weird STI that only infects tentacles. If you touch me, I hope you're ready to have your bits get sores and fall off!"

The world grew even hazier around me, so much that I wasn't sure I even got all those words out. A shadow fell over me, and I glanced up, ready to see the Lords.

They always managed to find me right when I needed them, to swoop in at the perfect time, to do the impossible.

Except, when I looked up, as the world darkened around me, I realized those were *not* my men. Instead, strangers, people I didn't recognize, surrounded me.

Well fuck, I suddenly miss Guardian…

Yazmor

I moved through the trees so fast it felt like a blur. Avoiding them was easy, since I gave myself over to the instincts inside me, to the *thing* I had once been so long ago.

My body had taken my true form when I could no longer hold the human shape. In some strange way, it felt better than it had in so long, like one of those dogs who lives its life in a tiny crate, unable to stretch out. Now, it seemed as if someone had opened that door and I embraced what I really was.

I lacked the time to think about that much. Nothing but Loch's scream mattered, but the way she'd disappeared when Guardian had grabbed her.

That creature moved impossibly fast. It made me appear slow, and I was far from that.

Or, perhaps because it was from this place, connected to this place, it could twist the world around it to cover more distance than I could.

Following was easy enough, because I could feel Loch still. Beyond that, the marks on the ground showed where Guardian had dragged her, the disturbed soil, the snapped twigs, the blood where she must have scraped over sharp debris.

Each thing drove my temper higher, especially because the logical part of my brain didn't seem to want to work anymore. I inhaled, drawing in the scents around me, letting them sink into me, sorting through them.

An almost metallic scent that had to be Guardian, the copper tinge of blood and beneath that? A subtly sweet scent I recognized immediately as Loch. That smell was burned into my memory. When I found her, I would bury my face in her throat and inhale it until it soothed me again, until I was sure she was safe.

Why did I keep almost losing her?

Because I have kept her at a distance.

If I hadn't been sulking, if I hadn't remained on the outskirts so as to avoid showing her how I looked, admitting that I could no longer hold my human form, I would have been close enough to stop Guardian. I would have felt it drawing closer, would have predicted what would happen and could have rescued her before she was harmed.

Instead, I could only chase her, hoping to catch up in time.

Never again.

I hadn't waited to speak to the other Lords, had left them behind. They could trail us, I was sure, but I could move fastest on my own. Time was of the essence.

The Path shifted, Loch's location more difficult to pin down. Was that because I'd located her before? Was the Path trying to outsmart us? It had been so focused on Loch already, so was it trying to separate us? To ensure we couldn't find one another again?

As plans went, it was a good one.

However, the Path had never dealt with a creature like me—its little games wouldn't keep me from my prey.

Loch's scent strengthened as I chased it, and I came upon her so fast that I skidded to a stop.

She was on the ground, Guardian nowhere in sight. She didn't move, her clothing ripped, blood on her arms and having stained the back of her sweater. She had her hand closed around a large stick, and it took a moment to work out why.

Her leg…

Even without touching her, I could tell the problem. It hung limply, even when she shifted in her unconscious state. She had at least partially dislocated it. Had Guardian done that? Or was it an accident?

I crouched beside her, resting my hand on her chest, feeling the way she breathed.

In and out. Steady.

No signs of struggle, of collapsed or punctured lungs. Her heart beat regularly as well.

Which meant that the superficial wounds and her hip were the extent of the damage.

Why is she unconscious then?

I touched her leg, and she released a pained noise even when not awake. *Ah, it was likely due to pain…*

An uncomfortable tightness in my chest said I didn't like that.

Instead of focusing on that, I grasped her knee in one hand and pressed my other to the outside of her hip joint.

"I'm sorry, Loch," I whispered as if that mattered at all before jerking my hand, the pop both a relief and something I hated. The joint needed to be set again, but the idea of causing her pain, even if it was for her best, bothered me.

At least she didn't wake. I didn't want her to see me, to associate me with pain or fear. She shivered in her sleep, the cold of this place no doubt getting to her, especially with how her body had to heal the wounds she'd suffered.

A part of me didn't understand how I could touch her, how I thought myself deserving to be so close to her. I no longer had even the pretense of humanity on me, appearing every bit of the monster I truly was. Knowing I shouldn't didn't change that I struggled to release her.

I should set a fire to keep her warm. The heat would help her to heal faster. When I went to leave, to gather the items to set one, I found myself trapped.

A glance down showed Loch's eyes open, her hand wrapped tightly around my wrist.

I hated the sight of her skin against mine, of how different we appeared when she touched me. It showed off how incompatible we truly were…

She belonged nowhere near my true form.

"I need to start a fire," I told her. "In the Path, you won't heal as quickly as you would elsewhere. The cold here will only make that worse." I tugged at my hand, but she refused to let go. I could have yanked away, but

I couldn't bring myself to do so, to potentially harm her. "You need to let go."

Loch shook her head and tugged at my hand until I came closer. She pressed at my shoulder, making me sit, then crawled into my lap without hesitation. She rested her head against my chest and pulled at my arms until I wrapped them around her. "You're warmer than a fire."

I couldn't stop myself from laughing at the moment, at myself, at her. I shook my head and gave in, holding her and trying to ignore just how much I enjoyed it. My arms wrapped around her more, dwarfing her because of how much larger this form was. "You know, you remind me of that cat."

"What cat?"

"The one from Wayne's house."

She snorted softly and nuzzled her cheek against my chest. Her shivering had stopped. "You mean the one you chased instead of helping me?"

"I helped you when you needed it. Even if I don't seem like it, I'm always looking out for you. See, I had to chase that cat, and it was not a fan at first."

"I remember the scratches."

"Eventually, it crawled into my lap just like this, as if it decided I wasn't so bad."

"That happens a lot with you, doesn't it? Things don't like you, but they eventually come around."

I rubbed my hands over her arms, grateful to see the goosebumps disappearing. "Those things come around because they see only the mask I show them. I don't understand how you can do that, how you can be *here* with me like this when you know the truth."

Loch sighed and her breath blew across my chest. "You're too hard on yourself. I keep telling you, I don't care what you look like. I don't care where you came from or what form you have or any of it. Those things don't matter to me. I know everything I need to about you." She frowned and touched her leg. "Did you do something? My hip still hurts but I can move it now."

"I put it back into place."

"Well fuck, I'm glad I don't remember that." She relaxed in my arms in a way I never thought anyone would do, not with me in this form. It felt so much like when she'd cried, when I'd held her and she'd sank into me.

I'd thought that was gone forever, that I'd never experience that again.

Leave it to Loch to never do as I expected from her.

"Guardian is keeping his distance."

"Yeah, well, he's licking his wounds." She twisted her face to look up at me, the familiar smirk of a troublemaker on her lips. "I may have used a pointy stick and stabbed him in his goods. Well, I mean, I don't know if his tentacles are his goods, but still…"

"Both squid and octopus use a modified arm to impregnate females," I offered, the fact sliding from me without thought. As soon as I said it, though, I froze.

Loch didn't seem thrown by the odd trivia, though. Instead, she pushed at my chest so she could see my face clearly. "That's the first time in a while you've told me some weird fact I really never wanted to know."

I went to turn my face away at the reminder that I was strange.

She set a hand on my cheek to stop me, to make me look back at her. "I missed it. Please, feel free to tell me all the weird shit you want, because when you don't?" She stroked her thumb over my cheek, showing no signs that my real form bothered her, that the smooth, hard skin, the strange features threw her at all. "It makes me feel lonely."

Her words felt like a rope thrown down a deep hole, the first time anything she said really got through to me, got past the doubts in my head, the fears that had grown so much through the manipulation from the Path.

Before I could respond, she turned away and frowned.

"What is it?"

"Just before I passed out, I saw something."

"What?"

"People."

That put me on alert. I glanced around us, searching for signs of attack. "I don't sense anything. Are you sure you didn't imagine it? You were injured and lost consciousness. The mind tends to play tricks on us at those times."

"No, it wasn't a hallucination. I've had bad trips—I know what that feels like. I'm sure it was real. I thought it was Guardian at first, but just before I passed out, I saw them. Six people? Maybe seven? They all stood over me."

"Why would they leave you alone?"

She furrowed her brows, clearly searching her memory. "They turned their heads just before I passed out. I think they sensed something else coming. You? But you would have noticed them…"

"Not necessarily. I was focused entirely on tracking *you*. I could have missed anything else in the area." I extracted myself from her, peering around in the dirt.

I crouched and ran my hand over the ground to her left. *Footprints*. There was no mistaking this for anything else.

Judging from the marks she was right—at least seven individuals had stood here, and the depth of the prints, the way they pressed farther into the dirt at the toes, all said they had taken off at a run.

And it also meant I knew the direction they'd gone.

Loch let out a soft, pained noise, drawing my focus back to her. I grasped her arm and helped her up, letting her lean against me. Her hip may have been fixed, but it would still hurt until it healed completely.

Heavy steps came a moment before the other Lords broke through the line of trees, finally having caught up to us.

They must have sensed the mood, because they didn't carry on immediately. Instead, they flanked Loch and I, looking in the same way we did. The trails in the dirt would have been obvious even to an idiot— which meant even Hale saw them.

"Well, the murder house didn't end up so bad," Loch said. "So why don't we follow the creepy strangers in the fog?"

Gorrin sighed. "That idea would sound terrible from anyone, but somehow, when you say it, it sounds *even* worse."

"Then stay here," Loch said and limped forward, holding on to my arm to help her, forcing me to go as well. "I'm going to go say hello to the neighbors."

And again, Loch reminded me that no matter how fragile she seemed at times, nothing much kept her down.

If anyone could survive me, it would be this woman.

Chapter Twenty

Loch

"Are we ever *not* going to feel surprised by this place?"

"Probably not," Hale said as he pushed past me and toward the little village where the footprints had led.

It wasn't until we found this place that I truly believed I'd seen people at all. While I would have never admitted to my own doubts, they sure as fuck had run rounds in my head. Had I imagined it? Was it just a dream?

We had run into Koller, but other than her, we hadn't seen actual signs of other people in the Path.

Well, there was the murder house…

The more time I spent here, though, the less sure I was that anything could survive long.

Guardian had targeted us — or me, at least — and the traps showed how easy it was to fall here. We'd survived as a group, but the idea that others here might have grouped together?

I would have never believed it until this moment, when I stood at the end of a cozy looking little cul-de-sac with ten adorable houses sitting along it. They all had perfectly trimmed bushes and immaculate lawns, and even had mailboxes lining the street.

"What the suburban hell is this place?" Hale muttered.

I snickered at his look, and when he glared, I offered him a smirk. "You look more upset right now than when we were in that dive bar with the Sand Snakes."

"I'd *much* prefer to go back there. Case you are fucking *blind,* this ain't the sort of place where I fit in. Neighbors like this tended to call the cops the second they caught sight of me."

"Somehow, I doubt the cops are going to come all the way here." I lifted an eyebrow as I glanced at the houses. "Plus, given anyone here must have come from the Chasm, I don't think the sight of you is going to upset them *that* much."

Hale huffed and shook his head, but each step he took screamed of reluctance. He sure as fuck didn't want to be here, and I hardly could blame him.

If the murder house reminded me of a picture-perfect family home, this place was the setting of every old nostalgic painting that showed what good old America was like in the fifties.

And much like Hale, *I* had never lived at let alone been welcomed in a place like this. I'd grown up a city kid, trash through and through if I were being honest. Suburbs like this made my skin crawl as I waited for someone to come out and tell me that I'd better keep moving along because this wasn't an area for my sort of people.

So I understood Hale's reluctance.

Gorrin and Yazmor hadn't grown up on Earth—assuming they even had a childhood, which I realized I had no idea about—so neither of them would have any feelings about this sort of place.

I glanced at Tyrus, but he seemed at ease.

At my look, he shrugged. "I told you my father was in my business before me. I grew up in a neighborhood such as this. It was older, of course, but the close homes, the community feel? I understand those things well. If anything, I feel more comfortable in a place like this than in a penthouse high-rise."

"Well color me shocked. I would have figured you for preferring the bright lights of the big city."

"The city is noisy. It is a necessary evil for someone like me, but that doesn't mean I prefer it."

"Why would you open a bar in a big building and take the top floor, then?"

"Because the top floor is the best. It only made sense I should live there." He shrugged as he took a few steps forward, pausing to glance over his shoulder at me as a panty-melting smile. "However, I believe I would be satisfied to call any place home so long as you were there. As it turns out, my only real requirement is you." He didn't wait around for a response, instead turning and walking away as if he hadn't just thrown out that smooth AF comment.

What an asshole.

It was entirely unfair for anyone to know exactly what to say in order to fluster me, and worse, to say something like that without the least bit of embarrassment.

If he'd blushed, if his ears had reddened just a bit, I could have accepted his nonsense, but *noooo*. He had to look as unruffled as he always did while I stood there like an idiot.

A press to my back got me moving, especially because the last thing I needed was to make any more fool of myself. I still wasn't moving that fast, my hip complaining, but my body had rebounded enough that I didn't limp much. Another few hours and it should be good as new.

"You shouldn't let him see you sweat," Yazmor said. He still was in his other form, but at least some of the familiar personality I knew had returned. I didn't doubt that he struggled, but just a glimpse of the man I loved helped reassure me that he was there no matter how different he looked.

"Easy for you to say."

"You don't let me fluster you like that, and I'm pretty sure I can be *far* more random."

"Yeah, but I'm *used* to your randomness! You can't shock me anymore because everything you say is weird. Tyrus doesn't pull out lines like that often enough for me to develop a tolerance for it." I knew I was pouting, but fuck it, I didn't care.

I wanted the upper hand for once! I wanted to be the badass who saved the day, the one who threw them for a loop. Instead, I was always playing catch-up, always reacting to all four of them.

I used to think it was because of their ages, but after so long together, I was pretty sure it was just *them*. For the first time in a long time, I cared what they said, cared what they thought of me. It meant their words mattered in a way few others did.

As we approached the first house, I had a moment of 'now what?'

We were in some weird little pocket of the universe. Was knocking appropriate? I had no idea the etiquette in a place like this.

Thankfully, we didn't have to question it long, because as we turned off the street and onto the first walkway, the door to the house opened. A woman walked out wearing the sort of dress that fit in perfectly with the surroundings. It was a pale blue with pretty little pink flowers and buttoned up the front. A tie cinched it at the waist and tied in a bow at the small of her back. She had her hair pulled up into a bun and even had fucking pearls at her neck.

Part of me wanted to poke her to see if she were even real.

"Welcome!" she said, a big smile on her face.

Still, something about her made it impossible to let down my guard, to believe that she was actually as innocent as she appeared. After all, if she came from the Chasm, if she'd survived the Path thus far, it would be foolish to underestimate her.

She took a step toward me, but before she could get any closer, Hale moved into her path and crossed his arms over his chest. His stance made it clear she wouldn't get any closer.

Still, the woman didn't appear startled. She smiled at Hale, showing no signs of finding his appearance questionable. "Don't worry. I have no plans to hurt her."

"Well for-fucking-give me for not believing that. After she got dragged off by that fog beast, you all showed up. Seems like a pretty big coincidence, don't it?"

So much for playing nice…

Still, the woman didn't look concerned. "Are you thinking we're in league with The Guardian? That's a silly idea."

"Then explain why you were there."

"We heard screaming and went to investigate. We don't run into many people, so signs of them will make us want to see what's going on."

"So why did you leave her?" Gorrin asked. "If you were so worried, why run?"

She put her hands together, fidgeting slightly. "I sensed something coming." Her gaze shifted to Yazmor, but just as quickly, it leapt away as if she couldn't bear to look directly at him. "I'd never felt something like that, and forgive me, but I didn't want to see what it might do to us. I'm sorry that I left her to fend for herself, but since it seems you know each other, it all worked out, right?" Her smile then seemed forced, but I got the sense it was because she wanted to convince us that everything was okay.

I couldn't blame her for her actions. I'd learned plenty of times in my life that to survive, people needed to watch out for themselves first. If I saw Yazmor and had no idea what he was, I was pretty sure I'd have taken off, too.

Yazmor tilted his head as he stared at the woman, but he showed no defensiveness. He really didn't care what most people thought of him, did he?

And why does that make me feel special?

I shook away the stupid thought to focus. "What is this place?"

The woman waved her hand at the ` small community. "This is our home."

"And who is '*our*'?" Tyrus asked. "Because as far as I was aware, nothing survived long in the Path. I am curious how you have."

"There's time for all that later. My name is Nona, by the way."

"Loch," I offered, lifting my hand in an awkward wave, then nodded at the others to introduce them. "Yazmor. Hale. Tyrus." I gestured toward Gorrin, but she interrupted me before I could say his name.

"Gorrin, of course. You have a hard face to forget."

"And yet I don't recognize you," Gorrin responded.

"Of course you wouldn't. You may have owned my soul, but I was far too low on the rankings for you to take notice."

If she knew Gorrin but *not* Tyrus or Hale, it meant she must have left the Chasm sometime before Tyrus had taken over. It at least gave us a *very* general idea of how long she'd been here.

"We have a place set up for guests," Nona explained. "But first you'll need to meet the others. This way!"

"Aren't you worried we might be dangerous?" Tyrus asked.

I tried to reprimand him with a sharp look. When someone was helping us, it was *not* the right time to be rude and suspicious. I'd learned my lesson on that when some nice strangers had once let me stay the night with them when I'd still been a teenager. I'd made the mistake of asking them how they knew I wouldn't steal from them, mostly because someone being that that trusting made me uneasy.

As it turned out, normal people didn't like questions like that. It made them think I had something planned, and I'd ended up having to spend that night on a bench in the park all due to my big mouth.

If I miss out on a soft bed and good night's sleep all because of Tyrus' big mouth, I'm stealing his blankets and making him sleep in the dirt.

Nona didn't seem bothered as she passed by us and started to follow the walkway toward the large house at the end. "No, I'm not worried. If you all made it here, you're clearly dangerous. We all came from the Chasm, so judging who's good and bad is a silly idea. It's like figuring the good and bad prisoners. They are all bad — it's only a matter of degrees."

"You don't get many visitors, then?" Tyrus asked.

"Occasionally, but it's still pretty rare."

"Did you get here at the same time, then?" I asked.

"Oh, dear, no. People don't come to the Path in groups, after all. No, our little place here is just a stopping point, so the few who survive this far always end up here. I wonder if the Path guides them here." Her steps slowed a bit, as if she'd gotten herself lost in thought about it. Her eyes blanked, her expression flattening in a way that was beyond unnerving, as if all the emotion inside her had frozen in the blink of an eye.

As quickly as it happened, she blinked rapidly and that same old smile spread across her lips. It happened so fast I nearly felt dizzy. She went on with her conversation as if nothing had happened. "A few leave from here and venture farther, but most who make it here stay, at least for a while."

"How many are here?" Gorrin asked.

"Currently? Twelve. Well, actually, I guess with you, it brings us up to seventeen! I don't think we've ever had so many. People only show up here one at a time."

"We ain't staying," Hale snarled.

"Most people say that, but they don't mean it. A day or two here convinces them to stick around." She opened the front door to the largest house at the end of the street, but when we walked inside, it appeared more like a lobby or communal space than an individual home.

I paused at the doorway, something telling me to be wary.

She turned back toward me, but the smile on her lips felt more dangerous than it had. Or maybe that was my own doubts, my own fears…

"We use this house for community meetings."

"So no one lives here?"

"Well, the first of us lives upstairs here."

"The first?" I asked.

"Yes. The one who founded this place, who created a safe place here in the Path for those of us who wait."

"And what are you waiting for?"

Nona widened her smile, reminding me *far* too much of Yazmor. "Why don't we discuss that over dinner? We'll have a meal with the entire group, you can meet everyone, including the first, and ask all the questions you want. Until then, follow me."

She headed to the left of the first room, and somehow the house seemed larger inside than it had outside. Was that some magic bullshit or was I just really bad at estimating sizes? Maybe a lifetime of men telling me that four inches was really eight had skewed my perceptions.

"There are open bedrooms here, changes of clothing inside them, and a bathing area. Please clean yourselves up and rest for a while—I'm sure it's been a tiresome trip here. I'll come back and get you when everything is ready for dinner." She didn't wait for us to agree before turning and leaving the house, closing the door behind her.

Yazmor made a low sound in his throat before he grasped the handle of the door and tried to open it.

Nothing.

He swung his arm at the door next, but it didn't so much as groan beneath the hit.

Which meant that Nona had managed to lock us in here.

"I knew this place was bad news," I muttered, then turned around.

"Where do you think you're going?" Tyrus called out to me.

"If we're trapped here anyways, I'm not missing the chance for a bath or a change of clothing."

"You know we might die, right?" Hale asked with so much sarcasm I was a bit shocked he didn't slice his own mouth on those sharp words.

"Yep, but if I'm going to die anyway, I might as well get to soak for a while first."

* * * *

"They may be nutjobs who locked us in, but they have a pretty good sense of style." I came out of the bathroom, brushing my hands down my front, over the incredibly soft fabric of the dress that I'd found in one of the closets.

Or maybe it was better to say that there were so many different types of clothing that *something* had to fit with my personal like.

I lifted my gaze when no one said anything to find all four men staring at me as if I'd come out naked.

No, wait, if I'd been naked, it would have been more lust—hopefully—and less confusion.

I glanced down at my front, wondering if I'd broken some unwritten rule. I'd picked a boho-style maxi dress because why the fuck not? It was made of the softest cotton I'd ever felt and was a mix of black and grays. I'd paired it with some boots, lined in fur. The whole outfit made me want to plant my ass in a hammock and nap in the sun.

But, given where I was, I had a feeling that both the hammock and the sun were far outside of my reach at the moment.

"What's wrong?" I asked when I couldn't figure out what I'd done this time to spoil the mood.

"You look different," Hale said. "You don't wear clothes like that."

"This isn't that weird…"

"It's not weird, no," Gorrin said, speaking slowly as if searching for the right words. "It's just not your usual style."

"And what is my usual style?"

Tyrus, Gorrin and Hale all exchanged looks, as if they'd sensed the minefield they currently were trouncing through.

"Normally you wear things that barely fit you and are often wrinkled and dirty," Yazmor chimed in.

I opened my mouth to argue, but fuck it, he wasn't entirely wrong.

"Well, then enjoy this because it might not happen again!" I crossed my arms in a huff. "Also, FYI, Mr. *She's our girlfriend,* you should know that the rule is you always compliment whatever your girlfriend is wearing."

"That's a rule?" Yazmor stared down at the floor for a moment, then nodded as if accepting it. "You should write a manual for me. I don't have enough experience to know these things and you'll get mad at me far less often if you write it all down." He pointed one of his long fingers at me. "I said *less* often, so expect to still get mad at me."

His words were so direct that I couldn't stop the way it stole any annoyance I'd had. While their reactions hadn't made me feel good, something about Yazmor's honesty chased that negativity away.

It also gave me a moment to look at the four of them. They'd washed and changed as well, and while I'd gone with something different, they'd picked clothing in their more common styles.

Hale wore black jeans and a black T-shirt along with a large black hoodie sweater. Tyrus had found a suit, though it wasn't all back as I'd grown accustomed to for him. Yazmor remained nude—though since he didn't appear human it didn't look strange. Gorrin was the one who gave me pause.

I mean, he'd worn such a weird outfit before, and that wasn't the sort of thing that they'd probably have here, after all. Still, seeing him dressed in a suit, much like Tyrus, had my mouth almost hanging open.

"What?" he asked, his tone defensive.

Right, I'm doing what he did to me, aren't I? Instead of apologizing, I went up to him and reached for his tie. He lifted an eyebrow but didn't stop me as I straightened it.

The door opened, silencing anything else we might have said.

Nona looked just as she had before, a bright smile as if she hadn't just had us locked in here.

298

Though her appearance at least eased some of my worries. It meant they hadn't planned to lock us in here until we starved to death or something.

"You all look wonderful," Nona said. "I bet you feel better after washing up. The Path isn't as dirty or dusty as the Chasm, but it still feels wonderful to clean up, right? I remember my first bath when I arrived here, how I just soaked for hours until the water went cold." She moved away from the doorway, waving for us to follow.

The room outside of the ones where we were locked in appeared different. The seating that had been there was gone, and in its place was a long formal table and chairs, all set with fancy china and crystal glasses.

Part of me expected someone to show me to a kids table, because I sure as fuck didn't belong in a place like this.

In addition to the changes of décor and furniture, others moved around the room.

They startled me as much as anything else. Sure, Nona had appeared normal enough, in a Suzy-Homemaker sort of way, but I'd figured she was the exception, not the rule.

That didn't seem to be the case, since every person I saw looked just as normal as she did. They wore a variety of clothing, but it was all clean, well-tailored, and fitting to the individual. Furthermore, the people all appeared human.

I turned a look on Gorrin, my eyebrow lifted in question.

They were from the Chasm, right? How could *none* of them be damned? Why weren't they twisted into monstrous forms? Were they all demons?

"You look confused," a man said who left a group of people and approached us, a kind smile on his face. He wore a suit, but it appeared an old style, made of a thicker, light gray fabric like wool.

"Why do you all look human?"

He didn't answer immediately, as if my words surprised him. After a moment, he let out a soft laugh. "Forgive me, but your bluntness surprised me. I am used to people who prefer to temper their words with honey, but you don't seem to do that."

"Sadly, that is a skill Loch has never quite learned," Tyrus said.

"Loch?" The man moved his gaze over me as if he wanted to connect the name with me. "You are a Demon Lord."

I took a step backward, his words feeling like a threat.

"Do not worry yourself. I am rather old, so I can usually tell the power level of a person. Yours is quite high. Given you are here beside Yazmor, Hale and Tyrus, it would only make sense that you were also a Demon Lord." He tilted his head when he looked at Gorrin. "Of course, that makes Gorrin's presence even more surprising. I would have thought stealing a person's power and position would leave soured feelings, but perhaps the story is more complicated than that."

He gestured at the table. "Please, sit." He went to move away, then paused. "Forgive me—I failed to introduce myself. My name is Cain, though they often call me the first." With that, he bowed slightly and retreated.

"He doesn't ever ask questions," I whispered to Gorrin. "Did you notice that? Despite all of that, he never actually asked anything."

"He's also a lot more informed than I would have thought if he has been here longer than the others. How would he know about Hale and Tyrus?"

I had no answer to that, but there didn't seem a way to refuse the order. They might have talked about dinner as if it were just an offer, but I knew better than to think that.

No doubt, if I checked the front door, I'd find it locked.

"Please, sit," Cain said, his voice rising above the general hum of conversation. He'd pulled a chair out, staring at me and waiting. "I saved you a place here, beside me."

"Hard pass."

He didn't move despite my not-at-all-kind rejection. In fact, even his smile didn't dim. Had he even heard me? "Do not fear. If I wanted to harm any of you, I could have done so already."

"You could *try*," Hale answered.

Cain still didn't move his gaze from mine, and I almost felt lost in his dark eyes. "I wish to speak to you, to hear about you and your companions. For that reason, I ensured I would sit close enough to make conversation possible. Now. Sit."

His command left no room to misunderstand that he would not take no for an answer. And really, who the fuck wanted this to turn badly over a stupid seating arrangement?

I suddenly recalled an old friend planning her wedding, when she'd fought with her fiancée over where everyone would sit, when she'd told me that a poor seating plan could ruin an entire event.

She probably meant ruined as in a few drunken arguments and maybe someone hooking up, whereas *ruined* here would no doubt turn bloody.

So I lifted a hand when Hale took a step forward to intervene. I could hold my own, and if that meant sitting next to this fucking weirdo, that was fine by me.

I'd done far worse in my life, after all.

The Lords took other seats around the table, none of us right beside one another. As uneasy as it made me, I tried to think like Tyrus. I could almost hear his lecture in my head, reminding me that information gathering was vital, and that the best way to do so was to insert oneself into the group who had the information.

Thus, us sitting apart would increase the odds of us getting a clearer overall picture than if we'd all banded together.

A few others brought food out on large trays, placing them along the center of the table, then took their own seats.

I counted twelve others, which meant if Nona was told the truth, everyone in the community sat at the table.

"How long have you been here?" Cain asked.

"No idea. None of my clocks work and there's no day and night cycle to judge time."

"Fair enough." Cain gestured at one of the plates. "The food is simple, but it is good."

"I'm not hungry."

He tilted his head. "You fear it is poisoned." He reached out and took a piece from the plate, something that looked like chicken, and popped it into his mouth. He chewed it slowly, then swallowed. "If I wanted you dead, I wouldn't go through the trouble of allowing you to wash and dress just to poison you."

When others at the table served themselves food from the plates and ate it without worry, I cast Tyrus a questioning look. He nodded, the motion so subtle others would probably not pick up on it.

Guess it's safe enough to eat.

I went to reach for the serving fork, but Cain took it before I could. He went about serving food for me, not asking what I liked but instead giving me some of everything. No doubt he did that so he didn't have to fight over each and every dish.

Afterward, he filled one of my glasses with water and the other with a red liquid, doing the same with his own cups from the same pitchers.

"Nona said you were limping when you arrived."

"Had a run-in with a hentai monster."

He frowned for a moment, his expression flattening a bit as Nona's had earlier. It was beyond strange, the way they seemed to freeze for a moment before resuming as if they hadn't paused at all. "You mean The Guardian."

"Yeah, that bastard. He's had a hard-on for me since I got here, and he's not great at taking no for an answer."

"Perhaps it sees you as an easy target."

"First—*rude.* I'm not an easy target. Secondly, yeah, it's targeted me. Even when I'm not the easiest to get to, it swipes at me. It grabbed my leg and dragged me through the forest."

"But you survived."

"Let's say I taught it a lesson in consent. It doesn't seem to care for things shoved into it without asking, so I'm hoping it applies that pretty liberally."

"Hmm." The sounds he let out would have made me think that he wasn't paying any attention, that he cared little for my answer, but when I looked up from the food to his face, his expression said that was *far* from the truth.

He stared at me with an intensity that would warrant a restraining order for most people.

"How did you make this place?" I asked, desperate to change the conversation.

"The Path is like mud. It is created around those who exist here. If there is no one here, nothing exists. Once someone understands this, they can control the form it takes to some extent. I arrived here a very long time ago, and I created this place as a haven. Over the years, others have come to me, and I have taken them in."

"Why stay here though?"

Cain tapped his finger on the table. "The Path is a raging river. On one side of that river is the Chasm, and on the other, the Plains. This place is a log resting in the center, a place for the lost to rest. We have no way forward, have not discovered how to pass from the log to the riverbank. We wait until we find it."

"So why not go back to the Chasm? It has to be better than this?"

"The Chasm is a dead end. It is chaos and it is violence. This small haven may not be much, but it allows us to be closer to the Plains than anywhere else. It is the best chance we have to make it through, to find the way past The Guardian and into Paradise."

"But you've been here so long. How can you still believe there's a way? I mean, if you haven't figured it out yet, why do you still think it's possible?" I shut my mouth before I went on, before I insulted him by basically asking how the fuck he hadn't given up on this stupid idea yet.

And given I was here in the same exact position, that was probably a pretty unfair thing to ask.

Cain leaned back in his chair, his fingers drumming over the armrest. "I know because I can *feel* it. I know it is possible because if there were no route through, they wouldn't need The Guardian to protect anything. I learned long ago that the larger the beast that protects something, the more valuable the treasure must be. The Guardian is a very large beast, and the only thing worth protecting with that is the Plains."

I shook my head. It was probably stupid to think someone as old as him as naïve, but that was exactly how it struck me. Still, his information might help. If he'd failed a hundred times, well, that was a hundred theories I could mark off my list.

"So how do you think you get past Guardian then? If you think it's possible, how do you think you do it?"

"The Guardian is connected with Hubis. It kills without mercy, though it toys with its prey first."

"That doesn't sound promising."

"The Guardian is not mindless. It is connected to Hubis but it is not without its own personality. I didn't realize it at first, of course. It took so many years here, so many deaths from others, for me to understand. It does not cross here, into this town, I believe because we do not leave the town. Its purpose is to prevent others from gaining access to the Plains, so as long as we remain here, it pays us no attention."

"Lucky you."

"Indeed. Your arrival has changed that, however. While you were resting prior to dinner, I walked the boundary of our town, and The Guardian prowled there. It did not enter the grounds, but it has never ventured so close nor stayed so long. Even now, it sits just past the clearing, as if waiting for something."

"So apparently my lesson didn't stick."

He reached out and caught my chin, leaning in to stare into my eyes. There was so much desire in his eyes, but it wasn't lust. Instead, it felt like he was salivating over a meal, as if he saw the final piece to a puzzle. "You stir The Guardian in a way no one else has. We have had demons here — damned never survive this far — and we have even had Lords before, but The Guardian has paid them no mind."

"Let her go," Hale snapped a moment before he buried his fork in the top of the table, the threat far from subtle. Of course, Hale had never really done subtle.

Cain didn't look away from me, paying Hale no mind. "You come here with three Lords and an angel. I can *taste* Hubis on you, know that his powers touched you recently. What are you?"

"Right now? Mostly annoyed. Let go of me before this gets ugly."

He didn't smile, all that nice friendliness having drifted away. Now he only seemed intense, as if he'd locked in on something he refused to let go of. "I have spent longer than you have existed here, studying, learning, trying to discover the secrets of the Path, of how to get to the Plains. I had nearly given up hope of ever achieving my goal, had thought perhaps I was cursed to never leave this place. You, however, will buy my admission into the Plains."

"What does that mean?" Or that was what I'd intended to say. My lips tripped over the syllables as if I'd drank a bottle of whiskey. My tongue lay thick and clumsy in my mouth, incapable of the finesse required to speak.

I yanked away from Cain, my chair tipping backward. I grabbed the table to keep myself upright when the room spun around me, when coordinating my feet became a challenge in itself.

A crash to the left showed Gorrin on the ground, and across the table I could no longer spot Hale.

I turned toward Cain, who had pushed his chair out so he could watch me as I stumbled. He must have read the question on my face, because he answered without me needing to ask. "Your glasses were laced with a powerful drug. It won't harm you long term — will simply make it easier to deal with you. I dislike violence when it can be avoided."

Yazmor made a sound that chilled me, something angry and feral. Near the end of the table he stood, though he wavered. He bared his teeth at the others around him, his violet eyes locking on me.

He took one step after another, and when one of the people got in his way, he swiped one of his long arms, knocking the person away so hard, they sailed against the wall.

"Impressive." Despite Cain's praise, he didn't seem all that impressed. Perhaps he just didn't feel anything anymore, as if this place had chilled him down to his core, had killed anything inside of him. "I have never seen a remnant here, have never seen the effects of this drug on one."

Two others tried to grab Yazmor, but he wrapped a hand around the throat of one, snapping their neck without ever looking at them. He reached for the other but stumbled, allowing the other to dodge it.

"He has made a good effort. You must matter greatly to him if he can fight the effects for this long. Perhaps that can be some form of reassurance for you."

Yazmor tripped and fell, the ground shaking slightly beneath his weight. Even still, he didn't stop. He dragged himself forward, reaching for me, as if desperate to get to me.

My body refused to obey me, and I had no doubt I'd lose the battle quickly. I turned away from Cain.

"You plan to run? I welcome you to try. You will be unconscious before you reach the door."

Fuck running. Instead, when I took the two steps I managed before I collapsed, I headed for Yazmor. I stretched my arm out, toward him, my eyes locked on that familiar violet.

"You are such a strange little creature," Cain said, his voice coming from closer, telling me he'd left his chair and likely crouched beside me. "You have the power of a Lord, yet you cling to these men. Even when you know something is hopeless, you do not relent. You reach for something you know you will never touch."

My fingers nearly reached Yazmor, a breath between us, but I never made contact.

Instead, Cain grasped my arm and hauled me from the ground, pulling me away from Yazmor, all the strength in my body gone.

"Do not worry, Loch. No matter how much pain you feel now, you will not have to suffer it long."

My eyes closed, the drugs overcoming me, with his words ringing in my ears.

Chapter Twenty-One

My arms refused to budge. Fuck, even my eyes wouldn't open. No matter how much I screamed in my head for me to *JUST FUCKING MOVE*, my body wouldn't obey.

I hadn't passed out, not exactly. Instead, it was as if the drug had locked me inside my own body, had disconnected my brain from all my senses, from everything.

I'd felt trapped inside myself, unable to hear or see or feel *anything*. It was like I'd gotten lost in a dark ocean, and I had no idea what way was up.

"Are you finally waking up?" Cain's voice floated through that darkness, and I latched on to it.

Not because I liked it, but because hatred was one hell of a motivator.

Finally, I managed to get my eyelids to obey my signals, because the dim light of the Path made me squint.

I was on the ground, staring up at Cain, who stood beside me. He stared down at me, an almost peaceful smile on his face.

It felt real, and that made it all the creepier. It was like someone smiling while a plane went down.

I moved my tongue in my mouth, trying to wake my body from its slumber. I could do nothing if I couldn't even fucking move.

I opened my mouth to ask about the men, but the sound that escaped wasn't even close to words. In fact, if I'd heard it, I wouldn't have thought it human.

Cain crouched beside me and ran his fingers through my hair, the touch almost kind. "Do not worry about them. They are not your concern any longer."

I narrowed my eyes, wishing I could say, '*fuck you*,' more than I ever had before in my life.

Still, he didn't get angry, didn't pull away. It was as though nothing I thought or said mattered. That was the worst of it—he wasn't doing this because he hated me. If anything, the kindness of his touch implied he cared, in his own way, and it sickened me.

"They are alive," he finally said with a sigh. "I have no wish to end more lives than I need to. Given the way they reacted to you, they may wish I had ended them rather than being forced to live on without you. That will be their choice, though. I will not take that choice away from them."

The fact that they were alive, that he didn't plan to kill him, allowed me to focus more. If I'd heard they were dead...well, I had no idea how I could have possibly pulled myself out of that hole. I couldn't have kept struggling, kept trying knowing that they were gone.

Knowing they lived meant I had something to fight for, something to hold on to.

So I stared up at Cain as I wiggled my fingers and toes carefully, trying to gauge my control, to speed up the process without alerting him.

"I find you strangely relaxing." Cain stroked my head, calming me the way a person would a frightened, wild animal. "Maybe it is because I know you are the key I have searched for. I don't want to sacrifice you, have never cared for that method of success, but after so long…I can no longer see another way."

Sacrifice? Boy did that not sound good for me.

What exactly was he planning to sacrifice me to?

A rustling to my side answered the question. A familiar tentacle shifted in the fog, as if making its presence known.

Well, if it isn't my old friend? I sure hope you're not holding any grudges over the whole stabbing thing.

What was a little stabbing between buddies?

"Try to be at ease," Cain whispered. "Your sacrifice will grant me access to the Plains. After all these years waiting, after all I have given up, all I have lost, I will finally ascend to where I belong, and I will have you to thank for it."

"What sort of metaphysical bullshit are you spouting?" I said, the words slurred but mostly understandable.

He offered a kind smile, one that almost made him seem like a different man. Was this who he had been before insanity had taken him? Maybe it wasn't as obvious an insanity as others, not as explosive, but that didn't change that he was just as crazy as any of the lunatics who had made their way back.

Fuck, he was probably even madder, given he'd stayed here.

"I told you that The Guardian is connected to Hubis. The way the world works is always the same—

everything has a price. We sell our souls to gain what we want, we pay the price for what we are given. I knew The Guardian would require a payment, but no matter what I tried, it never accepted any gifts. You are the first thing it has focused on, which makes you the perfect payment."

"You think you're going to give me to that grabby octopus and that's going to get you into Heaven? Thousands of years here and *that* is the best plan you could come up with?"

He let out a soft laugh, seemingly brimming with life. Then again, in his mind, he was about to get to Paradise. What was a little demon sacrifice to gain that?

"It will work. The others you came with will free themselves, allowed to do as they please."

"And your followers? You're going to just leave them on their own?"

"If The Guardian deems them worthy, if it feels the payment is enough, it will grant them passage as well. They fear The Guardian too much to come with me. They have to walk their own path, as we all do."

"Except me? Who gets fed to the guard dog so you can get what you want?"

He pressed a gentle kiss to my forehead, the warmth of it sickening. "Be at ease, Loch. It will be over fast, and you will not have to suffer anymore either. You can pass from this world to whatever is next, and perhaps there you'll find real contentment."

Talk about empty promises.

A tentacle reached forward, through the fog, as if searching. It was slow, careful.

"Do you remember what I did to you before? Because I'll make that look like foreplay if you touch me again," I said to Guardian.

It hesitated, pausing as if thinking.

I let out a hollow laugh. "That's right. You remember me."

"Stop fighting," Cain said. "This is all done. There is no point in fighting against what cannot be changed. It will only hurt you more."

"Funny story," I said and looked up at Cain. "You're far from the first who has said that to me. The thing is, no matter how much easier my life might be if I just gave in, I can never quite bring myself to do so. It just isn't in me."

"So what will you do?" He asked me like an adult asking a toddler who was threatening to run away, like someone who knew the other person was bluffing.

"I think I'll fight," I said before using the little bit of control I'd regained to lift my head and slam into his forehead.

The action seemed to startle Guardian, who pulled back into the fog. Cain yanked backward, holding his head as he got to his feet.

"If you had simply accepted things," Cain said, the first signs of anger bleeding through his voice, "The Guardian could have taken you before the drugs wore off, before you had to even *feel* what would happen to you. Because you chose to fight, because you worked to rid yourself of the effects, you will now have to suffer through it all, will have to feel every moment of it! I tried to save you that agony."

"Yeah, well, I'm going to go ahead and return that gift. A quick and easy death has *never* been what I wanted."

I reached for my wrist, my hand wrapping around the handle of the dagger, the one I'd been unwilling to draw for so long. The weight of it, the feeling still made me sick, made my hand shake, but I refused to give in.

A horrible sound rushed through the trees, shaking them all, full of rage.

Ah, good old Yazmor. I smiled at the way it made me feel, the reminder that the same man who could let out that terrifying sound could smile so sweetly at me.

"It sounds like they're shaking off those drugs, too, and if you think *my* temper is bad, well, I seem like a sweet pup compared to them."

Cain stared toward where the sound had come from, pressing his lips together. After a moment, he shook his head. "It will take them time to get here, and when they do, it will be too late. The Guardian will take his payment and grant me my way to the Plains." Cain stood up straighter, his body shifting before my eyes to take on a form I'd never seen before.

He was like a dark angel, large wings spreading out behind him covered in black feathers. His eyes glowed red as they locked on me.

Except he didn't touch me. Instead, something slammed against my back, knocking me forward. My body still wasn't operating all that well still, so I couldn't right myself before I hit the ground.

Guardian wrapped a tentacle around my leg, much as it had before, but it didn't yank me. It was almost like it *wanted* me to feel helpless, wanted me to know exactly how little power and control I had.

I knew octopus were assholes, but I hadn't realized they could be sadists, too.

"I never wanted you to suffer," Cain said, his voice deeper and darker than before. "This wasn't *my* choice — it was yours. If you had only behaved, if you had only given in, you would not have had to suffer at all."

"The easy path has never been my way," I said as I swiped my blade toward Guardian, though it avoided my strikes.

Did it know what the blade was?

Would the blade even work if Guardian wasn't ever alive?

Well, a sharp edge is a sharp edge and that stick sure had managed.

I kicked at another tentacle when it reached for me, just as the fog seemed to thin around us.

Which gave me my first actual look at the beast that had plagued me since I'd arrived here.

I'd assumed it would be something like a squid or octopus, but fuck had I been wrong. Instead, the center of the creature resembled a spider, with ten legs — assuming I could still count right — and four tentacles that came off its back. It had jaws with rows of teeth, and it snapped them toward me in threat.

"Talk about a face only a mother would love," I muttered before I grabbed a stick beside me. I snapped it, but when I tried to pull the same trick as the last time, it swung another tentacle at me to knock the sick away.

"Just accept it," Cain said, the excitement in his voice almost vibrating. "It will be over faster if you just accept it."

"Loch doesn't accept shit." Hale's voice made me jerk my gaze over, though I hardly recognized the man there.

In fact, *all* the men were in their other forms, and standing together, they made quite the sight.

Hale was the only one whose demon form I'd never seen, and he reminded me of a wolf, his body hunched forward, his face having shifted to look more dog-like. His ears were long and pointed, and as he snarled, his sharp teeth shined even in the dark.

Cain only had a moment to react, to turn and look at them, before Yazmor leapt forward. He grasped Cain by the throat, holding him up so his feet dangled.

"I'm so close," Cain whispered. "So close to finally getting there…"

Hale and Tyrus moved behind Cain, each grasping one of Cain's wings.

Tyrus leaned in, his voice full of fury as he spoke. "I have no control over who gets into the Plains, but I can assure you, anyone who dares lay a hand on *my* woman will taste hell."

"Fuck you," Hale added on.

The two of them yanked hard, pulling Cain's wings from his back and throwing them aside like junk. The scream that left Cain chilled me, but I didn't have time to think about it long, not when Guardian yanked at my leg as if to take me on another ride.

Before I could go anywhere, a hand caught my wrist, wrapping strong fingers around me. "I have you," Gorrin said, "and I won't let go."

I gripped his hand back, holding tightly no matter how hard Guardian pulled.

Yazmor stared into Cain's face, not releasing him, not letting him down.

"Just kill me," Cain whispered, pain drenching his words.

"No." Yazmor tossed Cain to the side, letting him strike a tree before he fell to the ground. "You can live knowing you failed, that you will never even *smell* Paradise, that you sacrificed so much for nothing. You don't deserve death—I want you to live through the pain and the regret. I want you to suffer here forever knowing you are trapped."

A shiver ran down my spine at Yazmor's words, at the anger in them, the bottomless rage that I knew he had, that he usually kept so carefully hidden.

"Hey, you think you could lend a hand?" I snapped when I felt Guardian trying to grasp my other leg as well, as the dirt crunched beneath those creepy, spindly legs of his.

Things should have spider legs or tentacles, but not both!

Hale rushed over, raking his claws over the tentacle that held me, causing Guardian to let me go. It didn't retreat, however.

Instead, it seemed to grow before us, shifting its weight to its back legs, rearing up.

"Looks like it's done playing around," Hale said.

"Yeah, well, so am I," I said, getting to my feet, grasping the dagger tightly in my fist. "I've run from this fucker, been afraid of it, almost got *sacrificed* to it, and I'm done. This ends here, one way or another."

* * * *

"Who the fuck put this thing on steroids?" I held my arm against my side, having no doubt that the bitch had busted one of my ribs. I struggled to breathe in, but still, I stayed on my feet.

For once, I wished *I* was the loser in the situation. I would have been perfectly happy to look around and find that everyone else was doing great, to have the Lords sweep in like heroes.

Unfortunately, that was *far* from the case.

They looked every bit as beat up as I felt.

No matter what we did, Guardian never stopped, never rested. Even when hurt, it didn't even slow.

Hale used his claws to slice a tentacle, but before the blood drops could hit the dirt, it had already grown a new one. Even my blade didn't seem to work. No matter how I sliced it, it would heal almost instantly.

The dagger would kill anything living or dead, but it seemed Guardian was not quite either.

"Loch, you need to run," Gorrin said as he moved in front of me, catching one of Guardian's tentacles and tearing it free.

"I don't think we can outrun this thing."

"I didn't say *we*."

His meaning struck me, and I reacted by kicking him in the back of his knees. "Not a chance!"

"I am more than willing to make a stand even if I know we can't win, but there is no reason for you to die here as well."

I shook my head, my eyes burning. *That* wasn't an option. It couldn't be. Even the idea of surviving, of waking up alone, it wasn't one worth taking.

Some things have too high a price.

Hadn't I learned that over and over again? If the price of my survival was to lose the men I loved, then I didn't want it.

"Just fucking go," Hale snapped without looking back. "There's no good reason for us all to die here."

"Then *you* go!" I shouted back. "The thing wants me anyways! It'll focus on me the second it can, and you can all leave. If it's between one life or four, the answer is obvious."

"Not if that one life is yours." Tyrus caught my chin and forced my eyes to his. "We have all lived a lot longer than you have. I'm more than willing to sacrifice whatever I might have had left if I know you will get to keep living. Head back the way we came, focusing on getting back to the Chasm. The Path should appear, and you'll reach the walkway we took here."

I shook my head, ignoring how it made his fingers dig into my chin. There was no way. It was an impossible order, one I couldn't obey even if I wanted to.

Yazmor swiped his hand at Guardian, then knocked against him just as Guardian attempted to bypass Tyrus to get to me.

Fuck, even if I ran, I didn't know that the four of them *could* contain that thing. It wanted me.

Why?

I stared at it, at the way it snarled and hissed and never seemed to fully take its eyes off me.

It's connected to Hubis. Those words had come again and again to me, but I hadn't thought about it much. Hubis didn't control Guardian, but they had a bond.

Guardian was here to protect not just the Plains, but Hubis himself. It was here to ensure nothing passed.

No, that's not right…

It was here to ensure nothing that would hurt Hubis could pass. I recalled getting a finger trap when I'd been a kid, remembered how no matter how hard I pulled, I couldn't get free.

Each time we went harder at Guardian, it responded in kind. Every time we hurt it, it came back harsher, struck harder.

Guardian was the final trap.

Which meant there was only one way through.

"Go," Tyrus snarled and shoved me behind him before turning back toward Guardian, flanked by the others, all of them willing to die just to give me time.

If we were going to die here, then we'd go together. Though…I could only hope I was right.

I took a deep breath, then rushed forward, ducking through the small space between Hale and Tyrus, avoiding when both tried to reach for me. It was a benefit of being smaller—I was a lot harder to grab.

I didn't stop until I stood just before Guardian, but held a hand up toward the men. "Wait," I ordered them.

"The fuck are you doing?" Hale asked.

"Something stupid, as usual." I held my hand out with the dagger, then dropped it. It disappeared before it struck the ground, the burning on my wrist showing it had returned there. Still, my point was clear. "I submit." I dropped to my knees, unable to hide my shaking. In fact, it was good I was kneeling, because I doubted my legs would hold me anymore.

But, fuck, if I died here, at least it was an interesting story, right? I could have ended by getting run over or something equally boring, but this was a story worth telling.

The idiot who got on her knees for a beast.

Not the worst thing I've gotten on my knees for.

"What are you doing, Loch?" Gorrin asked. "If you think we will just accept your death, you are a fool."

I shook my head and dropped my gaze, closing my eyes. "Guardian protects the Plains, right? He keeps out threats?"

I said nothing else, breathing slowly, praying I was right. If I was wrong, it was the end of *everything*.

Guardian wrapped a tentacle around my throat, squeezing it tightly until it cut off my breath, but I resisted every instinct inside me that wanted to fight, that wanted to struggle.

I forced myself to submit, to prove I wasn't a threat. The world dimmed around me as my lungs burned, as my body was desperate for oxygen.

I heard the shouts of the men, but it felt so distant I couldn't hear it.

What a stupid idea... I chastised myself for a moment, thankful only that dying meant I didn't have to live down the massive failure. *Sure, let the monster kill me, that was just brilliant.*

Air rushed into my lungs so fast that it shocked me, especially when I hit something hard.

What the fuck?

I rolled, coughing violently as my body tried to recover. The light around me was so intense I could see nothing as I forced myself to my feet, ready to fight again, to face whatever was around.

Had I been wrong? Had Guardian thrown me for some reason? Had the others attacked and knocked me free?

Finally, my eyes adjusted enough for me to make out my surroundings despite the brightness.

Green fields stretched out around me, the colors so crisp that I squinted. The air was fresh and cool and cleaner than any I'd ever breathed before.

Is this...

A gasp came from my left a moment before a large body struck the ground. *Hale.* A moment later, Gorrin followed, then Yazmor and Tyrus. They seemed to appear out of nowhere, but their reactions told me they'd followed me.

They'd trusted me, or at least decided that whatever had happened to me was worth following, if just for the chance to find me again.

Gorrin crawled closer, pulled me to him and kissed me, stealing the breath I'd finally caught again. The others did the same, all of us desperate and panting and trembling. I had been *so* close to death, so close to a darkness I could never return from, and yet somehow, we'd come out the other side alive.

Gorrin looked around, his hand wrapped around mine tightly.

"Are we..." I asked but couldn't finish the question, too afraid of the answer.

He got to his feet, then pulled me up beside him. "Yeah, we are. Congratulations, Loch. You're the first demon to ever reach the Plains. Welcome to Heaven."

The Devil's Luck: The Devil's Due
Jayce Carter

Excerpt

"Huh, heaven is a lot nicer than I would have figured." I closed my eyes and tipped my head back, savoring the feeling of the sun on my skin.

Or, rather, whatever light source they had here. Given I was in the Plains, it wasn't the sun.

Which sure was the one place I'd never figured I'd get to.

With the life I'd lived, hell hadn't been a shock to me, but heaven? Good people ended up here, and I hadn't ever fool myself into thinking I belonged in such a place.

"I miss the Chasm," Yazmor said from beside me. "When you breathe in there, ash sort of coats your throat and tongue."

"And you think that's a good thing?"

He shrugged, tucking his hands into the pocket at the front of his hoodie sweater. "It makes me feel like I'm back home."

For Yazmor—a remnant from an old version of the world—home meant a place that didn't exist anymore. I recalled what I'd seen of his world, the universe that had come and gone so long ago that no one else remembered it. Smoke, ash and fire had filled the landscape, so I could understand how that might make him nostalgic.

"Well, I'm planning to enjoy this sun and fresh air. Who knows if I'll get a chance again."

"Are you planning on dying or something?"

"I didn't plan to die the first time, but that didn't stop it from happening. I've learned that no one really plans to die — it just happens."

Yazmor bumped his shoulder against mine, making me trip slightly from the impact. "Yeah, well, I don't plan on letting that happen."

From anyone else, that would have seemed like some empty boast. Coming from Yazmor, though? If anyone had the ability to keep death at bay, it'd be him.

I glanced at him and fought my smile. He was back to himself, and it was hard to believe just how awkward things had been so recently.

Our trip through the Path — the only way to get from the Chasm to the Plains — had twisted all five of us. None had reacted as bad as Yazmor. He'd lost himself to his other form, unable to keep his human one. Worse, he'd pulled away, putting distance between himself and the rest of us.

He hadn't been the only one to struggle. I'd been so quick to doubt myself, afraid to make any choices in case they were the wrong ones, in case someone else suffered because of it. Gorrin had turned even more over-protective than usual. I was lucky we were stuck there, because if he'd been on Earth, he'd have surrounded me in bubble wrap and never let me out of his sight. Tyrus had let his paranoia run wild, causing him to hoard goods and watch us all as though we were planning to fuck him over. And Hale?

He walked ahead of me, his jacket off, which showed his tattoos in the sunlight. He had been terrified that I'd betray him, had looked at everything I'd done or said, looking for proof that I would hurt him.

I could understand each of their behaviors, their fears, which the Path had played upon until they could hardly recall the uneasy trust we'd found.

When we'd finally gotten here, to the Plains, that heavy feeling had let up. Still, it was a lot harder to move past the things that had happened, the things we'd all admitted, the sides of ourselves and one another that we didn't love or want to examine.

Worse, we all looked like hell. Gorrin had warned us *not* to use our powers unless we had no other choice. Angels and Hubis could feel if we did, and while a little could get overlooked, using our powers too much would get us caught.

"So, this is heaven," I said for what had to be the hundredth time already. I just couldn't fully believe it.

"Were you expecting clouds and cherubs?" Yazmor asked.

"I mean, I wouldn't mind any of that. This just seems too normal, like we could be in any little town. Why does this place look like that? Doesn't it pre-date this sort of place on Earth?"

"Well, some of the Plains changes, just like the Chasm does. Areas can look different based on the people there. Also, since angels do a lot of work on Earth, they influence human trends."

"You're saying Hubis wastes angels' time by making them decide whether adobe or brick are going to be on trend? They've got nothing better to do than that?"

"Of course not—that would be crazy! Angels care more about style trends. Remember those super baggy pants with the tall platform sneakers that were popular in the nineties? Yeah, those were *all* Azael."

That was before my time, but I recalled seeing pictures of teens wearing them. "Well, now I'm even more glad he's gone."

"Right? If you have that sort of power, you should use it better. That's why I made those little keychain pet video games big."

I would have laughed him off—most people did—but I'd gotten to know Yazmor well enough to guess he was telling the truth. The more outlandish something sounded, the more likely it had actually happened.

We'd only been in the Plains for about an hour, according to Tyrus' watch. Despite turning my phone off in the Path, it had still ended up drained. *Leave it to the Path to still be fucking me over.*

Gorrin had taken the lead as soon as we'd arrived, his comfort here reminding me that this was his home, that he knew this place better than any of us.

Fuck, he knew this place better than any other place.

It made me glance his way, to see his wings out and pure and almost sparkling in the light. They'd appeared as soon as we'd arrived.

Were they harder to hide here? I didn't dare ask, because Gorrin had one hell of a *do not cross* on that subject.

Gorrin had been rather strange about his angel form in general, as though it made him uncomfortable. I had a feeling that being here, in the Plains, was the worst time to question him.

Something moved to the side of us, making the brush rustle. It was the sort of slight shifting that came when a person was trying hard *not* to get noticed.

After dealing with Guardian and his overly enthusiastic tentacles, my nerves were shot. It meant I reached out and grabbed for the person, then hauled them from the bush they hid in.

Instead of the weird shit I'd dealt with in the Path, however, I didn't at all expect to find a child in front of me, my hand wrapped around their thin arm.

It was a young girl, her eyes wide as she stared up at me. "I'm sorry," she rushed out, not bothering to pull away as if she knew it would prove useless.

And a glance around told me why she might just react that way. The Lords and I looked rough when we were at our best, and after barely surviving the Path?

We were *far* from our best.

Our clothing was tattered and dirty. Dirt and blood streaked our faces. Enough time had passed that our injuries had healed, but that didn't remove the stains from our fight with Guardian.

If *I* saw us somewhere, I'd have run in the other direction, too.

And that didn't even go into Hale and his tattoos and piercings or the tattoos on my face, along with my green hair.

Basically?

We were one hell of a hot mess.

I smiled, pretending that'd soften my appearance and our whole vibe. "What's your name?"

The girl swallowed hard, then answered in a small voice, "Emma."

She appeared to be seven, perhaps, and rather slim. She had long dark hair and matching dark eyes. In fact, she looked a lot like Tyrus. However, the most notable feature was the way her lip on the left was tucked up, toward her nostrils. I was pretty sure it was called a cleft lip, though I'd never really seen it before in real life.

I didn't take much to not react to her appearance. I might have been surprised if I'd still been alive, but after five years in the Chasm, with damned who were twisted into almost unrecognizable forms, nothing really threw me anymore. "Emma is such a pretty name. I'm Loch."

Emma glanced at Yazmor, her gaze suspicious and unsure. At least that told me she had some smarts.

"My name is Yazmor." He crouched in front of Emma, giving her one of those smiles that unnerved normal people.

Except she seemed taken by it. Maybe it was similar to how children liked cartoon characters with exaggerated features—that sure described Yazmor, after all.

"Why were you hiding from us?"

"I thought you might get mad at me."

"I'm never mad," Yazmor lied. "But you've been following us for the last ten minutes."

I turned my gaze on him, frowning because I'd totally missed that. In fact, I'd stupidly thought I'd done so well, that I'd managed to spot her when no one else had. *Turns out I'm a step behind, like always.*

"Not a lot of people live this far out, so I was curious who you were."

"I don't like a lot of people." Yazmor balanced on the balls of his feet, not wavering in the least despite the awkward position. "So I prefer quiet places. You look like the type of person who'd understand that. I bet you always have your nose in a book or your head in the clouds."

Some of the shadows fell from Emma's expression, a sure sign that Yazmor had won her over. It seemed he could charm anyone if he really wanted to.

Well, he sure charmed me, didn't he?

Emma nodded quickly, then reached for a book I hadn't noticed before, one clutched in her other hand. "I was reading this one when I heard you pass by. It's about a dragon and a princess."

"Does a knight come and save her?" Tyrus asked as he walked over, his tone somehow softer than I was used to. In fact, despite the way he could intimidate the hardest of people, he seemed almost kind as he spoke to Emma.

Emma shook her head, pulling the book against her chest. "Of course not! She saves the dragon from the knight, and her and the dragon live happily ever after."

A sharp bark of laughter escaped me before I could even think about it. I wiped my fingers under my eyes when the laughing fit made my eyes water, then leaned forward a bit as I caught my breath. "Sorry, but that is so my kind of story. Who wants the knight when they can have the monster, huh?"

I peered to the side for a moment to see Yazmor and Tyrus with similar grins on their faces, as though they understood exactly what I meant. If my men weren't considered monsters, then nothing deserved that title.

I stood back up, then winced when my stomach decided that was the right moment to growl, the sound loud, even above the chirping of birds and general relaxing atmosphere that sounded like a sound machine used for meditation.

Emma stared at my stomach in surprise, then looked up at my face again. "If you're hungry, why don't you come eat at our house?"

"Our?" Tyrus asked. "Who is 'our'?"

"Obviously it's her and her family," I said.

Tyrus lifted an eyebrow, as if telling me to think it through. Only when he did, did his point hit me.

This was the Plains—basically heaven. It meant people didn't grow up and live together and have kids like I was used to.

It also meant that Emma, despite appearing like a child, might very well have been impossibly old.

Emma didn't seem fazed by Tyrus' question or my stupid guess, which thrilled me. The last thing I wanted was to show up in heaven and make the first child I ran across cry.

"I live in a house with a few others. It isn't very far from here, and we have plenty of food there." She paused, then frowned. "Are you new? Most new souls appear in the center of the palace."

"Yes, we're new," Tyrus acknowledged.

"Did you get here together?"

"The five of us met out here," he said, the lie slipping from him so easily that it reminded me not to ever trust Tyrus. Even I couldn't catch it when he lied.

"Five?" Emma twisted, staring at Hale as if she hadn't noticed him before. Maybe watching me had so distracted her that she hadn't seen us all.

She showed no real reaction to Hale, despite how he looked. That wasn't even close to the case when she finally spotted Gorrin coming back, since he'd walked ahead quite a while.

Emma stumbled backward, her feet tangling into the brush that lined the walkway, so she ended up on her ass. "I'm sorry," she rushed out, her voice thin and terrified. "I didn't realize you had an angel with you. I would never have spied on you if I had, would never have done something so disrespectful."

Her words rushed from her so fast that I struggled to understand them.

Not that Gorrin appeared all that surprised when he finally reached us, where Emma still scooted away in the dirt without taking her eyes off him.

"Be at ease," he assured her. "I am not angry."

She went to speak, but nothing came out at first, as if her throat had tightened to the point where even words couldn't escape. She pressed her lips together then swallowed before trying again. "I'm sure you don't want to come to my place. It isn't what you're used to, and it isn't nice enough for someone like yourself to step into it." She didn't look at him, her gaze down, her voice trembling.

Gorrin sighed, his wings shifting to show how much he didn't care for this reaction. Of course, he also didn't seem surprised by it, which made no sense to me.

On Earth, people viewed angels as saviors, as holy creatures meant to protect and watch over us. Sure, I'd been dead long enough to know that was total bullshit. Angels were like every other type of being — some were good and some were absolute shit. Still, I'd figured that of all places, in the Plains, they'd be loved.

Instead, the terror in Emma's face told the truth.

Gorrin reached his hand out, bending down to offer it to Emma. "I would appreciate any food you could spare and some clothing if you have it."

Emma stared at his hand but didn't move to take it. "We don't have anything you would find worthy."

Gorrin let out a sigh then retracted his hand. He must have realized Emma wouldn't accept his help. "I assure you, whatever you have will be most appreciated."

Emma scrambled to her feet but kept Gorrin in her line of sight. His final words had given her no way out, no way to refuse. Even if it was clear she wanted him nowhere near her home, to deny him now would be to go against an angel, and even if I didn't know much about the Plains, I had a strong feeling that *that* just wasn't done.

"Okay," she said softly, moving around us, giving herself a large swath of space. "It's just up this way a little farther. Come on." She walked quickly, looking tiny and fragile compared to the five of us, especially with the way her shoulders trembled.

Yazmor, Hale and Tyrus followed her, leaving Gorrin and I a few steps behind.

"What was that about?" I asked him, keeping my voice low so it didn't carry to Emma.

Gorrin closed his hands into fists, and somehow, he seemed just as bothered as Emma was. While it was fear from her, he held on to frustration. "I told you before that the Plains are not the heaven people believe this place to be. That includes angels."

"She's terrified of you. Why?"

"Because she is smart. Anyone who wishes to survive in the Plains should avoid angels. If you believe Azael to be alone in his cruelty, you are sadly mistaken. The most dangerous things here are the beings who appear just like me."

He didn't wait for a response before he walked off, following Emma and the others, leaving me to stare at his back and his wings, which still fluttered as if to display his unease.

All the time I'd spent wanting to get here, and it suddenly didn't feel like the reward I'd hoped for.

Maybe heaven really wasn't all it was cracked up to be…

* * * *

The way Emma had carried on about her place not being good enough for Gorrin had made me think she'd undersold herself.

As it turned out, she'd oversold it.

The place could barely be called a house. The roof had holes in it, and the windows were all boarded up. If I'd seen a kid living in a place like this on Earth, I'd have immediately kicked the shit out of whoever should have been taking care of them.

Yet here we were, in fucking *heaven*, and they had a kid living in this?

"It's not that bad," Emma whispered, shame filling her words.

I tried to clear the look from my face. The last fucking thing she needed was for me to make her feel bad. How often had idiots offered me pity like that while not doing shit to help. "I've lived in worse places — trust me. All a person really needs is a place that keeps the rain and wind out."

Emma shrugged as she moved deeper into the single large room, with beds set up in areas along the outside edges of the space, almost like small camping areas. "We fix the holes when we can, and we've got lots of blankets. Before I found this place and the other people who live here, I mostly slept outside, so this is a big step up."

"And that was safe?" Tyrus asked, slipping into his, 'I'm going to fix this,' mode he usually was in.

"There aren't a lot of people this far out. Most people stay in the city, close to the palace."

I sure as fuck heard that evasion. She hadn't answered about it being safe, not really, which meant it wasn't safe, but she'd done it anyway.

I cut a glance Gorrin's way, wanting to strangle that asshole. This was *his* world, and from what little I'd seen, it fucking sucked. Might as well blame him for that.

Tension lined Loch's eyes, a sure sign the girl didn't like this shit any more than I did. Then again, Loch and I understood each other in a way the others didn't, had a shared background unlike the others.

Tyrus had been used to being in charge for a long time, had grown up with rich and doting parents. Yazmor wasn't even from this world, and Gorrin hadn't really grown up at all since Hubis had created him as the first angel.

Loch and I had been raised dirt-fucking poor, amongst the filth of the Earth, forced to cheat and steal and struggle just to survive. We understood one another—and Emma, it seemed—in a way the others never would.

The back door of the place opened, and a woman walked in, brushing her hands on the front of her pants, leaving dirty prints behind. "You're back early, Emma." She spoke as she moved, without looking up, as if it never occurred to her that it might not be Emma there.

Which really sold the fact that not many people were out here.

She sucked in a sharp breath when she finally did look up, when her gaze settled on Gorrin—or more specifically, his wings—first. She didn't run the way Emma had tried to, and I liked the woman immediately when her first reaction was to grab Emma and yank the young girl behind her.

"What are you doing here?" the woman asked, her voice careful but strong.

"My stomach," Loch said, and right on cue, it grumbled as if to make the point for her.

"I said they could eat here. I met them out on the road," Emma said from behind the woman's back.

The woman tried to look at each of us, but her gaze kept returning to Gorrin as if he were the only one who could hold her attention. Then again, to her, she had one angel and three souls. We were chump change in her eyes. "I can't believe that an angel doesn't have better places to go than here…"

Her words made me snort, a balancing between respectful and rude as fuck. I could hear the battle, the desire to tell Gorrin to get the fuck out of her place, but her fear of what he might do if she didn't treat him with the utmost reverence.

"I told him that," Emma whispered. "He still said he wanted to come here."

The woman twisted and crouched, staring straight into Emma's eyes. She lowered her voice, but it wasn't nearly quiet enough for me to not hear what she said. The benefits of being a Demon Lord included fantastic hearing.

"That isn't just any angel, Emma. That is *Gorrin*, the first."

"I didn't recognize him," Emma said.

"He's been gone since before you came here, but he's the strongest of them. You should know better than to invite strangers here, especially angels." The woman grasped Emma's hand, holding it tightly as if she wanted to pull her away from all of us immediately.

She seemed smart enough to know that she couldn't outrun us, though. In fact, I could almost see in her eyes the plan forming as she worked out what to do.

If I had to guess, I'd say she'd feed us, give us what we wanted and needed, play nice until we turned our backs just long enough for her to grab Emma and bolt.

"I am not planning on harming any of you," Gorrin said, his voice the same flat one he used when talking at underlings. It might have seemed mean, but fuck knew I understood.

People as terrified as Emma and that woman wouldn't listen to reason. They saw Gorrin as an enemy, as a threat, and him reassuring them wouldn't change shit.

It was like a man-eating tiger swearing up and down that it wouldn't eat someone. History showed the tiger's true nature, and only an idiot would believe what came out of their mouth.

The woman rose and kept Emma behind her and out of sight. "Of course—our home is yours. I'm afraid we don't have much, but what little we have you are welcome to."

"We don't need much," Loch said. "And we aren't freeloaders, either. I can help cook."

"We need some clothing as well," Tyrus added. "We're strong, though, so please allow us to complete some chores to repay you."

The woman pressed her lips together, all the refusal bright and clear in her expression. Still, she couldn't outright say no, so she nodded. "We don't need any help but thank you. I'll have Emma go and see what clothing might fit you while I get food from the garden and pantry. I'll have something cooked up and ready in the next hour or so, so please rest until then." She leaned in to talk to Emma, whispering something that I couldn't catch.

I didn't really need to hear it to know it was a warning, though. Emma nodded in response then headed out through the back door. Only once she'd left did the woman take her first real, deep breath, as though without Emma in the crosshairs she could finally relax.

"Please, take the time to rest here," she said, then turned and left through that same door.

Loch took off after her, but Gorrin caught her arm. "Where are you going?"

"To help."

"She said not to."

"So? She said that because she's terrified of you. What better way to prove we aren't as bad as she thinks than by making ourselves useful?" Loch peered around the large falling-apart building. "I mean, obviously they could use some help."

Gorrin released her. "Okay but be cautious. Angels are rarely out this far, but that doesn't mean it can't happen."

Loch nodded before following the woman out of the back door, leaving the four of us in the place alone.

"Aren't they worried we'll steal something?" Tyrus asked.

"Nah," I answered. "They know there isn't anything here worth stealing. If they've got shit worth anything, it'll be hidden somewhere else."

My words took me back to my own childhood. I'd lived in group homes as far back as I could recall, and we'd all learned early that anything of value needed to be fiercely guarded. I still recalled a hollowed-out area of a wall in an abandoned building where I'd stashed my valuables.

Of course, being only six at the time, those *valuables* were less than twenty bucks in cash, some non-perishable foods and an extra set of clothing. Still, that was important in that world. A little bit of food could mean the difference between life and death back then.

I'd stored them away like a squirrel, making damn sure no one knew about them in case I had to take off for some reason.

Tyrus turned toward Gorrin, his expression severe. "Should we expect similar reactions to you while we're here?"

"Most likely."

"Can't you just hide those fucking wings of yours like you do in the Chasm?" I asked.

"No. Being here makes it almost impossible to hide them. Besides, even without seeing them, the spirits here can sense my powers. They can spot me as an angel even if I could hide my wings."

"So fucking much for being able to sneak around," I muttered. "You didn't think to mention before that we'd be that fucking obvious with you here?"

"I had been considering that," Gorrin answered. "The thing is, in the Plains, what you just saw is common. The spirits avoid angels whenever possible. They are likely to spot me and take little notice of anything else. That may work in our favor. Terrified people ask fewer questions."

"And you don't think anyone will gossip about Gorrin strolling around with four others? That they will not think that is rather strange?" Tyrus asked, crossing his arms and cocking up one eyebrow.

"Why would they? You could walk through the Chasm, and no one found that strange. Seeing an angel in the Plains is normal."

"What if they see *us*?" I gestured at myself. "I don't isn't exactly have a normal, blend into the background look. You don't think anyone's going to recognize me?"

Gorrin shook his head. "The spirits here have never been to the Chasm, so they will have no idea who or what exists there. Most will not even know that there are Demon Lords let alone who they are or what they look like."

"What about angels?"

"Azael handled trips to the Chasm prior to his death, and since then, it has only been a single angel who has done so. That limits the people who have seen any of you to only Hubis himself and that single angel, and since that angel took over Azael's position, he will stay in the palace. Until we reach the city, we should be safe. I would suggest you remove your piercings, at least."

I grumbled, even if I knew he was right. Since I'd died with the piercings, the holes wouldn't close up, but fuck did I dislike the idea of not wearing them. Those bits of metal felt like a part of me, an armor I really enjoyed having, but that didn't matter. They'd call attention to me.

Instead of arguing, I went about taking them out.

"And when we get to the palace?" Tyrus asked. "What then?"

"I cannot give you specifics yet, but I do have a plan in the works." Gorrin's expression was so flat that it would have given nothing away to any other person. I'd known him for a long damn time, though, so I could read him better than most people.

That is a lot of uncertainty there. Doesn't seem like he's too confident in whatever plan he's got.

I peered up to try to release the anxiety inside me, the part of me that wanted to know the plan so I could do *something*. A ray of light poured in, making me flinch against the brightness.

Gorrin headed toward the front door.

"Where are you going?" I asked.

"As if you planned to allow them to continue living in this state. We should fix the roof first." He didn't wait to see if I agreed, and that annoyed me more.

I didn't love that he felt as if he knew me, even if he had been right.

Tyrus didn't move, so I paused to look at him. "Not planning on helping?"

He undid the buttons at his cuffs, then rolled up his sleeves. "I don't care for heights. You two handle the roof. I'll see what I can do about the windows. Yazmor can…" Tyrus looked around as if realizing for the first time Yazmor had disappeared on us.

The sound of a pissed-off bull from outside made me sigh. *Sounds like Yazmor is once again petting an animal that isn't all that into it.*

Of course, as annoying as he was, I had little doubt that after getting himself gored, he'd do some chores out there.

Who would have figured Demon Lords would end up as handymen? Part of me wondered what Emma and that woman would think if they knew the truth, if they realized that the demons who ran the Chasm were here fixing up their place? I even found myself craving that credit, wanting to see Emma smile when she saw it, wanting to see that woman let down her guard and see me as…

I shook away the idea as soon as it occurred to me. I knew my place, had accepted it. I was a scary-looking delinquent, and it didn't matter what I did — the world would never see me as anything else.

About the Author

Jayce Carter lives in Southern California with her husband and two spawns. She originally wanted to take over the world but realized that would require wearing pants. This led her to choosing writing, a completely pants-free occupation. She has a fear of heights yet rock climbs for fun and enjoys making up excuses for not going out and socializing.

Jayce loves to hear from readers. You can find her contact information, website details and author profile page at https://www.totallybound.com

Home of Erotic Romance

Sign up for our newsletter and find out about all our romance book releases, eBook sales and promotions, sneak peeks and FREE romance books!

www.ingramcontent.com/pod-product-compliance
Lightning Source LLC
Chambersburg PA
CBHW030402030726
47497CB00002B/442